Bronté Woodard

MEET ME AT THE MELBA

G.K.HALL &CO.

 Boston, Massachusetts

1978

Library of Congress Cataloging in Publication Data

Woodard, Bronté.
  Meet me at the Melba.

  "Published in large print."
  1. Large type books. I. Title.
[PZ4.W883Me 1978] [PS3573.0613] 813'.5'4 77-19316
ISBN 0-8161-6543-2

Published in Large Print by arrangement with Delacorte Press.

Set in Compugraphic 18 pt English Times

To my parents,
Eva Mae Terhune Woodard
and
Myron Bronté Woodard, Sr.,
and to my aunt
Georgia Josephine Terhune Paul
with love

Prologue

If life had been as easygoing as he was, Doc Vacalis would have gotten along fine. When he was eighteen, life was as clear before him as the glassy waters of Tarpon Springs, Florida, where he and his brothers dove for the sponges that put bread on their table. Their father made them outsiders, sitting on the waterfront sipping bitter coffee, talking with his Mediterranean cronies, despairing of the new world, remembering the old, skipping over the reasons for having left it. Somehow the old man's journey had been a gargantuan mistake, and all the things that had befallen him in America — wife and children included — were like the visitations of Olympian retribution that had befallen other wandering Greek heroes. And so he sat, day after day, along the waterfront, watching his sons sail into the dawn and home with the setting sun, with little praise and less thanks. They were his sons. It was an honor for them to do for him.

The honor had long ago paled on Doc, who was the oldest. He had no love of the sea. By night he dreamed of drowning, and by day he swam among the reefs, his hands growing cut and callused reaching out for spiny objects that the water made look soft. So, one night early in his eighteenth year, an hour before his mother would come to rouse them, he slid out of the bed he shared with his two brothers, grabbed up his clothes, tiptoed naked through the tiny house, and dressed in the sandy yard, beneath the old palm tree, whose fronds crunched in the pre-dawn breeze. He crawled under the house, jimmied a loose brick from one of the pilings, and took out the twenty dollars it had taken him three years to hoard. He was about to leave when a light went on above him, sprinkling golden slivers through the boards.

He slid down on his haunches and

waited for the alarm to be sounded. He heard the Old Man's heavy-footed stride. He took about ten steps, then stopped. There was the screech of a window being raised. Doc went dry inside. All his moisture had gathered into a single, pulsating knot in his stomach. Then he heard the steady rainlike noise, and almost gasped with relief. The Old Man was pissing out the bedroom window. He claimed he gave back to the land what the land gave to him. The last Doc ever saw of his father was a strong, colorless arc that hit the sand with a hissing sound and was absorbed without a trace.

Doc made it to Atlanta, Georgia. It seemed to be where things were happening. It was 1905, and there was enough hustle and bustle in the streets to make you think you were a part of the world, not just an alien diver in a place where things never changed.

He got on, just like that, conducting a streetcar, his uniform shiny, with buttons tight around the stocky physique as hard as the black glint of his eyes as he approached the proper young ladies, schooled to blush, who took their seats and primly handed him tokens or asked for change.

Melba Eubanks always asked for change. It gave their hands a second time to touch. Melba took typing, her proud stenographic hopes as high as the pointed breasts that attracted Doc Vacalis's attention. She thought it was her curls, as dark as his, that caught his eye, and she tossed them as she turned from him, her breasts jiggling with the effort.

They spent months staring at each other with no words except "Tokens?" "Change, please." "Thank you, ma'am." "You're welcome, sir." He thought of her, his uniform growing tighter. At night her breasts hung invisible before his open mouth as his spit-greased hand pumped him on to the relief his landlady frowned upon on sheet-changing day.

Then the day each had counted on arrived, and she was late the afternoon he changed his shift. There were only three in the car when they approached what they both knew to be her stop. They could have built a bridge between their eyes when she made no attempt to get up. When the car emptied and the end of the line arrived, he nodded to old Milton, the driver, who lived for bowel movements at the end of the line. Old Milton left, and they were alone.

Melba rose from her seat and started out past him. He could lose his job from what he was about to do — or, worse than that, his life, judging from what he had heard of the high price for Southern pussy. Still, he extended his hand as if to help her, and when she gave him hers, he pressed it down against his crotch.

She was filled with terror, but she squeezed. He took her off the trolley, leaned her against a bank of dandelions while she thought of grass stains and hell, then forgot both as he was on her, in her, around her, humping her goatlike and sucking through cloth the tender breasts that tried their best to get to him as they shot from fear to pain to joy to greater joy, then slumped beside each other in the dying day. Old Milton came back and, tired of waiting for Doc, left with the trolley.

She ran her hands through his thick jet hair and knew what beauty was. He removed her clothes and knew the same. Never was their passion so beautifully spent as the evening they lay in the dandelions and first loved. She opened herself to him again, and he filled her, lying in her arms while she took a dandelion and softly blew it into his hair.

"Melba," she said.

"Doc," he said.

"Sarah," they said later in the year, holding the baby of that afternoon.

Of course, things were never the same again for either of them. They lived in a furnished room, the conductor job having expired. Then they spent a year in Birmingham, Doc going into the coal-mining trade until his leg got wedged between the elevator and its destination. He got two hundred dollars for that, along with a crutch he was never without for long and directions back to Atlanta, where Melba sewed, a convenient occupation when, after four fallow years, she ran fertile again at fifteen-month intervals — first with Preston, then Royal, then the three girls, Araminthia, Maybelle, and Louise — and Doc stood in line for the bits and pieces of work that came to those who didn't walk so well. Drinking came to him, too, though it was strictly medicinal. He never liked the taste or the feeling, just the quiet, foggy place it took him to. He thought of going back to the underwater world he had left, but his breath had gotten short. Diving was a young man's work, and he was old at thirty-four, with six mouths to feed and one more in the spring.

He had been working as a checker at Lawson Steel, 6 A.M. till 7 P.M., at wages he'd have spit at had he the two good legs to walk away on, but he had to take their guff with thank yous while bosses in suits with watch chains had high old times in brand-new cars that waited for them all day long, shined by Peg Leg Willie, too crippled to be of any further use. Doc knew he would end up there one day in Willie's place, when the leg he hobbled on finally had to be taken off. The leg had never got its color back: It was yellow below the knee, and scaly, as though the blood had to wedge its way through the crushed veins. Melba rubbed it nightly, sometimes kissing the dry toes as if her moisture could bring new life. And with her kisses came the old idea that he could do anything, but what he did was make love to her, forgetting the rest.

When talk of a union came to Lawson's in 1920, Doc went along with it. Indeed, he became most vocal, envisioning a contract clause that would save him from Peg Leg Willie's job.

"I can take some time off if it comes to a strike," he told Melba. "This union's got Northern money behind it. They got a strike fund. They got a food fund. They got a car pool. You never heard of that?"

Melba smiled and lay back on her pillows. She ached. What could be more merciless than an unborn child? She was glad to hear that everything would turn out all right. She had been discouraged, no denying, but she had been a Baptist before Doc Vacalis, and they were trained to look on the bright side of an industrious God who would provide for those who did their share. She had been fallen away from the Church too long. When this baby came and the union had made Doc secure in his job, she would take them all back to church, walking down the aisle with a humble air the first few times. The Baptists loved a good penitent.

Word of their imminent good fortune leaked out to the children. Melba confided in Sarah, her first-born, like a close friend. She had talked early as a baby, and, oddly enough, her baby's world was not limited to her own needs and wants. Melba felt that she was in Sarah's eyes the way she wanted to be seen. Sarah was never a child.

Preston, her second-born, was a child. Preston Marlin Vacalis. He had big, blue eyes just like Melba's own. Of all her children, he was the one who had given her the fondest memories. It was as though something of Doc had settled in her second child and he would always know how to bring her pleasure. She felt like a young girl when she was with him, and he could wipe away all the lies the mirror was beginning to tell her.

The year of the strike Preston was ten years old, and he peddled papers on a downtown street. Before that he had shined shoes, but he had learned that he could sell a paper quicker than he could shine a shoe, and he had long since learned that money was the cause of all their problems.

The strike came in November, but not as many left their jobs as the union had hoped. Still, it was a little over a third of the work force, and the men gave one another courage with tales of production schedules lagging far behind. They set up their lines outside the gates and nodded in a friendly way to their former companions who chose to stay on the job. The Thanksgiving turkey with all the trimmings was provided by the strike fund.

At Christmas there was turkey with no trimmings. The Church had adopted a hands-off policy with the strike. They didn't think well of strikes in the South.

There was the scent of the Bolshevik about them, and you never could tell where equality would try to wedge its black toe in the door. "If it is new and different, you can count on the majority not to like it," said Doc, "unless it comes in a can or on wheels."

Doc sat by the window, his young/old face taking in the last of the afternoon's light. It was February now, and a cold wave coming. It was too cold to snow. Some of the men had gone back to work, getting back in when Mr. Lawson himself had come out to the strike line and made an appeal. "For the sake of your families," he had said, "I'm asking you to put down your signs and come back in. I'm not begging you. We can get along without you, have been quite well. But anybody's entitled to a disagreement. That's why this is the United States, but the war's over now. Jobs'll be hard to come by. Come on back in while you still can." He had nodded to them, turned, and walked away from the guarded steel fence.

There were no more than a dozen left on the picket line the next morning, their hopes as dark as the leaden skies that were supposed to take the weather down to zero. "The bastards gave in," somebody said. "Just a word from Old Man Lawson and in they went. Well, let 'em. We'll beat 'em yet!"

They received encouraging words from the union men who came around, but Doc knew that they had become a joke. He looked around and saw that he had stayed with the dregs of the job. Three were young and stayed out half the time drunk. Six had nothing to lose, as they were about to be too old to be of any use. And the others? They were misfits like him. One of the unionizers had brought a bottle. They passed it among them. Doc took his turn, and it burned him awake, a warm streak followed by the cold again, but in that he saw one thing as clearly as Peg Leg Willie could see his reflection in the cars he wiped — his life had taken a wrong turn somewhere and was so wound around in the wilderness that he didn't see how he would ever get it back on the right track.

Somebody started ragging one of the guards. It had been going back and forth for the whole strike, but the guards, on instructions, had kept their lips buttoned. Now, with only the ragtag ends left, they were answering back derisively, then going back to the warm guard shack while Doc hunched his shoulders beneath the coat the wind had got into and continued his grim parade, carrying the sign that read I CAN'T FEED MY KIDS ON LAWSON STEEL WAGES. That the statement was true made no difference at all. They had lost from the beginning. Doc Vacalis knew that now.

Preston still had twenty papers left to sell. He sometimes had as many as five left over, but never before twenty. It was five in the afternoon, and four degrees. The streets were empty, and likely to remain that way till the thermometer took an upturn. He had made about ten cents from this day, and that didn't put too much on the table.

Night was coming on when he gave up

and swung onto the end of a passing trolley, resting on the stingy edge just above the tracks. It was easy to steal a ride tonight, the conductors staying closed inside. But Preston got a little flash of growing up. He was about to be too big to ride the streetcar ledge — unless, of course, something stunted his growth or he died of lockjaw.

Feeling weary with age, he swung off at the Pryor Street Institute of Tailoring and Pressing, one of the few colored-owned businesses in the downtown area that was patronized by whites. Blacks and whites both lined up at the Institute. First come, first served.

Elmo Flagg, a shiny patent-leather man wearing a green eyeshade, owned the place. He let Old Stitt, Preston's supervisor, drop Preston's papers off on his covered back stoop, where the rain and the pigeons wouldn't get at them. Whenever Preston had any extras he left them there, so that at least he had a witness if Old Stitt suspected him of keeping a penny or two extra.

The Institute was a basement operation.

An uninterrupted flight of thirty-two steps led from a pipe-clogged ceiling through a maze of new and ancient hand-lettered religious announcements to an awesome view of clothes — old, new; fine and shabby — come together like penitents to be made clean and whole again.

The blast of heat from the presses almost sent Preston reeling. He had not known how cold he was, and now he was stinging. He bounced down the steps, feeling all the bones in his feet.

The place was thronged with people. Elmo, all three of his tailors, the pressman, and Bessie Loomis, who did the buttons and collars and measured the ladies, were chugging back and forth among the swaying lines of paper-wrapped clothing. Bessie had Scoe, her boy, with her. He was about Preston's age. They knew each other — not well, but well enough to fight, in gangs on the vacant lots of Summerhill, the deadly tussles of childhood.

Preston ducked under the counter, taking the privilege of a shortcut to the back stoop. Elmo turned and watched the white child with his unsold papers. "Hey, you, Preston," he called, determined to keep his voice as level and uncaring as he would have liked it to have been.

Preston stopped, his eyes as wide as those that were on him. Being singled out sent imagined transgressions through his head.

"There gon' to be trouble out to the Lawson. If yo' daddy out there, you best be seein' if you can get him home." The eyes looked away again, as though his trouble embarrassed them. They all knew Doc, liked him when he was sober, his plight not so very different from theirs, and stayed out of his way when he had made his load, spewing it and his anger that he was the way he was.

"I don't know if he's there or not," Preston said.

"If there gon' be trouble, he gon' be there," said Elmo. "You got a token?"

"I don't need a token."

"You need a token more than you need pneumonia, which is what you gon' get if you plan on riding the side of the trolley like I seen you do," said Bessie Loomis, digging into her apron pocket and coming up with one, which she handed to Scoe, giving him the rough shove she was sure he needed.

Scoe advanced wordlessly and stuck the warm token into Preston's icy hand, then pulled his own warm hand away, stunned by the chill.

They looked at Preston as though he had to take it, so he did. "Thank you," he said to no one in particular, and started toward the back to drop his papers. Elmo took them from him.

"Never did think you'd show up with them papers. Folks been asking for them. Too cold to buy 'em in the street tonight. Waited till they got down here." Elmo took the papers and walked to the counter. "Here they are, folks. Cold off the press. Step right up. This boy's in a hurry."

There was hesitation; then a black man with red-shot eyes stepped up for the first one. Then another — lining up now — until the papers were gone and the first warmth Preston had felt in hours came to him from the coins he clutched tightly.

"Get on," said Elmo. "Don't let yo' daddy get into anything."

"I thank you," said Preston. There were things to say he hadn't the wit to say, and sharp, definite things to be felt he hadn't the time to work out. He almost added "sir" to his thanks, but he overruled himself as he headed for the steps.

He swung off the trolley after another stolen ride. He would either use Bessie Loomis's token for a rainy day, to save the papers, or drop it somewhere on the lot where Scoe would find it and think he'd had a little luck.

There was a gathering crowd in the front of the gates at Lawson: a group of well-dressed afternoon drinkers from the Kimball House, smartly bundled against the weather they usually encountered on their New York trips; men in ill-fitting handout clothes from the Union Mission, with its watery stews and Praise Jesus suppers in return for a night out of the wind on pews as unyielding as the Ten Commandments; a few women, the kind that Preston had been told men had no respect for. They were mainly milling about, on the edge of getting bored. It was almost the first hour of night, the darkness translucent.

Preston dashed across the cobweb of tracks at the trolley turnaround, looked at the crowd, then stopped, scanning the faces. He was frightened, filled with the kind of dread that ghost stories bring. For all the people, there was no sound; it was as though the air were too frozen to carry words. There was no color, either, just blacks and whites and a tattered brown or two.

The guards had German police dogs they had been longing for the chance to use. Now they brought them out. Preston saw their faces against the fence, teeth bared. Beyond them, on the loading dock, stood three men in overcoats, one of them with his open, a gold watch chain shining magically in the last of the light. Preston pushed his way through the crowd, his eyes on the shining chain. There was power with it.

Before he got to the fence, the siren

began, far enough away at first to be like a nagging thought. "Hey!" yelled one drunk. "They're coming to get you. They're gonna take you in anyway. Put up a fight why don't you!"

Doc was the first to turn and look at the crowd. Preston saw him, but that was no Father there. It was just somebody as scared as he was. The crowd was urging Doc and his buddies to get fierce and fight, but they had waited too late. The gentleness of despair had settled over them.

The crowd hated them for their weakness. The people looking out the factory windows hated them for their stubbornness. The guards hated them for the opportunity that was going by for the dogs to make them look good. And, like Doc, the pickets hated themselves for the lives that were sliding through their fingers while everybody else seemed to be holding something.

The Black Maria pulled up, and five policemen, billy clubs drawn, rushed between the crowd and the pickets. Their captain, a portly man, born for desk duty, pulled a sheet of paper and began to read. "Any form of picketing, marching, or the carrying of signs outside places of business calling for the disruption of labor and commerce . . ."

A bottle came out of the crowd, striking the captain on his pasty forehead, sending him against the fence, where a snarling German shepherd took a plug out of his gloved hand, prompting a terrified squeal that was an overture to what the crowd had come for. They began to shout, and the policemen took out their vengeance, not on the crowd, but on the pickets, swinging their clubs through them as they backed toward the fence.

Doc was hit twice; the blood pouring from a cut over his eye was the warmest thing he had felt all day. He swung on a cop, and the cop slammed his club where Doc's smile had been and never was again.

Preston rushed toward him as he fell. "Don't hit him! That's my daddy!"

Doc's shame was overwhelming. His son had seen him down. "Oh, God, Preston. Go home!" He stepped forward and was hit again, mercifully this time, taking him away from the embarrassment of the moment and putting him face down in the sharp gravel, which left little marks on him as though he would need to be reminded.

When Preston tried to touch him, he was shoved away, and Doc, unconscious, was dragged into the depths of the Black Maria. The other pickets were put there, too. The crowd, disgusted at the short and sorry show, broke up. The workers left the windows. The man with the gold chain left the dock with his companions. The guards began to feed morsels of meat to the dogs. The Black Maria raced, yodeling, down the street.

Preston stood alone in the cold. There wouldn't be a trolley for an hour or so. He began to walk slowly, following the tracks, keeping his eyes on them all the way into town. The wind stung when it hit.

It had gotten well into night. The sergeant at the desk had told him they'd be letting the pickets out soon. "Might as well," he had snorted," "they got nobody to stand bail for 'em, and no use adding them to city expense." Lawson's wasn't pressing any charges. It had been worth it to them for the ones on the inside to see what happened to the ones on the outside. It made them feel lucky, thankful, and glad.

Preston took up a stand across the street from the station house, wedging himself against a soaring Doric column, one of six that boosted up the courthouse roof and gave the impression of classic justice. The wind was off him here, and the stars in plain view. Preston forgot his vigil for a while, absorbed in the wonders of the night. He felt as though he could leave himself, be out there with the stars, rising above a world of duty and . . . But he could go only so far. His drifting reveries left him feeling small and limited because he could not reach the heights he had no name for; his was a pole vaulter's dream of soaring given by error to the star low hurdler.

They were letting the pickets out one by one, not wanting them to congregate in the streets. Doc was third out, and Preston was ready for him.

Doc looked into the gutter, as though

the answer lay there. He didn't even turn around at Preston's footsteps, was startled when the hand pulled at his sleeve. He gave it a shake with the practiced defensiveness of those who are pushed aside or moved along. "Go 'way. Ain't doin' nothin.'" Then he saw Preston's blue eyes, those eyes that didn't miss a thing, straight and sure.

"What the hell are you doin' here? Go home."

"I . . . I waited on you."

"You don't need to wait on me no more. Get on home."

"Why don't we go together?"

He was like his mama. You could hand it to her for that. Melba had come down through all her children. The one she was carrying now would be her, too. They were so unswerving, so adapted. They understood everything that eluded him. All their eyes were blue, and his were brown. God, he thought, deliver me from blue-eyed people who know it all. Nothing seemed to hurt these blue-eyed people, nothing but himself; he knew that much. All he'd ever done was give them life and drag them down. He was a Jonah to them, an evil charm.

Preston's newspaper pennies lay cold against his thigh, rubbing through the thin pocket. He stuck his hand inside, jingling them to a sleigh-bell sound, nervously, yet with a sense of power. Doc heard the noise and knew the lure, always following the jingling sound of money like a donkey after carrots.

"I got nothing to take home tonight," Doc said.

"I got something. We'll get by."

"Sold your papers, did you?"

"Yes, sir. Sold them all." Once again the jingle. The thought went through Doc's head: Just knock him down and take it. He raised his hand against those big blue eyes, saw them closing, bleeding, falling, saw himself tearing off down the street with a child's pennies that would have fed his house tonight. He lowered his arm, half smiling in the street light's glow for the big, blue, all-seeing eyes.

Doc made a fist, the cold going through his hand in splinters, rubbed a stubble of his bony chin, and decided it was time to leave for points unknown — a place where those like him could go and stay and forget what had gone before; a regular place for irregular people. The thought was the first nice thing that had happened to him all day.

"Let's go home, Daddy."

"You've got that manly knack, don't you, son."

"Sir . . . ?"

"A manly knack. It's the thing to have. Make good use of it."

Doc turned and limped out of the street light's reach.

"When you coming home?" Preston was almost crying, but he managed to control it. The tears would freeze.

The corner was before Doc. If he could make it there, he could get away; no looking back — he could turn to salt that way. What's wrong with salt? he thought. He turned. Preston stood his ground. He was manly.

"When you coming home?"

It came again. Doc heard the voice almost break, then reached out and ground his knuckles down the granite

26

building's heartless edge. He could take that pain all day.

"Bye and bye," Doc said. "Bye and bye."

It was so easy. Two halting steps and he was forever out of the line of their blue-eyed vision.

Melba never gave up. "He'll come back," he said. "Things will get better and he'll come back. He's loved here, and you always go where you are loved." It became her faith, so strong that she gradually faded into it like the lace and satin sachets she hoarded beneath her pillows, a gentle sweetness on the air. She spoke frequently of love, structuring for herself a gingerbread palace where they lived on goodness. Soon after Doc left, she modestly delivered her final child, a boy named Jimmy after a long-ago baker who handed out sweets to her in the childhood to which she rapidly returned, the promise of her life run out at thirty-three. From then on she divided her time between the porch swing and the sweet-smelling bedroom.

Chapter 1

He called it The Melba. To the twenty-seven-year-old Preston it was as beautiful as she had been in the crystal moment of his childhood when she was all the world could offer. Melba. It was a magic name.

He had decorated the place with Sarah's help. She in turn had been inspired by engravings in history books she had read. If there had been choices in her life, she would have liked teaching history, where things were safe and frozen. She had grown to love the speed with which eons had passed.

* * *

Doc's departure had taken the sweet out of Sarah's sixteen. She had ended her

28

schooling and run the house. She was an excellent student, but there were unquestioned duties, and sixteen was the magic age when truant officers ceased to be a threat. So she ran the house off the paper-boy earnings of Preston, eleven, and the shoeshine money of Royal, nine.

It was Sarah who started the fiction that Doc had wandered back to Tarpon Springs and was sending them money. Though the three younger girls were small, they were not without their instincts, turning it into playground gossip, where it was dropped, picked up, and carried to other homes and believed as truth by those who knew the value of the word overheard.

Then there were the ones, mostly black, who knew the truth, divined it, for they held on from hand to mouth themselves, had their men disappear from hopelessness or hope. It was the same. The women had to stick it out, earthbound by children — except for those like Melba who at once stayed on the earth and left it.

* * *

There were several civilizations represented in The Melba Cafeteria. An enormous Grecian fountain dominated the room. The man who sold it to them said it had been modeled after one that was thousands of years old and only recently come to light, preserved by one of those lava flows that seem to close the pages of time like sealing wax. Preston had wanted a white marble floor like the one that had been danced on in a picture show he had seen, but he settled for linoleum. The tables were black, like the chairs that went with them. Both stood on gilded legs. The customer lines were on either side of the room, and on one side stretched a continuous black leather couch. It curved at either end, and gave great flourish to the room.

DINE DELIGHTED OR YOU DINE FREE. Preston's motto was lettered in gilt near the revolving door opposite the huge Toledo scale, YOUR WEIGHT FREE. He hoped that soon the tradition in Atlanta would be "Meet me at The Melba by the scale."

Ferns hung from the ceiling. No place else had that, though Preston could have done without them. He hated the idea of fronds falling into food. Still, they were lovely reflected in the mirrors that hung floor to ceiling on either side of the room, interspersed with reproduced works of art. It was beautiful. It never failed to take his breath away, though things had been in place for only a week, with the opening tomorrow, June 14, 1937. The date sang in his head. He would be established as an Owner. From B.C. to A.D.

It occasionally dawned on Preston, with more of a pang each time, that he would not be the lone, undisputed owner of The Melba. He had backers, three of them, who, as backers are prone to be, were in late middle age and had unyielding philosophies of their own. At one time or another Preston had worked for and been taken advantage of by each of them. P. W. Waller he had worked for first and longest, beginning on the sly in the stockroom of Waller's Haberdashery when he could still be categorized as child labor. But he had made his way to a tie-wearing job at the front of the store, and eventually became its manager. He had moonlighted as night manager for Mr. Hildebrand, who ran the Red Wing Roller Rink. Hildebrand had dabbled in many things; Preston admired him as much for his Shriner's pins and fraternal rings as he did for his business success. Rasnake was the third and most recent of his former employers, owner of Rasnake's Fine Foods, an operation Preston had entered on the ground floor. Preston had learned the food business as he had learned everything else — the hard way. He believed hard work paid off. It was the only thing he had ever heard that made total sense. Now hard work seemed to be starting the long-awaited payoff. The three men he had worked for had invested in him.

It was Rasnake who unearthed the organ. Preston thought it shabby, but the carpenter put it in an empty space, built a shelf over it, and added a display of ceramic food. If it wasn't quite artistic, it looked delicious.

The serving lines shone with newness.

The kitchen was inviolate. The pantries were cleaned and painted, as were the storage rooms and restrooms. It was his moment of extravagance. It was his. And Waller's. And Rasnake's. And Hildebrand's. And the bank's.

"We think you went a little overboard in the decoration department," said Waller as he, Hildebrand, and Rasnake gave the place a final inspection on that balmy Sunday night before its Grand Opening. Preston's heart would have opened The Melba with a brass band, but his mind had a say in it and opted for a humble Monday. There was no need to go highfalutin on people.

"You can't serve mirrors," Rasnake said.

"Not that it's not fine-looking," Hildebrand said. "But it's a bit . . ." His hand drew spirals in air, indicating that he had no useless knowledge of decor. "You got that money where it's not doing a bit of good."

It was the first time Preston had hated them. Here they had made him one of them by their investment; now they were taking it back, hacking at his world, seeing dollars and cents, oblivious to beauty. He had been good with their money, too, sparing of it because it wasn't his. That was his own hard-earned money on the walls and hanging from the ceiling.

"I beg your pardon," he said, "but that's my money you're looking at. I used my savings. I figure it'll give folks something to look at and talk about while they're eating."

He said it earnestly but firmly. He was still a bit hot around the eyes when his partners smiled at him, shook his hand, and patted him on the back, heading toward the revolving door. They made chuckling references to tomorrow being the "big day," and Preston found he suddenly loved them again for giving reality to his hopes.

"One thing about investing in a cafeteria," Waller said as the four of them stood on the street in the heavy summer night, "we always know where to go to get a free meal."

They laughed appropriately, and Preston watched them walk away. He stepped back to the curb and looked up. THE MELBA — jeweled in big blue neon letters outlined in dancing golden stardust. It made his head spin around as neatly as the revolving door spun him back inside.

Scoe had set up the easels of flowers that had been sent.

* * *

In those first hard days after Doc disappeared, Bessie Loomis had sent Scoe, reluctant, timid, half angry, down to the Vacalis house with a scrawny, naked chicken she had wrung. He held the bird by the loose skin that had covered its neck, keeping it barely above the hard dirt road, dragging an instant here and there to show he wasn't afraid to do it.

Preston had seen Scoe coming, and waited until he climbed the steps, then opened the door, giving a look as hostile as that he received.

"What you want?"

They faced each other in the cold. "My mama Miss Bessie Loomis. She know yo' mama. She know you."

"I know her. Know you, too."

"Hello, then."

"Hello."

"She sendin' y'all this chicken."

"What for?"

"Say y'all needy."

It wasn't the truth that had hurt him. It was the idea that others knew it. He and Sarah had made a world for Melba and the children in which they were not poor, just hard-working and economical. They believed this themselves from time to time, wanting it, willing it, waiting for it to be.

"We ain't needy from niggers."

"This chicken as white as you is."

It would feed them. Sarah would stew it in a pot, and they could get by two days if you counted the broth. But Preston was imprisoned by his pride.

"Just leave it there," he said, nodding to the planked porch floor.

"I ain't leavin' it there for some dog to get. If I'm gon' leave it, you got to take it." He shook his head at the sense white folks were without. How did they get to be white if they were so dumb?

Preston extended his hand and took the

chicken. That's how easy it was, and how hard. "Thank you" wouldn't come.

"Maybe I'll see you sometime," he managed as Scoe started down the steps.

"Maybe so," said Scoe. He went across the yard and down the road.

Preston stood on the porch and held the chicken. Behind him in the house were the noises of children fretful with evening, about to be tucked away by Sarah, who was calming them with promises of Melba's good-night kiss. When I am grown, Preston thought, I will live alone where it is quiet. I will have a bed to myself, and a big clock that chimes. He looked down at the chicken. It was greater than all his wishes. He went inside.

* * *

Sarah came out of the kitchen carrying a bouquet of flowers which she set on the canopied cashier's booth that was to be occupied by Miss Fan, a bottle-blonde, kewpie doll lady whose voice was firmly nestled in her nose. Miss Fan had been at Waller's Haberdashery when Preston started there, and though her voice never failed to set his teeth grinding, he had found a place for her in his jobs since. She was one of those people who had probably been born middle-aged and powdered. If he had passed her on the street, he would have thought her funny-looking, but right from the start she had been one of his people, and where he went he took her.

Sarah smiled at Preston and held up two pairs of crossed fingers.

"Watch out we don't get double-crossed," he said.

She quickly put one hand behind her back, as if to annul any omens. She was in her thirties now, but she had already lost her chance to bloom. She had been too busy at the time to notice, had set aside expectations until she could spare the time, but now that she had the time for time, time had no time for her.

There was a card on the flowers. She opened it, gave a little start, then covered it with a smile. The flowers were from Robert Pascal, who sold fine jams and jellies. Were there any other kinds?

At about the time the girls were marrying off and Jimmy was going away to school, Preston had thought to introduce her to Robert Pascal. She was always amused at Preston's idea of matchmaking. It had nothing to do with suitability. It was primarily based on availability, like a farmer corralling a cow and a bull. Any old cow and any old bull. No wonder Preston was a devout bachelor. He refused to see the inside of things. Surfaces seemed to be enough for him.

Preston looked around the flowered, spotless room. "Let's have a toast," he said.

Sarah smiled in surprise. Her brother was no drinker.

"I don't want anybody to get the idea I'd serve liquor, but got a little stock for whenever my partners or anybody that's somebody comes in. I put it in the cream pitcher. They can put it in their coffee cups and nobody'll be any the wiser. They used to do it in speakeasies."

"That's the cleverest thing I ever heard of."

He poured brandy into two coffee cups. "If this place is the success I think it's going to be, I'm going to buy us a house. Maybe across town in Buckhead. Then you could start cooking Sunday dinner and everybody would come."

They regarded each other nervously, neither equipped for intimate moments.

"Mama would be so proud," Sarah said. "She worked hard all her life, and now she's got a cafeteria named for her. If only the dead could come back from time to time and see how things turned out."

"The Melba Cafeteria," she said, lifting his cup with a jaunty slosh.

"The Melba Cafeteria."

It was toasted. Opened. Successful.

The days unraveled like gold thread. He was up before dawn for each of them, watching them begin and watching them end, a steward for the sun. There were thirty people who worked for him: cooks, counter girls, waitresses, busboys, dishwashers, Scoe, and Miss Fan. A time clock was installed, more for their benefit than his, he told them, though overtime pay was not yet in the scheme of things.

The Melba opened for breakfast at seven, its gears shifting into lunch a little after ten, though if you were keeping bankers' hours and straggled in before the eleven-thirty rush, Mattie or Sadie or Elvira or one of the counter girls would scramble you some eggs on the clean-scraped grill behind the counter. The rush eased off by two o'clock, everybody tired but exhilarated at having fed nearly twelve hundred people. The lines closed down at three, when the cooks, who had been there since before six, went home. Miss Fan had her final money tally in by three thirty. By five the kitchen gleamed as though it had never been put to use. By six the chairs had been upturned on table tops and the floor was mopped mirror-smooth, the ferns that hung above it given back like phantom stalagmites. By six thirty Preston had examined the work for shiftlessness and told the boys whether they could go home or had to do something over and this time do it right. Then Scoe would pop his head around a corner or out of a door to see if Preston needed anything else. By seven the place was Preston's again. That was when he did the books, checked the larder, and made out the orders, sitting alone on the huge leather couch, surveying his domain. He never tired of it.

They put his picture in the very paper he used to sell. "An innovation in dining," they called it. Sarah had it framed. They were going into profits, too, not enormous ones, but a steady trickle that would allow him to buy his partners out, perhaps within five years. That was his goal. By 1942 it would be all his.

Sometimes he felt like dancing in the night; once he took some stumbling steps when he was alone and the lights were out. Then the thought came to him: He would use his skates. He could get back to the pantries quicker for his countless nightly inventories. So Preston went back to skating.

* * *

He remembered when he had first found the Red Wing Roller Rink. It had been an airplane hangar till complaints zoned it obsolete. Then Hildebrand had planked the flat earth floor, had it planed smooth, sheathed it, stocked a slew of skates, picked up some recorded waltzes cheap, and opened up for business under the sign of a continually flapping neon wing.

It was 1929, and Preston was nineteen and work was all he had ever known. He spent long days managing Waller's Haberdashery, and nights were spent studying for a mail-order high-school diploma. Then he had it, and found himself at the tip of loneliness.

The Red Wing was a foolish place, he thought, evil with wasted time, but one of the memories of his childhood was of children whizzing by on their skates while he lugged either a shoeshine box or a bundle of papers. So he paid a dime at the door and a dime for the skates and off he went, his mouth flying open in surprise at his own velocity.

Preston had always looked on his body as a vehicle to get him where he was going. Now he found that his body was doing things he had never imagined. He moved, one foot after the other, with grace, passing everyone on the floor, negotiating turns effortlessly, the spinning wheels a part of him as though they had been waiting to turn his tread to dancing.

There was a manager in the center of the floor, a young man, graceful, too, and full of pride with it, a chained whistle around his neck. Preston watched him, picked up his movements, shifts in weight, glides and turns; he took them on and made them effortlessly.

His opened mouth turned to a smile. He had never received this much pleasure from himself. Preston was a virgin still to all except his wicked hand.

He found himself in the center of the rink, receiving the notice of the man with the whistle, who decided that fancier footwork was needed to put the newcomer in his place. "Roses from the South" was playing, as scratchy as the metal wheels against the hardwood floor. Other skaters began to stop, the music growing louder as the jostling, falling, laughing ceased and the metal-on-wood whirr was reduced to the sixteen wheels of the two moving men.

It became a competition, the manager carelessly executing figure eights, frontward and backward, Preston following, making each movement a little faster, giving his moves an edge and a flourish. He did not notice the staring crowd. His vision was blurred, yet nothing had ever been so clear to him as the movements that he made.

The record stuck. The table on which the victrola sat was kicked by Margaret Whitehead, twenty-five, big-busted, generously hipped. She handled the concession stand, her cola-sticky fingers going to her big pink mouth in humble ecstasy as she watched the men glide by. She dreamed of pencil-hipped men with pile-driving asses who would come and rescue her from the world of Baby Ruths and Almond Joys, or at the very least make it more bearable. And there were two in front of her, the essence of her dreams.

She wore no skates, flatfooted as she was, and trudged the fifty feet to Hildebrand's office, where he sat deep in the favorite pastime of his ledgers.

"There's a guy out on the floor," she said, "skating good as Tom. Maybe he'd take the night shift if you asked him."

Hildebrand could never remember her face, just the icecream mounds of her breasts. He liked big women, and they usually liked him — that was how this one had gotten her job — but she was not fulfilling for him, with her icy ways and lofty airs. "What's that you say?" He spoke gruffy to put her in her place.

"Somebody out there can skate. Maybe he can take Tom's place."

So Preston could and did: four nights a week that ended his aloneness, gave him money for the time he spent, and brought him for the first time within range of love.

The Red Wing was open Wednesday nights through Saturday nights. Preston cordoned off an edge of the rink as a bullpen for kids; he was good with them, knowing how to make them behave without tears and screaming, letting them out onto the big floor when they could hold their own. He didn't mind the counter work, either, making change and keeping records so perfectly as to make

Hildebrand think that all his other workers had cheated him. Gradually Hildebrand left the place to him at night.

And Margaret longed for Preston. She, who had never come to work on time, showed up early and stayed late, watching with joy as, on skates, he swept the rink with a pushbroom. He was her figure of romance.

At first he did not suspect the passions he aroused in her, did not know that the odors of his sweat when nights were hot and busy could drive her to rubbing herself in tender places as she foraged among the ice blocks with a pick, making snow cones. He was more intent on watching Hildebrand, for he was a Shriner, a man of the world, a joiner of clubs, an attender of football games, fifty-yard-line seats and out-of-town trips with wagered money, a man with a fur collar on his coat and a master key to the good life when the demon Depression had most everybody else down and out. Hildebrand's life was flint to Preston's stone. He was no longer thankful just to hang on, secure in obscurity. He wanted a "Mister" to his name from neighbors he would have calling from across their gardens, smiling, keeping their distance respectfully, which was more than he could say for Margaret Whitehead, bumping up against him now behind the counter as he loaded ice into the cooler.

"Gimme a little room, willya?"

"I'll give you all I got." She giggled.

He looked up, startled. The place was closed, the evening opening an hour away.

He had been drinking a NuGrape. He licked a purple lip, then bent again to the cooler, and she pressed herself against his butt as though their equipment were reversed. The touch of her seeped into him. His brother Royal was the ladies' man, not him. He sometimes saw where lips had been along the collars of Royal's shirts, and though he said nothing, the thoughts were there. The hot summer streets were full of bare-armed girls who dawdled outside Waller's Haberdashery windows and gave him one-syllable thoughts that had to do with lust, though his face was waxen-calm, like the window dummies he undressed. But Preston's dreams were alabaster, and Margaret was the all-too-solid flesh.

He plunged past her, destined for the attic fans, which were slow to cool. He climbed the ladder. Margaret waited a moment, then started after him.

The attic was a furnace, holding the heat the tin roof gave it during the day. Preston shed his shirt, laid it at the ladder's top, and began wiping the week's accumulation of dust and grime from the blades of the giant fans. There were three of them. It was a job he hated doing, wouldn't do when his dreams took life, when he found the job he was looking for.

Margaret heaved herself to the top of the ladder and gripped it, gasping for a moment.

He had not heard her. One of the fans was already on, causing a draft that was rapidly drying the sweat that had poured out of him. She blew on his neck, and her breasts swayed near his back where clinging drops of sweat were about to shiver into air. He swatted, suspecting a gnat, connected with flesh, and almost fell into the fan.

"What the hell!" he yelled, turning, eyes fired.

She took his grease-smeared hand, placed it on her breast, closed her eyes. The hand withdrew; its greasy prints remained.

"Margaret, I think the heat has got the best of you."

"It's not the heat that's got the best of me."

Then he looked at her. The world to Preston had been like the inside of a watch, just moving things doing their assigned tasks. Dreams were things that didn't happen, and he had sent them all his longings. Now one of his oldest longings had winged back to him.

"I'd like to walk you home . . . one night."

"Tonight's a night."

"I have to talk to Mr. Hildebrand first."

"I'll wait outside and cool off." She was all modesty with him now, smiling in that forgetful way women have when things are settled to their satisfaction. They went down the ladder.

At first the night wore on endlessly, eleven o'clock too far away to count on. Then in came his brother Royal, drunk with the kind of reckless confidence that comes of having too little of it sober. He was holding a beer and a girl, someone pretty in a summery way, with blondish, marcelled hair. There was a quality of morning about her, something fresh that expected or hoped for the best. She wore an elaborately knitted sweater in the colors of sunrise. Preston noticed all of this, though he was not a person who noticed people who entered his life on somebody else's arm. After tonight he would forget her until the time that she came back and made sure he never did.

She was laughing. Drunk or sober, Royal had charm. Charm, to Preston's way of thinking, was not an integral ingredient for anything. Royal was his brother, and he loved and hated him with the same ferocity. He was a bit over a year younger than Preston, and they couldn't have been more opposite. In their early, hungry years, when Preston had handed down his shoeshine box to him,

51

the seven-year-old had objected. "It's heavy," he had said. "I don't like it."

"You like to eat, don't you?" came Preston's reply.

And that was the difference between them — Preston had encountered grim reality.

Preston regarded his brother. Royal had been in drinking a time or two before, had probably been everywhere that way. Usually he skated himself sober, but of all nights to come in here three sheets to the wind! Well, maybe he'd just skate and that was all.

"Hi ho, Presto," Royal said, looking away an instant as the girl saw someone she knew and went to say a word. "Can we get some skates?" He meant free.

Even if Hildebrand knew he was letting his brother and a date in free, he wouldn't care, but it made Preston feel furtive, as if he were giving away something that wasn't his to give. Still, the money Royal would save by coming in free would leave a little more that he could help out with at home.

Preston set the skates on the counter. Royal wore a nine and a half. He judged the girl to be a five. "Girl friend or friend girl?"

"Hoping for the best," said Royal, taking the skates and going toward her. Royal approached people his own age so easily. To Preston there were three kinds of people: employers, employees, and customers. To Preston the Promised Land was where people moved as equals, falling in and out of love or simply knowing each other, learning the way that people are.

Jimmy Newton skated up. He was one of those boys who hung around and seemed to know people. Preston thought of him as a leaner, because he was forever slumped against something — the wall outside Mundy's Drug store, the bicycle rack outside the Temple Theater, and now here against the counter, reaching over in a too-familiar way, taking a wrench and tightening a skate just as Royal came back.

"How ya doin', Royal. Sorry to hear about today," Jimmy said.

Royal's thin, beery smile slid away, replaced by guilt.

"Hear what?" Preston knew it

was the worst.

Royal held on the counter, pulling himself back and forth on the skates. "My career as a telephone lineman came to an end this afternoon." Royal shrugged as if it were of no consequence, ran a hand through his long hair, then shook his head as though that would clear his field of vision. He was like Doc, from profile to propensities. He looked back toward the girl, who was making her way toward them slowly and gigglingly, unused to wheels beneath her but determined to conquer.

It was all that Preston could do to keep from grabbing his brother by the collar. Instead, he slammed a pair of skates into a rack, looked grimly at Royal, and demanded, "What happened?"

It was the tone that set Royal off. "What is this? Confession? Forgive me, Father Vacalis, for I have sinned. I got tired of their guff, so I told them what they could do with their goddamn telephone lines. By the spool."

"When you work for somebody you have to do what they tell you with no back talk.''

The girl's name was Palmetto. She had been born charming and raised polite. She came skating up, prepared to be both. She was smiling.

''Yeah?'' Royal was sneering. ''I've had it with 'Yes, sir' and 'No, sir.' I'm through dancing to somebody else's tune, and that includes yours.''

''You're not through eating, are you? There are some things that don't change. We got responsibilities.''

Palmetto held on to her smile with the same desperation with which she held on to the counter.

Royal and Preston stood looking at each other, hating each other as only brothers can. ''You're looking at somebody who's about to make a big change,'' Royal said. ''A big one! You have such a good time being the family martyr that I don't think you could ever be anything else . . . or even want to!''

It was as though he was telling Preston he was doomed to begin with, sneering at the very dreams that had kept him plodding along when plodding along was the best that he could do. Preston felt that he was being jeered at. Royal's words were hammering him into the ground. But his life had to change, too. He had to do things he had never done.

That was why he grabbed Royal's collar and lifted him onto the counter, slugging him methodically, the way he did everything.

Royal's initial astonishment quickly faded, and he fought back, getting a hold on Preston's belt and yanking him up onto the counter, where they rolled an instant like a couple of beached fish. "The Merry Widow Waltz" was playing, and they struggled in time to it.

Margaret Whitehead saw what was going on and pushed the buzzer that set off an alarm in Hildebrand's office; it was to guard against young toughs who hung around. Hildebrand had a baseball bat on a chain that he thought would disperse a crowd. It had never been put to use. Margaret grabbed a couple of empty NuGrape bottles and chucked them toward the point of action.

Hildebrand had been dozing in a haze

of cigar smoke. The buzzer almost sent him over backward in the chair, and he rammed against the desk as he rose, overturning the ashtray and sending a dark layer of ash across his neat white ledgers. It took him a moment to put his hand on the chained bat, but he found it and charged out the door, ready to do battle, wondering why the hell the people he paid good money to couldn't take care of it.

Most of the skaters had stopped, watching the silent struggle as the brothers pummeled each other on the counter.

Palmetto had never seen such a thing. "Stop it!" she screamed. "Stop it!" But they went on as though they had never heard her. It reminded her of a moment when she was very young and two of her grandfather's stallions had gone at each other in ferocious battle. "They got to do it," Granddaddy had said. "It's in their nature." All her life she had heard how men had to do what they had to do, as though they were at the mercy of some electrical spark in the universe, while women were to do what was expected of them, neutralized somehow, no spark within them to ignite. Her spark was close to being ignited now.

"Stop it!" she screamed again. 'You damn fools!'' She reached out for the nearest leg she could find and gave it a yank. It yanked back and sent her crashing against the counter on her skates, knocking the wind out of her. She blinked her eyes and moved away, then stopped short, her eyes and mouth going as wide as they ever had. A strong blue strand of her sweater was tangling stubbornly around a skate wheel.

Palmetto was literally coming undressed. Preston and Royal had tumbled off the counter, and they were taking her sweater with them. The entire right arm was unraveled, and she could feel the shoulder loosening. Her face went as red as the thread that was now coming undone. She gave it a tug and tried to break it, but it was strong. "Oh, hell!" she said. If she was going to be humiliated at the roller rink, at least she'd get in a few licks of her own. She jumped into the fray and started pulling hair.

Preston had never been in a fight with anybody. He had never run away from one, but he'd always been smart enough to tiptoe around the edge of a conflict without losing either face or skin. Fighting to him was a waste of time. But somehow slugging Royal was like hitting out at everything that had ever outraged him.

Palmetto had hair in one hand and yarn in the other. The sweater was down around her breasts. She saw that it was Royal's hair she held, and when he turned to look at her, Preston took the instant and knocked him unconscious with a roundhouse right. There was a mild grunt from the crowd, as though something had been taken from it. Hildebrand reached around the counter and started the record over. Most of the skaters resumed their wheeled trudge around the floor.

Palmetto scooped up as much of her yarn as she could reclaim and gave Preston her most irritated gaze. "What you did was wretched," she said, then promptly ignored him as she bent to Royal. There was a cut on his forehead. His eye was going to be black. There was a gush of blood from a split lip.

"Should I get a doctor?" Hildebrand asked.

"I'm a nurse," she said. "Just get me some water and a towel."

Margaret hotfooted over to the concession stand, where she dipped a rag in melted ice.

Preston thought every tooth in his head had been knocked loose, and he figured his jaw was broken, too. He shrugged his shoulders, trying to see if anything was broken there. His nose was bleeding steadily, but he wiped the blood away with the back of his hand. He had won this fight, yet he stood alone, while Royal lay on the floor, no doubt possuming for tender love and care. Margaret was handing the girl a rag, then looking over them to him, sweat glistening on her upper lip.

"Come up into the office," Hildebrand said. "We'll do something about that nosebleed."

Preston sat on a hard chair with his head back. Hildebrand had placed a a gummy piece of brown paper under his upper lip. "Don't know if that'll do any good or not, but my mammy used to do that for me when I had a nosebleed."

"I appreciate it," Preston said, sitting up. He held his hand under his nose to see if there would be a drip, but none came. He started to spit out the paper.

"Leave it under there a minute. I think something in it must get into the bloodstream. A chemical or something."

"I'm sorry about the fight. I never got into nothing like that before. If you want me to quit, I'll understand."

"Quit? What in hell are you talking about, boy? That fight didn't hurt nobody 'cept you and your brother — mainly your brother."

"Yes, sir. I better check on how he is."

"That little gal he was with took him out. Hell, Preston, don't let it worry you. If I had a nickel for every time I busted up one of my brothers, or got busted up, this would be the Red Wing Auditorium instead of just a roller rink."

"I appreciate it. It won't happen again."

"Don't worry. Don't worry. I'm glad to know you can take care of yourself. Makes me feel safer." He reached into his desk and pulled out a pint bottle that bore no label. "Strictly medicinal. Not often you can say that and mean it." He handed the bottle to Preston, who hesitated, removed the cap, and drank bitterly, still swallowing after there was nothing left to swallow.

"I'm not too much of a drinker."

"Takes practice."

They stared at each other for a moment. Preston smiled, feeling foolish with the paper still against his upper gum now tasting darkly of liquor. He started to speak, but the paper got caught in his lips, and he had to reach up and take it out.

"Mr. Hildebrand . . ."

"That's what they call me."

"Well, sir . . . I'm looking to find out about a position I hear has opened up, and I was hoping . . . at least I thought I'd ask . . . if you knew anything about it." The man wasn't giving him any help. He just sat there staring straight at him. "It's with Rasnake's Fine Foods."

Scoe had told him about it. A wholesale chain that sold to restaurants was opening a branch in town. "Going into competition" was the way Scoe had put it. And that's what Preston felt he was ready to do. He had been feeling like a helium balloon knocking against a ceiling. He had to make that ceiling give before he lost his push.

"Hell. I know Snake. Known him for years. What do you want? A good word?"

"Yes, sir. I'd appreciate it."

"Shit, if there's a job you've as good as got it. Old Waller going to lose you, eh?"

"I figure I've gone about as far as I can go in the haberdashery line, but I haven't said anything to him about it yet."

"I won't give you away, son. Anybody who can fight like you did tonight can get ahead in the world. And you sure don't belong behind some counter selling clothes, or renting skates either, for that matter, though I'll hate to lose you."

He produced another pint bottle, and they took another swig. This time Preston held his eyes open and willed them not to run. That was the way men of the world did it. But it burned like hell all the way down.

The rink was empty when he came out, no sign of Royal or the girl. He began turning the switches that put the place to sleep. There was a final shoosh as the fans went off; then one by one the fluorescent lights went out, until the only light in the place came from beneath the closed door to Hildebrand's office.

Then Margaret was silently beside him, her insistent scent burning through him the way the whiskey had. His eyes were getting used to the darkness, and her face was the first thing to come out of it. There was so much in his head he had to say, but his chest was full with something else, and he couldn't breathe and talk too. She seemed to understand. Perhaps it was that way with her. She blended next to him.

They walked down Confederate Avenue, chaperoned by street lights. Ahead of them lay darkness when light and pavement both ran out. Though her hand was in his arm's crook, earthbound Margaret seemed far way. He had counted the street lights. Eight were left.

He mentioned to her the course he was taking at the Harold Howe Correspondence School of Law. He wouldn't actually be able to practice law from it, but a graduation certificate would credit him with a year of law school. There were seven street lights left.

He thought of his virgin days. He had never thought of them at all, since they were all he had; now suddenly there would be a dividing line in his life. He knew that Royal carried rubbers; he had scorned them as a waste of money. What if she got pregnant? What if she already was, and wanting to put the blame on him? He thought of leaving her then and running, but he saw the heave of her anxious breasts. They seemed to need him as much as he did them. Six to go.

He thought of his sisters — not Sarah, but the little ones. But they were not like Margaret. They were only like themselves, sweetly innocent, exempt from desire. It made him feel ashamed. That's what he needed now. He needed sin to save him when it could, not damn him when the dirty deed was done. She touched his arm and smiled. Her eyes were dark and gave the street lights back to him, all five.

He wanted her naked, not even air between them. His clothes were heavy on him: coat, tie, shirt, undershirt, pants, shorts, shoes, socks, and garters. Here it was mid-summer, and him bundled like a nun. Her dress was sheer. It showed her every move. He wanted to run his hand between her legs before she took her clothes off, wanted his hand to go into darkness at her knees and feel her secrets before he saw them. He imagined her touch. He wanted her to be smooth as she opened to him. He had to slow his pace a bit as the thought ran through him. He'd lived too long on little things. Four left.

He had once read a filthy book, something Royal had. It showed some popular cartoon characters gleefully involved in the most enjoyable of the seven deadly sins. One of the naked women kept pushing herself against the constantly erect men, saying, "Drop it in the slot." What if that was all it was? Just a drop in the slot like a bottomless coin changer needing a busload to fill itself up? He could fill her up. He could! His head was feeling light, all the blood from it having rushed into his cock. The three lights left were shining brightly, encircled by moths.

What if she changed her mind? Women did that. Then a story Sarah had told him came back. It was something he had not wanted to hear, something he had yelled at her about before stalking away. It was a story Melba had confided about Doc and a street car and a field of dandelions. There were dandelions where they were going. He was his father's son. Two shining, pointed lights were left. Margaret's breasts were just the same.

The final house had long gone by. The night was filled with crickets. Buttermilk Bottom stretched before them. He almost laughed. Here he was at the jumping-off place of his life, and he was tickled. What a fool he was. Who would have thought a silver moon could send down all that heat? He'd have spit if he could, but there was nothing there, just the dusty taste of bourbon and the bitterness the paper had left. Then he saw her bobbing breasts and knew that the saltiness of her flesh would start his juices running, too. There was a single street light, hard and glowing, pointed upward.

He twined his fingers within hers, pulling her along. They raced for the darkness of the field. The street lights ended, and the night began.

Chapter 2

Preston couldn't pinpoint when the tie-chewing had begun. He certainly hadn't done it in his haberdashery days, and on roller-rink nights he had kept his tie tucked into his shirt, military style. He had been open-collared most of his time at Rasnake's. It must have started in the nights when he hunched over his ledgers at The Melba. Sarah once asked how his ties got so chewed up, but he said nothing. He wondered if he was addicted to some chemical in the dye.

He and Sarah found a house on Howell Mill Road. It was ten years old and had eight rooms. They were awed by its vastness and the solid construction of its walls. They had spent their lives listening to other people's private noises. Now the lack of them was deafening. Sarah developed the habit of grunting to herself as she roamed the rooms, needing a noise to get by on.

Sarah went to Biggs and bought a few fine pieces that Preston stormed about, but she had her few little dreams, too, and some of them were mahogany. There was a highboy, and a dining-room set that was fit for anybody. She polished it every week and wiped it every day. Sooner or later she wanted a chandelier that could look at itself in the table. Every time she polished the table she thought of Robert Pascal, who had been so clean that he had reminded her of a piece of furniture.

He was shorter than she was, and had chubby, cherubic cheeks. His hands were in better shape than hers, manicured nails with glistening half-moons. His shoes were blindingly shined, and his suit was creased and pressed in all the right places. He looked as though he had stepped out of a magazine ad, except that he was too much of a dumpling and the men in magazines ran more to steak.

On their only date he had taken her to a fish place out on the Macon Highway. It was a place where everybody went, and she was excited about it. Her three sisters had come over to help her get ready — it seemed to be an event. She had laughed and protested and loved it. She had felt so much for others in her life that to feel for herself seemed unnatural.

They had eaten catfish, pulling out the bones with their fingers. There were hush puppies, french fries, and apple pie. He had brought a bottle in a paper sack, and they had setups. The restaurant was brightly lit, and the only place she had ever been that was louder was to a parade. Her hands got greasy and her bladder was about to pop, but she hated like anything to use a public restroom. The places were rife with disease, and there were some women in the restaurant she would certainly have hated to have to follow to the commode. But finally it was that or let the dam burst.

The pine-paneled restroom was cold and reeked of Airwick. She went into a booth, hiked up her dress, pulled her britches down around her knees, and squatted several inches above the seat. She was very careful not to touch anything, but just as her stream began, she swayed uncertainly on her new slingbacks. She caught herself on the side of the booth, but dropped her skirt in the process. Unfortunately, the stream continued, and she peed all over the back of her dress.

If she could have chosen a moment to die, it would have been then. She took the dress off and rubbed it and blew on it, but it was a silk dress, and it was hard to hide pee on silk. When she couldn't stay in the booth any longer, she set a pleasant expression on her face, went back to the table, and sat down. The dress was still wet.

Robert Pascal remarked that the onions in the hush puppies sometimes acted up on him, too. She kept her smile but was mightily offended. If she ever had a romance, she wanted it to be like the ones in the magazines, where you didn't pee on the back of your dress and onions didn't act up on your date.

Later, when he called, she told him she was busy. Strangely enough, she liked him over the telephone, and several times a year they would have long conversations in which she laughed a lot.

The others were curious at first, but gradually it died.

The only thing Preston ever said about it was "You missed a good catch."

"I wasn't fishing," she replied.

So Sarah had settled into primness and developed a slight catch in her voice, as though trembling on the verge of something, blaming it on allergy when anyone asked, but knowing it was something else, some cry within that never got cried.

They joined the First Methodist Church on Peachtree Street. Mr. Waller went there. The Sunday school was filled with businessmen who welcomed Preston, made him feel he honored them. He joined the Lions Club. Could the Shriners be far behind?

It was through Sunday school that he came by Drew Whitnall, an energetic man with a face full of broken veins who played the organ. He was in his fifties, with eyes so watery blue they threatened to run down his face. He was a reformed drunk. He proudly proclaimed it, turning it into his greatest accomplishment, though the telling was stronger than the actuality. For a pittance and his food, Drew played the lunch-time organ at The Melba. If Preston never saw God, he came as close as anyone had a right to, standing behind his stainless-steel counter at the height of the lunch rush amid the clockwork clatter of his workers and the hungry buzz of his customers, listening to a Romberg organ serenade piped over seven speakers. "Golden Days" was his favorite selection. He was in them.

There were, however, some warts upon these days. People never did exactly as he meant them to. If customers were always right, someone had to be wrong. That's where his employees crossed his path. They weren't as much in love with the place as he, were mysteriously unfulfilled, spent their nights doing God knew what. Sometimes the phone began to ring as he got up at five: He'd have to stop by the jail to bail out a cook or a busboy. The Melba was closed on Sunday, and at first he paid off on Saturday night and spent Monday morning bringing them, bleary-eyed, from jail to work. Was everybody crazy but him? Did he have to tell them how to live as well as how to work? He supposed he did. Since he had accumulated a store of wisdom, he saw no sense in not sharing it at length. He also changed payday to Monday. There was less temptation then.

If perfect love didn't flow between him and his employees, a great deal of respect somehow did. The Melba was much more his life than theirs. They became his family, to be fought with, abused, and helped in the way of families. He concerned himself with their sick and their dying as well as their happinesses. He learned to deal with their creditors and the sneaky arms of law that had to do with non-support.

Nearly all the faces in his employ were black, but neither he nor they found it unusual. A labor force had to be some color. They had been raised to serve, to stand and wait. Just because slavery was long dead did not mean that servitude had ceased.

They laughed a lot. He envied that. He had never found much to laugh at in the world. Life was a serious business to him, annoyingly full of worthless distractions. For instance, there were the girls who came through the lines, gently pushing their trays, eyeing him with ripe smiles across the steam tables. They were bare-armed, like the girls he had dreamed of. Now they seemed to want him. "Hello, Mr. Vacalis," they would say, putting twists into the syllables of his name, pouting with him sometimes or coyly pausing with breasts that gently heaved above crisp fried chicken and Sadie's famous chess pie. He smiled at them, forced himself to learn a line of chatter. They were customers, after all.

But in late afternoons, when the tables were only sparsely filled with regulars — businessmen with the luxury of a rest and trusted, dimpled secretaries allowed to run errands — Preston would come through the kitchen's swinging doors carrying a round tray full of hot sugared biscuits with butter sliding down them. Drew always played "I'm a Ding Dong Daddy from Dumas" with just the slightest bit of fanfare as the doors swung open. It was getting to be a tradition, and it wasn't cheap, either, but it pleased Preston as much as it did the customers, and he caught himself smiling too much above the scented smoke of the biscuits.

Some of the girls started calling him the Ding Dong Daddy from Dumas, with an emphasis on the "Ding Dong." They were brazen, these working girls, looking right at him when they said it, flicking their pink tongues against white teeth that often had traces of lipstick on them. Preston could stare them down; he had developed what he liked to think of as a smoldering look. But he was under control in that department. Sarah kept his home for him, and he was satisfied with that. They were as used to each other as a pair of well-worn shoes. There was no need for any change.

Preston had had his fill of changes — from having a daddy to having none; from shining shoes to sweeping alleys; from Waller's Haberdashery to Hildebrand's Red Wing Roller Rink; from

Rasnake's Fine Foods to The Melba Cafeteria. He had a house now, and he had a way of life. He wanted to stay where he was. Like a tree, he would grow in place. He always wanted to see the same man when he looked in the mirror.

He never allowed himself to be clouded with views of why he was the way he was or thought the way he thought. He was as he was, and other people had their quirks and their own ways whether it suited him or not.

* * *

Take for instance, Royal. A fight was a fight. It had long built between them, and Preston was sorry it had to happen. He liked to express his emotions in private, as though they were somehow related to the bowels. But when things were over and done with, they were over and done with. Preston could build and explode, but grudges weren't for him — except for Doc, but that was a special one that grew harder with time. Royal, on the other hand, had reacted to the fight at the roller rink in an unexpected way: He had disappeared that night in 1929. Eight years ago.

While Preston had been plowing up half of Buttermilk Bottom with Margaret, Royal had gone home, packed up, looked in on the sleeping Melba, kissed the rest, and told Sarah he was off to see the world Sarah had cried half the night, but dried her eyes and made the coffee for Preston when he finally dragged in as the sun was about to rise. He looked like Doc to her that morning, but she didn't tell him, only knew that he was his father's son and hoped that whatever had happened hadn't changed him and left them to put their load on little Jimmy. Sarah had never worked except around the house. She could have managed without the men, she supposed, but she didn't kid herself about her chances.

Preston had downed his coffee in irritable silence when she told him of Royal's departure. "He'll come back," he said, recalling their childhood days, when Royal had once run away for almost two hours. But there were days and then months without a word or sign. "Just like Daddy. Sorry as hell" was all that Preston ever said about it, though sometimes a stranger made him start with a sideways likeness to his brother.

Then there was Margaret. She seemed to think that it was going to be a regular thing, him and her and Buttermilk Bottom. And, as much as he had liked that forbidden night, he wasn't going to pay for it with his life. She had started using words like "us" and "we" and "our." He had one family on his hands. He didn't need two. He didn't mind lying down with her, but getting up with her was a different thing.

He asked advice of Sarah about women and their ways. Sarah knew what he was after and told him straight out, wondering why so many people always got in on what it just took two to do. Preston was polite to Margaret, even courtly, kept her devotion while keeping her away, then learned than her period had arrived. "I'm off the roof," she called it. He considered himself lucky that nothing else was on the way to chain him down further. Life was loosening itself about him.

He left the rink and Margaret behind him when he went to Rasnake's. He also left Waller's, and the old man hadn't liked it at all, looked startled as though Preston had stepped on him. His chipper, ruthless eyes had clouded over like a child's. "Why?" was all he asked.

"I don't feel there's advancement here."

"There's better things. Security. Rasnake's opening up new. You could be out tomorrow. There's a Depression going on, in case you haven't heard."

"Yes, sir. I know it. But I've got this chance. I want to do something that makes me different. I want to do something like you done."

"You think you can get to be somebody working at Rasnake's Fine Foods?"

"I can take a step that way. He ain't set up yet. There's a lot needs to be done that somebody's got to find a way to do."

"I know all about it. Your time has come."

There was a rush of sarcasm in Waller's voice, but Preston passed it by. "If you say so, then I know it has." He reached out with his shaking hand, which Waller, after an instant's pause, grasped.

Preston had soon found out Rasnake was a wheeler-dealer. He rode around town on charm. He had iron-gray hair and Indian-looking features. Sometimes, when nobody was watching him and he'd let the smile fall off his face, a stern, sorrowful look would creep over him. The first time Preston saw it, he had been loading hundred-pound sacks of flour onto a huge wooden tray that lay just outside the office. He and Scoe had been heaving for over an hour, side by side. It was their first delivery. They were excited and tired and pitching in, riding on their hopes as much as Rasnake was, counting on Fine Foods to lay the track to choo-choo them into the wonderful world of competition. Preston thought they had a crackerjack team — him and Scoe and even Miss Fan. There were a couple of other by-the-hour workers, but Preston didn't consider them a part of the force. He had always been paid by the hour himself. Now he was a salary man. It was another step. He'd gotten a salary for Scoe, too — not as much as his, of course, but he'd bet there weren't a hundred Scoes in town who knew the money was coming in every week without a dock. And Rasnake? Well, he was a pistol ball. Anybody could tell that. He could shake a hand with style, look you right in the eye, and get you to give him your business while he was giving it to you. Preston had never seen anything like him. It made him feel humble to watch his boss at work.

Doc had had the family charm, with some sliding down to Royal. Preston knew the difference between a show horse and a work horse, and he had always felt it was his duty to pull the plow, but now, once in a while, he longed to learn the high-stepping that others seemed born to do. Yet there was Rasnake, seen through the streaked glass of his office looking tired and weighted down as anybody waiting for a streetcar at the end of a long day. It made him seem human, and Preston didn't like that a lot. He liked the men above him to be gods.

But they did well. One year sped by, and another was ticking away. Orders were taken, trucks were loaded, deliveries were made. Preston learned it all and he did it all. He had, as Doc had once told him, a manly knack. He never walked into a room and looked for something to do. He saw it right away and did it right away, his job or not. And when he was working he wanted everybody else to be working, too.

"That Mr. Vacalis beats anything I ever saw," said Miss Fan one hot August day as she walked out of Rasnake's tiny office, removed her wire spectacles, which had left a ridge in her nose, and began to clean them in the folds of the white smock she wore over her crisp cotton dress, starched almost to cardboard but making the rustling sound she thought a lady ought to have.

"What he done now?" asked Scoe, below her on the dock, pulling his sweat-stuck undershirt from his stonehard belly. He would have liked to work bare-chested, but Preston drew the line at undershirts for whites as well as blacks.

"He put up this notice we got to work Sunday."

It was to be the third Sunday in a row they had worked.

"Well, vegetables is fresh and folks is buying."

"I don't see how they eat them in this heat. I seem to have been living on iced tea and salmon croquettes all summer."

"I like a big meal to get by on," said Scoe.

"Well, men, of course, need more than women do," she replied. "I wish a breeze would spring up from somewhere. I believe the winds grow absent-minded in August and forget there's such a place as Atlanta where people are sweltering."

She would have gone on dropping listless words into the afternoon, but Preston was walking toward them, bringing the personal breeze he carried with him, stirring people to action where he walked.

"Why, Mr. Vacalis, how cool you look. I would say you are impervious to the heat. That's a state of grace in the dog days."

"Mr. Rasnake's coming in this afternoon," Preston informed them.

"How nice," she said. Scoe rolled his eyes. Preston ran the place like a battleship anyway, but when Rasnake made one of his increasingly rare appearances Preston behaved as though it were a battleship under fire.

"Everything is shipshape," Scoe told him.

Preston gave that remark the cutting look he thought it deserved. Nothing was ever shipshape. He picked up a routine order sheet, stopped the two men who were about to drive the order away, and quickly, methodically checked it. He took particular interest in a side of beef that was going out.

"That side of beef going down to Brisbane's Cafeteria?"

"Yes, sir."

"Who told you to put it on here?"

"That Scoe, he did."

Scoe shrugged. "It was ordered."

"Then why in the name of God aren't we billing them for it?"

Miss Fan could have used a fan. It was her mistake, and her cheeks mottled with discomfort.

"For the Lord's sake, Miss Fan, can't you keep up with a side of beef going through here?"

"Don't you start on me this afternoon, Mr. Vacalis. I am simply not up to it."

"And I am not up to having a side of beef going out of here unbilled."

"Well, you are the supervisor, you know. It is your job to catch the little mistakes. And it's rare I make an error."

"But when you make an error it's a rare one, all right."

She laughed. Scoe laughed. The men holding the side of beef laughed. Preston allowed himself a little smile at his own joke. He hadn't meant to say it. He didn't know what got into him sometimes. Now they'd be larking around, and he would have to yell to bring them to their senses and get them to the work at hand.

Miss Fan went back into the office, then stuck her head out. "Maybe we ought to hold that side of beef. Brisbane's is a slow-pay. They're over six weeks behind."

Preston did collecting, too. "Let it go. Think I'll make this delivery myself, though. Come on, Scoe." He started toward the cab of the truck.

"What about Mr. Rasnake?" Miss Fan called.

"Just tell him the place is shipshape," Preston said as he swung into the truck.

Miss Fan shrugged. Some days there was no telling about anybody.

Preston had had his eye on Brisbane's Cafeteria. It was on the corner of Peachtree and Cain, right next to the Henry Grady Hotel, in the heart of things, where Preston longed to be himself, tired now of the outskirts of town, with open collars and sleeves rolled up and hunkering down with hayseed farmers who thought a fart was a social grace.

He looked at himself in the rear-view mirror as he swung the truck onto Stewart Avenue. There were lines in his brow and around his eyes. Time was tracing itself on him, and he was not tracing himself on it. His skin was tanned, too, getting leathery, and his hair was going dry — thinning, too, he thought.

"Look in the glove compartment," he said to Scoe.

"What you want?"

"That bottle of Vitalis."

Scoe grinned, unscrewed the top, and passed the bottle.

"Take the wheel," Preston said promptly. He poured the strong liquid into his palm. He liked the smell.

"That stuff does cut the air," said Scoe.

"Good smell."

"It strong enough. I heard it so strong it go down into you head and lets the skin open up so more hair can grow."

"I never heard that."

"I didn't say it was true. I just said I heard it."

Preston reached behind the seat and pulled out a tie, turning up his collar and beginning to put it on.

"You gettin' mighty dressed up for a delivery trip."

"Think I'll leave that to you today. I'm going around front and talk to Mr. Brisbane."

There was no slight in what Preston said. It was a fact of their lives, one that Preston never noticed and one that Scoe never let on that he did.

Scoe saw himself in Preston sometimes, had to, there being no place else to see himself that did any good. Scoe had no one else to follow, though following was not to be his destiny, according to Elvira. That's what she whispered to him at night, cradling him in her plump, firm arms and giving him back the things that were taken from him in the day. "You won't be bowing and scraping all your life. I tell you that right now. You gon' be up there with them big shots, and you ain't gon' be opening no door or driving no cars for them, either. You gon' be somebody, Scofield Loomis." And, so saying, she led him. She knew she was going toward something, only she had to have a man to get there. She wanted to live a better life, to be somebody with respect. That was her mission. She clung to it and loved it as she did Scoe. They were indistinguishable.

Brisbane's had a revolving door. Preston

thought it elegant. There was one at the Biltmore Hotel, too, and down at the Ansley. It was like a carousel, not just "Come in" through an ordinary door, but whirl into something vital and important, even if it was only lunch. Brisbane's went downhill from the door. There were a couple of mirrors and paper flowers, but beyond that the place was as flat as the food Preston ate, sitting at a table that hadn't been too well wiped, looking out over other tables where dishes still lay bearing bits of uneaten food. If this were his place, he would sure put a stop to that. There wasn't a waitress or a busboy in sight. It was a good building, too, and a huge room. Somebody could make a killing here, though at the moment the place seemed to be killing Brisbane, a medium-sized nondescript man who walked into Preston's contemptuous gaze.

Brisbane was a hand-wringer. First he'd wring yours, trying to tell you with a grasp how glad he was to see you. Then he'd wring his own hands, as he did now, sitting across the table, saying how bad things were going but how good they were just ahead and if Rasnake's Fine Foods could give him just one more thirty-day extension, well, then fall would be here, wouldn't it? People ate more in the fall, when things were brisk.

Preston thought of the fall and of Brisbane's and of what was going to happen. He saw the place empty, then open again and him inside. He finished his cherry pie, feeling the jab of too much baking powder in the crust, and gave Brisbane the extension. Indeed, agreed so wholeheartedly with the man's assumptions of the future that he ordered more than his usual amount. Preston smiled, doing him the favor. Brisbane walked his mentor to the revolving door, wrung his hand once more for good measure, and watched as he went down the street.

Preston stopped a moment on the corner of Peachtree and Cain. In winter this was the windiest corner in town. Lots of people lost their hats here. Brisbane would lose more than that.

But before he did, Melba died. Sarah found her one November morning in 1935 as she tiptoed with her coffee into the darkened, sachet-scented bedroom at the back of the house. Sarah knew she was dead the moment she entered the room, even though nothing was amiss, not even the trace of a smile Melba had slept with since the day some years back when she had imagined Doc had returned to her. Sarah had set the coffee down as she always did on the tiny secondhand table with the cracked marble top. The steam from the coffee gently misted the glass on the photographs of the children. Everybody smiles in pictures, Sarah thought. She stared over Melba's corpse to the histories of the lives depicted on the table top, each caught in a timeless instant, locked forever in a single breath, the expression of their essences converged into a single word: "Cheese."

Outside the door, Sarah's brothers and sisters were noisily and impatiently foraging into the day. They were hardy, rambunctious people of careless intensity who knew that life waited on them at other places than that small shabby house. Sarah loved them all, had been their mother in all but birth. She knew that they would react to Melba's death with wails and grief that would immobilize them, putting them directly in the way of things to do. She searched for a trace of pain in Melba's face, found none, and was relieved, clinging to the hope that the physiology of her end had been as merciful as her mind had been, shutting her away from all but remembered happiness. She had no tears for Melba now, though she felt a mother to her, too.

Sarah turned and left the room, putting on her morning face of brisk efficiency, hiding as she always did behind the rush in other people's lives, serving breakfasts, finding coats, laying fleeting kisses across departing cheeks, standing in the doorway at long last an hour later, holding the smile and looking into the bleak November morning that was unable to rain.

They couldn't find Royal, had no idea where to locate him, though Preston had suspected for a time that Sarah was in touch with him and kept it quiet. He waited for her to own up to her deception, but the proof of his suspicion did not come. He was sorry he had suspected her, tried to be nicer to her as he held her arm when they walked from the black touring car the mortuary used to take them to the cemetery the day they buried Melba. Preston had some savings now — not much, but he dipped into them to buy an eight-grave family plot. His little sense of irony was strong enough to bring a shrugging smile to him when he realized that the only thing he owned in life was a place for death.

The Vacalises were not churchgoing people. So they were surprised to learn that Melba had become Greek Orthodox somewhere along. To Preston's way of thinking, it made no difference what religion she had been. She was gone; that was all. But Sarah had gotten in touch with a bearded priest, who stood before them in the rain, robed under umbrellas held by soaking acolytes. The man brought more mystery with him than comfort, seemed to be chastising them as heathens as he spoke from a Bible, not always in English. He was stranger than the death.

The sisters gave each other tears and hugs while Preston tried to be his manliest for little Jimmy. Scoe was there with Elvira, and Elmo Flagg had come. Preston could never remember seeing him away from the sewing machines and presses of the Institute of Tailoring and Pressing. They huddled respectfully to one side. Rasnake was there, standing, to Preston's amazement, with Hildebrand and Waller. The three of them — men he had dreamed to be — were saluting a woman they had never met to honor him. He nodded to them, fearing it was a sin to feel such pride instead of grief. They must consider him a man of promise to come out in the rain. Waller and Hildebrand, whom he had left, remembered him. How odd. He always assumed himself to be forgotten when he was out of the range of others.

One of his sisters — Araminthia, in her early twenties now, and lovely; courting, too, a young man nearby throwing her glances over the open grave — carried a dark blue umbrella that the sun hit for an instant, turning it to purple. Melba had had a lavender satin nightgown when he was small. "Light purple," she had called it. Lavender was a scent. He had liked the feel of satin and the soothing color, liked the touch of it as it sifted through his baby fingers. She had abandoned it to him. His childhood was laced to countless nights of caressing it until he fell asleep. In time the gown had disappeared. He had outgrown his need for it, and then for her, but not his love, which now came rushing in out of nowhere.

Ashes settled damply over the flowered casket. The sun withdrew. Araminthia's umbrella lost its color. The priest was speaking kindly to Sarah, then to Preston and on down the line. The mourners walked toward them to speak. Neighbor women were back at the house with too much food, assuming that sorrow ended in the belly instead of beginning there. Preston smiled in spite of himself as Hildebrand, Waller, and Rasnake approached to shake his hand and offer consolation, as well as the hope within him that they were men together. He introduced Sarah, then the others, proud that they looked so good, something he had never noticed, just as he did not notice a white carnation that twisted loose from the casket as the gravediggers stood by impatiently. It skittered, windborne, across other graves, growing muddy as it went, until it came to rest at the base of a stone woman, too voluptuous to be an angel. Preston, standing taller now, manhood shining, helped his sisters to the car.

Melba's death had seemed to Preston to unlock a series of events concerning his family. They began to go away, not drifting but rushing pell-mell in all directions, anxious to be done with their collective past and on to futures full of promise in the distance.

Preston was left with Sarah and little Jimmy, who had his future, too, but needed them awhile. He was fourteen, a baby Preston thought, then remembered his own fourteen, when he had been a year in the stockroom at Waller's. He had considered it a position, off the streets and into a building. Later, Preston had gotten his mail-order high-school diploma — six months before Royal had gotten his. He had presented the diploma to Waller, not asking for a raise, but letting him know that his place in the world had improved. He was made a sales clerk. He had to wear a suit. Waller called a clothing manufacturer, and within a week Preston received two new suits, neither of which fit. "This is not a gift to you, son, but an investment in your career in haberdashery. I do not expect to be repaid. You seldom do in this world anyway, but I want to see you neat and clean. Clothes make the man." Waller was profound. He let Preston buy the shirts and ties on time. Elmo Flagg had fitted the suits, charging just for alterations, never telling Preston that he'd practically had to remake them.

Preston had brought Scoe into Waller's to take his place in the stockroom. Scoe was a good worker, made no difference if he was a friend or not. Preston never thought in terms of friendship anyway. There were those who let you down and those who proved themselves. Nobody had ever given him anything but a chance to prove himself, and that's all he'd ever give anybody else. He was a graduate of the School of Hard Knocks. He had a preference for that student body.

And here little Jimmy wanted to be a doctor. Foolishness, that's all it was. A gamble. He might get there and not take to medicine at all, and all that money gone to waste. After all, Preston's own legal ambitions had fallen away, though he never told himself the reason, just blamed it on time and space and things at hand, but it was still there to mock him sometimes when days were long and fruitless. Still, Jimmy would have college. Preston had decided that. If he did well and proved himself, they'd see about later things later, but he had to take business courses. That was a magic word with Preston. A businessman was what he was, and business was what he meant. He had a tailored image in his mind of a bright young man with glistening eyes and clean-combed hair walking briskly down the streets of life, perhaps carrying a briefcase.

A year after Melba died, Preston stood across the street from Brisbane's, watching the paltry evening business while people were lined up around the block at the nearby Georgia Theater to see something that would make them happy and take them far away. That was the trouble with Brisbane's. There was nothing in it to take you anywhere, just basic bad-cooked food that you could get more than enough of at home.

The picture show was fifteen cents. A waste, he told himself, but he wanted to see why the others went there. He bought his ticket and went inside. It was paradise.

It was the lobby that got to him first. It was a castle with an island in it where they sold candy, popcorn, and Coca-Colas. He regarded it suspiciously. A uniformed usher showed him to his seat. He didn't like the darkness, that was sure. No telling what kind of things went on in there. He looked up, and there were flickering stars in the ceiling. It took him a moment to realize the clouds were gauze and the twinkling stars were blinking lights. It was like real sky, only better, like the sky should be.

He looked at the screen. There was the girl he had dreamed of. In dreams her features had eluded him, yet here they were, perfectly realized by a goddess who seemed to have no idea she was more than human. She sang and danced with such exquisite unawareness of her charm that Preston wanted to speak out to her, almost did for an instant, making that sharp intake of breath that precedes a nervous declaration. The lady in front of him turned with a sharp look, and he was stunned to silence.

He could have loved the movies. He knew that. From the first black-and-white moment, his nameless, formless longings took shape. These people were as tall as buildings. The audience around him was slack-jawed at the miracles before them. They are little people, he thought. He identified more with what was happening on the screen, and he knew that he was one of them, someone whose life should take on size, only the size would have to come from him, not some blade of light above the balcony.

He never knew the name of the picture that he saw. He got there in the middle and left when it was over, not thinking to sit through it again. It would have been dishonest in a way. He had known the show had started, just wanted to take a gander.

He walked out of the theater, still lightheaded, having to force himself to earth. He knew what he would do when Brisbane's came his way. He would make his customers think their dimes bought banquets. People wanted to be delighted. He rolled the word around in his mind. "Delighted . . . Dine delighted." That was it. The kicker came, and with it the shiver of success that was to be. Dine Delighted or Dine Free. He took one last look at Brisbane's and walked rapidly down the street, his footfalls sounding to him like movie footfalls. If he could have danced, he would have.

Brisbane's failed ingloriously that July of 1936. Bankrupt. Preston's moment greeted him. His plans had become such a world for him that the reality of the time at hand left him for a moment weak as though someone had slugged him in the gut, then punched his kidneys for good measure. It was that bad. A trickle of fear slowly began to eat through his picture of success. What if the word he heard was "No?"

He sat on the dinky porch of the house they had shared with Doc. They could have moved some years ago, but it was home. It bore a shiny coat of paint, and there were spring flowers along the concrete walk that Royal had put in before the fight. He'd have talked his plans over with Royal, at least that's what he told himself. Perhaps they'd have been partners. But alone was a man's way, and that was his.

Sarah was fixing supper in the house, humming in her fractured voice that never seemed to hold a key. Jimmy was studying, putting his eyes out in the failing light, a lamp beside him. "Turn that light on," Preston said. "Electricity's cheaper than glasses."

"Supper'll be in about twenty minutes," said Sarah, coming out of the kitchen and wiping her hands on a cloth.

Preston rose and stretched. "Think I'll take a walk."

"I don't want it to get cold," she said.

"I'll be back on time."

It was beginning to be shirt-sleeve weather, but Preston wore a coat. It set him apart, he felt, showed there were things on his mind. A little spray of mud kicked up onto the cuffs of his severely creased trousers.

The sun was going down as he crossed the caked-dirt road to Scoe's. A tiny, naked black child swung in an old inner tube from a tractor tire that had been tied with rope and hung from an oak branch. There were few porches here, but there were rough stoops, and on them sat black men, their shirts open to catch a breeze. A few women were out, too, just to watch the dying sun. The air was full of frying. Preston waved and spoke to a few, scattering first names in the air and getting "Mister" back. He liked it on this side of the bottom. There was nothing to prove to anybody here.

Scoe and Elvira were sitting on their

porch in a rickety swing Scoe had constructed out of crates. They were big people, not yet stout, but headed there in middle age. The swing creaked beneath them, and Preston eyed it dubiously. Elvira laughed. She had a way of picking thoughts like lint off people's shoulders.

"It ain't gon' fall."

"I didn't say a word, Elvira."

"You don't have to," Scoe answered for her. "She knows it 'fore you says it. She does the same to me."

"Hush up. I don't want somebody to think I'm a conjur."

"They already do."

She laughed. They caught the laugh from her, but Preston wondered if she was.

"I got lemonade to fix," Elvira said. She didn't want to get in the way of the purpose of his visit. It was only once a year or so that they received a call from Preston.

Preston leaned against the porch. He had unbuttoned his coat and let it fall open. "Cooling off," he said.

"Look like there might come a shower."

Preston nosed the air like a bird dog, something he had learned from the hunkering farmers. "It'll blow off." He tore out a single weed that had escaped Elvira's vigilance and chewed it meaningfully. "Been thinking."

" 'Bout what?"

"Moving on."

"From here?"

"Sooner or later, I hope, but that's not it."

"I can guess all night. Got nothin' else to do, but you could tell me right off if you will."

"Been thinking about opening up a restaurant. Not a restaurant exactly. A cafeteria."

"Where you gon' get the money?"

"I don't know."

"You ought to be able to get it."

"Think so?"

"I don't see why not. Depression's over, so they say. Money's coming back. Saw the other day where they was parading up in New York City. Coupla million folks paradin' for the NRA."

"If it's over up there, it'll take a year or

two to work its way down here."

"That don't necessarily have to be. Things is lots faster than they used to be."

"Too fast if you ask me."

Scoe nodded, and they faced each other with the air of men whose dreams were still dreams, with the numbers of their days racking mercilessly up on them. Scoe chuckled, drawing a small laugh from Preston, close in the pain of their mortality.

"What about Mr. Rasnake?" Scoe asked.

"I dunno. I thought of him. He's well off, but I don't know if he's got enough to go the whole hog."

"You know some others."

"Who?"

"If I gots to tell you who you knows, I might as well not say a word."

"Hildebrand and Waller."

"Them's the two."

"I quit them, though."

"They got more respect for you quittin' than they would've had for you staying."

"You sure?"

"Nope. But I think it. You did yourself

one better every time."

"It's a chance."

"That's all you gon' get."

"What do you think about it? I mean, do you think it'll go?"

"I ain't never known you to do nothin' that didn't come out all right."

"I don't mean me. I mean the idea."

"Feedin' folks is a hard business. You got to feed 'em good and charge 'em fair, and sometimes that don't work. Didn't work for Mr. Brisbane. I guess that's where you thinking of."

"Brisbane didn't know shit from Shinola 'bout running a place to eat."

"It ain't my place to speak on him, but I think you'll do a damn sight better."

"I'll drink to that."

Elvira had been listening from the living-room window, holding three glasses of lemonade on a plain wood tray Scoe had fashioned from a plank. She timed her movement to his remark and swung onto the porch through the prized screen door, the only one on that side of Buttermilk Bottom, which had little clumps of cotton stuck on it at random to ward off mosquitoes.

The sun had gone. The bruised sky was fading into night. They drank Elvira's lemonade with aahing sounds.

Preston thought to drop the weed he fingered, then thought it would be somehow rude. Elvira's house was as neat as a white's. He stuffed it into his pocket, buttoned his coat, made his excuses and good nights, and went toward Sarah's dumplings.

Elvira leaned against Scoe's arm. The day had lost its warmth. She needed his. "How you think he'll do on that?" she asked.

"He'll do all right. He got to get the money first."

"He'll get the money. He got the look of a man who ain't about to be denied. It'll be good for him, and good for us."

"Why you so sure he'll get the money?"

"He ain't got nobody, Scoe. All he got is himself, and he got to get something."

Chapter 3

June Bug, Fat Boy, and Scooter were the three dishwashers at The Melba. Scooter did pots and pans, June Bug did glasses, and Fat Boy did plates, occasionally gobbling a morsel before the plate was dunked in the sink.

Scooter had his eyes on better things than pots and pans. He wanted to carve meat out front, as Ed did, wanted a high white hat and a crisp white apron, to flash the sharp steel knife against the carving fork as he worked his way from well-done to rare.

When The Melba had been running for two years and things were settling into place, Ed let Scooter fill in for him occasionally. Scoe knew about it but said nothing. He was enough like Preston to want things in their places; still, there were times Scoe had to look the other way.

One lunch rush when Preston was gone, Ed allowed Scooter to take over behind the counter. This did not sit at all well with Sadie, the dessert girl, a stocky woman who took pride in the array of sweets she set out. She didn't care too much for Scooter, whom she was sure had stolen a quart of strawberries she had washed and cored.

She watched him carve. "Mista Preston catch you on the line, he gon' run you off from here."

"You do yo' work. I do mine."

"Yo' work in the kitchen. Scrubbin' pots. Scrubbin' pans." She let out a high-pitched giggle as Scooter turned to her in a rage.

Several of the customers who had been docilely pushing their trays along the line saw Sadie jump back in fright just as Preston came in through the swinging doors, carrying a vat of vegetable soup. "Hot! Hot!" he called as he approached the line, then stopped short as he saw the flash of metal. It was Scooter holding the carving knife and fork.

Nobody was sure if anything had happened or not. Sadie was untouched, and Scooter later claimed he was only twirling a piece of meat on the fork the way he had seen Ed do. Preston had Elvira send extra dessert over to the people who had been in line. He wanted memories of The Melba to be sweet. The South was full of lurking violence. It seemed to rest on that. It had just better not rear its head at The Melba Cafeteria.

He resolved that Scooter would have to go, and it hurt him in a way, because no one had been let go and it would be a mark, a little crack in his perfect wall. He sat out front that night, doing his books. Payday he would let him go, and, so deciding, he sighed.

Saturday-night revels were going on outside. Cars cruised past the plate-glass windows like orderly, instinct-driven salmon. Occasionally a rebel yell could be heard, loud and meaningless.

Scoe and Elvira came out of the kitchen.

"We gone," Scoe announced.

"What's your hurry?" It was a joke.

"We don't hurry up and get out from here, we ain't gon' get home in time to get to church in the morning," Elvira answered.

"Yeah. Well . . . I guess you better get on." They brought out smiles in each other. He knew their night was just beginning, not ending, the way his was. He wished that they would stop and talk, but what was there to say? His conversation began and ended with The Melba — that and a few disgruntled opinions on politics, but what would they know about that? They started to go out the back, but he rose. "I'll lock it behind you."

Elvira smiled. It wasn't always they went out the front. Preston had his skates on, gliding easily ahead of them. Elvira laughed. Scoe gave her a nudge, but she persisted. "You and them skates."

Preston put a swirl in the turn as he stopped by the door. Elvira applauded. He gave a mock bow. Just don't take it too far, Scoe thought. Just don't take it too far. Preston wasn't the first lonesome white man he'd seen. They could be right loose when they had the need, but when the need was gone it was the black man who paid for it instead of them, as though they had seen too far into something that only whites should see. "You ought to go home yourself," he said.

"Don't bother about me."

"Somebody ought to, and that's a fact," Elvira said.

That was women for you, all opinions and advice, not content to let things stay in the air where they belonged. "Come on, woman." They would fight all the way to the but stop, ride home estranged in silence, speak across each other to neighbors along their street, then come together in passion behind their closed door, slamming against each other with needs greater than their knowledge, and love greater than that. Elvira would voice a pang about missing church, and Scoe would tell her he'd build her a steeple of her own. "Oh, Scoe Loomis," she'd whisper, clutched fast in his strong black arms. "I ain't no better than you are." "No, ma'am," he would tell her, "you ain't. But you still pretty damn good."

And that would be Sunday.

Preston watched them as they walked away. It occurred to him that he was always watching things. Nobody watched him. He was feeling low until he began to skate among the tables, gliding in and out among the upturned chairs, circling the fountain, which had become a wishing well lined with copper pennies. After a moment he was smiling. The place was his. He was skating in his own place. He watched himself flash by in mirrors, and was for an instant so close to happiness that he thought he was there. But it passed, and he stopped short. What if somebody had seen him from the street? He sat down and approached his books in a foul humor.

At midnight, when he hadn't come home, Sarah nervously phoned the cafeteria.

Preston was asleep over the ledger, his arms folded under his head. He was snoring almost as loudly as the phone that jarred him awake. He awoke in a panic. He thought it was a fire bell. His eyes were red. He had worked eighteen hours.

Then he fixed on the shrill phone, knowing he had to get it to stop. He lurched away from the table, his mouth flying open, and the place turned upside down around him. He had forgotten that he was still on wheels. The last thing he saw was the disinterested gaze of a perpetually damp cherub in the fountain as his head slammed against its edge. The ringing stopped.

Palmetto Russell sat in the chart room on the third floor of Piedmont Hospital, looking at the hem of her formerly white uniform, now spotted with Mr. Ewig Stone's urine, splashed when the old man tried to relieve himself in the stainless-steel urinal and missed, striking it on the side, sending a spray on her as she stood there torn between compassion and homicide. He was so old and pale and elegant that he could have been her mistily remembered grandfather. But instead of apologizing, the old devil had grinned and given a hearty laugh. ''I didn't expect such a gusher,'' he said. ''Like a firehose.'' She had looked at the flaccid hose and almost laughed. Men and their cocks, she thought. They were worse than boy dogs and trees. Anything their cocks touched they thought they owned.

It was 4 A.M. — three hours to shift change. She would have liked a cigarette; the thought of a Lucky Strike sent a contraction through her mouth and throat. They could smoke in the chart room, though it was frowned on, but Palmetto didn't like the smoky smell that clung to things, didn't like to carry it with her on her rounds when she was being an Angel of Mercy.

She was twenty-nine years old, a fact she hated to think about and did constantly. She was an old hand at Piedmont. New girls were coming out of training every year. Seven years had flitted by since her training. The days had piled up like unpaid bills. Sometimes, like tonight, she wanted to scream, to throw out her arm and pull a cord to "Stop this machine!" That's what she'd done once as a little girl, sleeping alone in an upper berth, train-bound for Fernandina Beach. She woke up scared, saw the cord, and pulled it, thinking it would bring her mother, Mamie. And it did, along with many others, as the train came to a rail-squealing stop. She had been very calm under the accusing faces. The eyes of storms never bothered her — not so it showed, anyway. That was why she was a good nurse. She responded calmly and efficiently to crises from without. It was just the ones within that were on the verge of getting the better of her.

She would get off the night shift. That was sure. She was doing it only as a favor to Miss Jenkins, anyway. "Honey," the spindly spinster supervisor had said, "I just can't get these married girls to come on at night, and somebody's got to come on for Darcy while she has her hysterectomy." Poor Darcy. She was thirty-five, and had to go and lose her female organs before they'd had any use. God might as well have saved her the trouble and let her be born without them. There was Darcy, a patient now down on the second floor, saying she didn't feel any different at all, and laughing louder than anyone else when harelipped Dr.

Dunbar twanged, "Well, honey, I took the baby carriage out, but I left the playpen."

It's easy to go bats on the night shift, she thought. The afternoon nurses had given the patients their sleeping pills an hour before she came on. The serious cases had nurses of their own. She was going back to private duty, that was certain. And she'd do it in the daytime. There were too many scary things in the night.

She took a chart off a wall hook and left the room. Asleep or not, she could at least check on them. There was one in particular she wanted to see. She had given a laugh of recognition when she saw Preston Vacalis's name on the chart. She had forgotten his first name, but the last name had stayed with her because it was foreign and she liked foreign-sounding names that were pronounceable. She was sure it was the same one who had gotten her in the brawl at the roller rink. She remembered Royal less vaguely, but still, that had been nearly ten years before, when she was in training. Nearly ten years. Dear God. And she had thought of herself as a grown woman then. She felt younger now than she had then, or maybe she was only more afraid.

She went briskly down the hall toward Preston's room, glad to be doing something to take her mind off herself. She paused outside the door, checked the chart, and wondered if he would recognize her. Not that he should. She probably wouldn't recognize him. All patients looked alike anyway, sweet and dependent on the white beds, the energies that propelled them through life taking either a rest or permanent leave. She entered.

There was a weak light burning. Preston lay like a sleeping maharaja, a turban of bandages around his head. His arms were motionless at his side, his chest rising and falling calmly. He looked like a young boy instead of his twenty-nine years. She studied him for a moment, not remembering him at all. But what was there to remember, other than the rage and embarrassment and the end of Aunt Eula's knitted sweater?

She put the fingers of her right hand on

his left wrist, checking his pulse. The coolness of her touch went through him. He opened his eyes, for once without the compulsion to leap up. She was looking at her watch, didn't see him staring at her. The light was at her back, turning her dark blonde hair to the gold she often wished it were. It put a halo around the starched white cap. She concentrated on her watch, nibbling an instant at her lower lip like a baby not long weaned.

She was the loveliest thing he had seen since the days when he had looked up at Melba as she shielded him from the world. He wanted to speak to her, to do something that would keep her from going away, but all he could manage was "Huh?"

She held up the little finger of her watch hand as though to hush him, looked at the watch a moment more, then smiled. She had dimples. "You woke up, I see."

He had no idea where he was. He was embarrassed by the lack of information. He smiled his Melba Cafeteria smile, serving courtliness with biscuits, gracious hospitality on the outside and toes curled up with shyness inside his shoes. His eyes had fickle focus; things were gliding by. The plain, sparsely furnished room was a galaxy to him, yet he had no orbit. He tried to sit up, his head heavy and lopsided.

She eased him back down on the pillow, a strong, gentle arm around his shoulders. "Not so fast, pardner," she said. There was a tease in her voice. He liked it. "Open wide. Mama bird's got a worm." She had whipped a thermometer out of the folds of her uniform and deftly inserted it between his open lips. It didn't even click against his teeth. Her aim was true.

She checked the railings on either side of the bed, chattering to him all the while, the melody of her voice going in and out like something on the radio during a storm. It was as if she were playing a game with him. Soon he would figure it out and it would be his turn, but for now he was content to grasp the shreds of her conversation: ". . . fractured skull . . . two days ago . . . your sisters . . . scared everybody to death . . . going to be all right . . . a week or so . . . nothing you can do about it but lie back and relax, you need that anyway . . . flowers in the hall . . .''

She took back the thermometer. He had forgotten it was in him. She smiled at what it told her, plumped his pillow, then stopped a moment, looking earnestly down at him. He wondered if she was having as much trouble keeping him in focus as he was with her. She touched his cheek, that same cool hand. ''Somebody needs a shave,'' she said. ''Sweet dreams.'' Then she was gone, and so was he.

Preston opened his eyes and looked around. He had been dreaming. There had been a girl, a nurse, but the dream had ended. She had been in white. Brides wore white. He was late for something, but he couldn't imagine what it was. Then he remembered The Melba, quit worrying about where he was and why, only knew he had to get there and save it. He didn't know what it was he had to save it from, but there was something the matter, something he should have known all along and hadn't. It was so obvious, so real. He'd had the answer in sleep so crystal-clear that it had calmed him even though the knowledge was painful. Something had risen from a deepwater part of his mind and told him a secret. His eyes had flown open with it; then he had lost it. It had gone out through his eyes rather than his mouth, and there was no one to give it back to him.

A radiator was gurgling on the far side of the room. He grasped the railings, pulled himself to a sitting position, and stared at it. The gurgling brought the fountain back to him; then he remembered the ringing that had brought him here in the first place. Was The Melba all right? Was it locked? He had to check on it. No one knew how to take care of it but him.

It was so strange to move. He was lighter than he had ever been before, more graceful than skate wheels had ever let him be. The floor was cold to his bare feet, but it was a good, calm cold that made him aware of his steps. He was wearing a funny gown open down the back. Instinctively, he closed it, holding it together with one hand and crossing to the radiator. He stopped there, warmed from feet to crotch. There was a window over the radiator. He leaned one arm against the sill and looked out.

A light from the parking lot illuminated the well-treed grounds. It was the verge of October. The leaves were still green but growing crisp. They swayed in the wind like enchanted multitudes, not knowing the wind had death in it. Autumn was a dying season, beautiful and longed for in the swelter of summer, but nevertheless an end to things, tricky, dazzling, giving the summer back sometimes for days and days as though it had changed its mind. Autumn wanted things too lovely, expected them to last. Nothing ever lasts, Preston thought, and with the thought he reached out toward the wind, but glass was there. There was always something between him and the place he wanted to be. But where did he want to be? His dreams were coming true, but maybe they were autumn dreams that would blow away. He had to get out of wherever he was and save The Melba. He turned in breathless panic and swayed an instant, like the trees outside. There was a sudden breeze. It was his falling, falling down between the gurgling, steaming radiator and the wall.

Palmetto had given in to a cigarette. She took a deep, guilty drag and concentrated on the bad taste it left in her mouth. She grimaced and crushed it against the metal side of a trash can. She would have to open the door to get the smell out. She rose, then stopped; something was the matter. She opened the door and looked down the hall. Everything was quiet. Shipshape. Four twenty-five, and all was well.

The hall was cooler than the chart room had been. Perhaps that was the cause of the icy feeling inside her. She folded her arms and gave a little shiver. She had a white cashmere sweater she brought to work in October and took home in May. But that wasn't it. It was something else.

She began to walk down the hall with no idea where she was destined. Mrs.

Davis, a stocky, Irish-looking practical nurse, shuffled by, the sides of her shoes slit open to accommodate gargantuan bunions. They nodded to each other, and Palmetto went, drawn on by something, irritated that it would not reveal itself.

Then she was outside the door to Preston's room, knowing it was his, hesitating, needing an excuse to be there, putting on her nurse's smile and pushing in. The bed was empty. She breathed deeply of the suddenly thin air, then saw Preston's naked legs sticking out between the radiator and the wall. Something was frying. It was his back.

It was all she needed. It was her purpose. She was in control. She rushed across the room, grabbed his right arm, and pulled. He was dead weight. Stuck. She pulled again, bracing her white-shod foot against the wall. He moved, but not enough. The radiator was leaving its marks at intervals in his back. There was nothing left to do but scream, and she found that she was good at that. "Otis! Mrs. Davis! Somebody help me!" There were two kinds of panic in her voice. One was for Preston, burning there. The other was because she was not strong enough to get him out, felt weak and limited, her femaleness getting in the way, as it always did when she needed to assert herself against the world. She kept on tugging and screaming.

Big, black, fifty-year-old Otis bounded through the door. Mrs. Davis, eyes gone as big as her bunions, watched from the hall, her hand to her mouth. Palmetto stepped aside with a tremble of relief. It was so easy for Otis. He plucked Preston from behind the radiator and held him in his arms, looking at Palmetto.

"On the bed," she said. "On his stomach."

Otis lifted him over the railings. "How bad he burnt?"

"I don't know yet." She took her scissors and cut the gown away. There were six marks from the radiator. Maybe they were only second-degree. The pale skin was already growing dark and crusty. "Get Dr. Atkinson, and tell Mrs. Davis to get down here with a salve tray and a hypo."

Otis left. Preston stirred, turning his head to look at her. "It's about time you woke up," she said. "Now hold still."

"Am I naked?"

That was a man all right, thinking women were to be seen nude but never them. She patted his upturned, unburned rump. "You're naked as the day you were born."

"Oh Lord," he groaned. "Things are getting out of my control."

How sweet he was. How plaintive. As tender as his smooth, burned back. She wanted him to be all right. "Poor baby," she said, leaned forward, and blew softly on the welts.

Later, in the last moment before the earliest of the day-shift girls began to arrive, Palmetto stood in the door to the chart room, looking down the hall. Preston had been treated and bandaged, and the burns were only a little more than superficial. She had given the hypo, and he was snoring peacefully.

All her life she'd heard stories of the unexplained snow-white doves that appeared out of nowhere to light a moment on the crib where a baby lay dying, and flying away when the life ran out as though winging it to Heaven; mysterious lights that appeared to guide the way across perilous swamps; omens, whisperings, ghosts, and portents. She came from country people. They were susceptible to such things. She had always scoffed. She had medical knowledge. Now something unexplained had touched her, but she wouldn't be thought silly by telling it around. "Just passing by," she said when Dr. Atkinson had asked her.

"Lucky," he said.

She nodded in reply.

There was a window at the far end of the hall. It was quickly getting light. She tried to recapture the moment she had sensed something was wrong, tried to find a rational explanation for it. It eluded her. She hated limitations.

Otis walked by. "Thanks," she said.

"Some night," he replied, and kept on going.

Preston remained in Piedmont Hospital

another week. His improvement was rapid, his disposition sour. Scoe came to the hospital three times a day, and Preston ran The Melba from his bed. Hildebrand, Waller, and Rasnake came by daily, as did Sarah. "The fall hasn't changed him a bit," they all said. And Waller always added, "I hoped it would knock some sense into him." Preston accepted their comments and visits with an irritated grace. The help took up a collection and sent gladiolas. He was embarrassed by the attention, and aghast at the waste of money.

When he was sure The Melba had been put to bed each afternoon, he slept, snoring softly through the supper tray and waking up at eleven thirty, when Palmetto made her first rounds, stopping by to see him last. They delighted each other. He took her lonesome terror away, and as a result received the considerable force of her undivided attention.

She was a lovely girl, convinced, as most lovely girls are, that the loveliness was on its way. He didn't have the words to reassure her, and wouldn't have wasted them on flattery if he did, but he had something better: He showed his awe in his eyes, and it made her feel incandescent. She thought him sweet and inadvertently funny. She blamed his peculiarities on the fall, and felt that they would pass in time.

He was an intelligent man, convinced, as most intelligent men are, that his thoughts had been thought before and put to better use by smoother men. But she seemed to hang on his every word, and he addressed her with the oratory with which he had once hoped to persuade juries. "The Greeks had a word for everything," Doc had told him; "when you got nothing else, you got the words." He found himself wanting to see her and laughing with her. He blamed it on the fall.

The night after his fall, she had come on duty expecting to find him asleep, but his light had been on when she came in. He was lying on his stomach, looking out between the bars at the foot of the bed. He had thanked her gruffly, formally, for her assistance of the night before. She sensed that he was a man who hated to be helped, and therefore needed it most of all.

She had rubbed his back, gently changing the dressing and keeping up a running stream of meaningless conversation to take his mind off the skin rips of adhesive tape. There were no blemishes on his back, and the burns looked as though they would fade. His shoulders were strong and smooth. Some men had hair that grew on the shoulders and down the back. She didn't like that, had always considered it animallike. Fronts were for hair; backs were for smoothness. She had rubbed no farther down than his waist, but she was thrilled by his buttocks. They were pale, defenseless things, yet firm. She thought fondly of the big, brave, wrongheaded men who had torn through her life like knights on their eternal quests, taking on things beyond them, sometimes losing but always valiant, rushing furiously ahead, pursued by their bouncing, sun-lost buttocks that held their tenderness.

On the third night Preston wore pajama bottoms and hid his better nature from her. That night she told him about their unremembered meeting. "How is Royal?" she asked.

"That was the last time I ever saw him."

"You don't mean it!"

"He left that night, and nobody's heard a word from him in almost ten years . . . He ever get in touch with you?"

"To tell you the truth, I didn't even know him. He was a blind date. I'd just come to town to go into training. A girl down the hall . . . Rita Moore . . . she got killed the next year in an automobile accident. It was the saddest thing. She had a date with this friend of his, and they both came to the lobby and he asked her if she could please come upstairs and see if anybody wanted a blind date. Well, I had never even had a blind date before, and I was scared to death, but I think I was even scareder of people thinking I was a hick, which I certainly was at the time, so I said, 'Yes, I'll go.' And I put on the sweater Aunt Eula had knitted for me. It was one of my first sophisticated moments, and I'd like to thank you for making it so memorable."

"I want to apologize for that. It wasn't like me at all."

He was so serious she laughed. "I thought you were the strangest person I'd ever seen."

Preston had never heard himself referred to in those terms. "I'm not strange."

She thought he was even funnier. "Then you'll just have to take my word for it."

He let her get away with some little things without correcting her. What good would it do? She was only a nurse at night. In a few days he wouldn't be seeing her again. Ever. Or would he?

"I'm dazzled," she said, getting out of the cab with him across the street from The Melba just past noon on the day he got out of the hospital. He wore a gray suit and carried a black suitcase. It was the first suitcase he had ever owned. Sarah had gotten it at Rich's and brought it to the hospital with the first robe and slippers he had ever had. Palmetto carried a bouquet of sweetheart roses the Jewel

Tea Company had sent him. It had embarrassed him. It was bad enough to send a man flowers, but roses? He told her she could have them. She seemed delighted. She stood beside him, sniffing them as they waited for the light.

He suddenly wondered what she was doing there. He had work to do. She was part of the hospital, not part of the cafeteria, but when he had told her he was going home, she had looked so sad. "I'll have to start sleeping nights again," he had said, and laughed. She had laughed, too, only it was short and hollow, not as natural as the breeze, the way it had been. Then, for unexplained reasons, he had felt sad. He couldn't wait to be out and back into his world, but he felt as if he were losing something, something he had looked forward to, and there was nothing new that he had looked forward to since The Melba had opened. So he had invited her, a slight, spur-of-the-moment thing that had kept him nervous all afternoon. Dates and going out were probably the most casual of things to her. Maybe she would give him a fleeting, toothy smile and forget all about it before the words had finished coming. What would he do then? It was so hard to save your honor with a woman. They found the most serious things amusing, and the most amusing things an outrage.

"They tell me I can get outta here 'round eleven o'clock tomorrow," he had told her. "Too bad you won't be here. You could help me with my suitcase."

"If that's some kind of invitation, it's the most left-handed one I've ever received."

She had forced him into a declaration, and after it was made she said only, "That'll be nice. I'll bring my appetite."

The light changed and they were in the street, not standing out from the noontime crowd, but feeling as though they did. "You're so tall," she said. There was wonder in her voice. She tossed her head, and the waves of hair moved dancingly, like the leaves he had seen before his fall. She was a different person away from her uniform. Now he was afraid she would be different, like those long-limbed girls he had dreamed about who seemed to have no destiny involving his touch. "I don't know why I'm so excited," she said. "I haven't even tasted any of the food yet."

"I'm going to start keeping it open at night. I want to see if I can build up a dinner trade."

"What a wonderful idea!"

"Do you think so?"

"I wouldn't have said it if I didn't mean it."

There was a bond between them after all. He never lied, hadn't had time to acquire that subtle art and had no patience with it. He had known that there was something in her that he liked. How good that it was truth.

They paused before the revolving door, watching the surging crowd. His absence had not hurt business at all. He felt overwhelmed. The tide of people ebbed and flowed whether he was there or not. How strange to have created something that could go on without you.

He was standing there, lost in the wonder of himself, when Palmetto grabbed his arm and yanked him with surprising strength into the revolving door with her. They were jammed together for an instant, whirling the several feet inside while she laughed as though she were on a carnival ride. The flowers were crushed against her breasts, and he held his suitcase in his arms. Then they were inside, and he jumped, almost sliding on the polished floor, and she was hanging on to him, her laughter heard above Drew's lunchtime concert. He was in the midst of "My Hero" when a sudden silence fell, ended by the commotion of their arrival.

Preston's dignity kept on revolving in the door. This was no way for a businessman to return. He was about to be sorry he had invited her. It didn't pay to take anybody anywhere. You never knew how they'd act, though she was luminously pretty above the clutched roses.

Elvira was cleaning a table when she looked up and saw them. Several customers turned, charmed by the sight of the exuberant young. "Mista Preston!" Elvira's voice had weight to it; even behind the counter several employees looked up.

Miss Fan looked up from the cash register and shrilly twanged the first thing that came to mind. "Dear Fathers! He's got a bride with him!"

Sadie, setting down a tray, brimmed over. "Mista Preston is married!" she squealed.

Drew deserted "My Hero" for Mendelssohn's "Wedding March," playing sonorously and weaving his head.

Mr. Tilden, a regular customer who always got three glasses of water, the free lemon, and the free sugar and made his own lemonade, began to applaud with his big, callused, lemon-stained hands. It was taken up. Preston and Palmetto received an ovation.

She just died laughing while he blushed in rage.

"Cut that out!" he yelled. "Nobody's married! This is my nurse!"

Palmetto continued to laugh, but waved a gloved hand in gretting. She still hung on to his arm. He wanted to shake her off, but he couldn't do that, so he let it go limp, hoping she would — for the love of God! — take the hint.

If she took the hint, she paid no attention to it. Some people! he thought, then disengaged himself, looking like a lightning-carrying cloud.

Drew had segued to "Humoresque," still nodding with the melancholy glow his mid-morning brandy had given him. Miss Fan went back to making change as though she'd never said a word. Sadie smiled brightly at the customer she had been helping, and Elvira turned with her loaded tray and started for the kitchen. "There going to be war in the camp," she muttered as she passed Sadie, who held on to that smile for dear life.

"Go ahead and get in the line," Preston told Palmetto. "Get anything you want. I got to tend to some things." He left her standing there, taken aback and uncertain. She started for the counter.

She slid her tray down the line and was met by a row of curious faces. Elvira had already spotted her, and met her on the other side with no introduction, just started off like a carnival barker, proud of the food they had to offer and telling it to her the way it was.

"Everything looks so good," Palmetto said.

"That's 'cause it is good," Elvira answered. "Get anything you want. You like pork chops? We got haddock. We got chicken à la king. We got fried chicken. Veal. We got vegetables. Any kind you want. How 'bout some corn and greens?"

"Okay."

"Dish it up, Mattie. Put a little okra on the side."

There was pride about this place. It fairly glistened with it. They were doing something everyday yet wonderful, and they seemed to know it.

"Got hot rolls and cornbread. Give her one of each." Elvira looked around and saw Preston and Scoe through the glass porthole in the kitchen door. Men didn't have any more manners than dogs on the street. "Mattie! Make up Mista Preston a tray."

They paused at the desserts. Palmetto's tray was loaded. Elvira picked up a wedge of peach pie. "I'll hold it for you and get it à la mode. What you drinking?"

She carried Palmetto's tray to the table

143

and set it down, arranging the little plates of food as if she were going to eat them herself. "Mista Preston don't know nothin' 'bout ladies," she said, "so don't you go getting put out with him. All he know is work and that's from can till can't. If there's anything you need, just holler."

"You've been so nice."

"Sit down and eat," Elvira said, and headed for the kitchen.

Preston and Scoe were in a corner, going over an order list. Preston was determined to find something wrong.

Scooter entered the kitchen with an empty pan and tossed it into a sink, where it landed with a clatter. Preston looked up angrily. The submerged irritations of The Melba were still there. He had forgotten about them. He had forgotten Scooter, who would have to go. Perhaps not, though. Maybe he had changed.

"Everybody run wild while I was gone?"

Scoe had heard all this before. He had done a good job of running the place, was angry at being asked the nigger-simple questions he was too good for. "We works just as hard when you're out as when you're in."

"Yeah? Then why are those boxes by the door not unpacked?"

"They have just come in."

The men stood staring at each other. Scoe was not about to let Preston get the best of him. He'd stare him down if he had to keep on staring till it thundered.

Preston broke away first. He looked around just as Scooter leaned up against the sink, lit a cigarette, and flipped the dead match toward a box.

Elvira swung into the kitchen just as Preston started for Scooter. Scoe caught her with her mouth wide open and motioned her to silence.

Preston stood in front of Scooter and pointed to a framed restaurant seal from the Board of Health. It boasted an "A" rating.

"You see that 'A'? I don't want to lose it. *Won't* lose it!"

Scooter blew the smoke out and spoke in an irritatingly easy way. "Don't get so heated up, Boss.''

Preston was being pushed, could feel himself going with the push. ''If somebody from the Health Department had walked in here, we'd be looking at a 'B.' ''

''Ain't nobody seen me.''

It was the unconcern that did it. ''Yeah. Well, I did, and that's all it took. Scoe, how many days he got coming?''

''Two.''

''Get changed and see Miss Fan. She'll give you your money.''

Scooter shrugged and headed for the door.

Preston could feel his heart beating, causing a breathless pumping in his neck. The throbbing vein must have run behind his ear, he could hear it so clearly. Then there was a silence, and he felt their eyes upon him. He had done it, cut someone away, but it had been asked for, you couldn't say it wasn't. He had been within his rights, would have been worse off if he had let it go. That was the trouble with being boss, you couldn't weaken. Ever.

Scoe felt the chill that Preston felt,

couldn't name it, didn't know why. He would have done the same to Scooter himself, but would it have been the same? No matter how close Preston came to them, he was still an arbitrary, order-giving world away. It wasn't Scooter anybody cared about. It was themselves. If one could go, why couldn't two or three?

"I've got no truck with the shiftless," Preston was saying to the kitchen at large, knowing he didn't need to justify his act, but doing it just the same. "What is it, Elvira?"

"You got company."

"Don't bother me with that!"

"She fixin' to walk outta here . . . so she say . . ."

He never should have brought her here in the first place. He must still not be himself. Well, he would get over that. There was nothing wrong with him that an afternoon at work wouldn't cure. He stormed out of the kitchen, almost running into Fat Boy, who swung through the door with a load of plates.

Elvira looked out of the window as he

crossed the cafeteria.

"You fixing to put your nose some place it ain't supposed to go," Scoe told her. "And it's gon' get chopped off."

"Anybody wants to chop me can see me," Elvira answered, and gave him a look that told him she made no allowances for husbands.

Preston walked through the cafeteria, giving orders as he went. "Getting low on cups at counter two." "Get Mattie out here with coffee refills." "Tell Elvira to make up the biscuit tray. I'll pass 'em when they're ready."

Elvira came out of the kitchen and watched him pause and sit down at the table. "Mattie. Sadie. Keep an eye on his ice-cream dish. Every time it gets low, slip him another. As long as he got ice cream in his dish, that man ain't moving."

She was right. Preston was a fool for peach ice cream, and the season for peaches was fading fast. Old Nola, back in the kitchen icing cakes and putting whipped cream on pies, would turn the crank on the ice-cream freezer for another couple of weeks, then shut it down when the peaches went and they returned to vanilla, which could be better bought.

"Miss Russell," said Preston, sitting down, his voice starched in formality.

"You must stop calling me 'Miss Russell.' I take off the 'Miss' when I take off my uniform."

"I don't know what your first name is." He blushed. He hated to admit when he didn't know something.

"Palmetto. It's a kind of palm. You know, palmetto fans. They always had them in the hymnal racks in church. The kind of rustling sound that they make can be very soothing. My mother said that when she was carrying me she would sit in church and close her eyes and just listen to the rustle of the palmetto. And since our last name happened to be Russell . . . I'm the only person I know who's named after a noise."

"Bet you have a lot of fans." He said it before he even thought. She made things be born in him that weren't there before.

She rolled her eyes in pain at his pun, but she gave a gleaming laugh and tilted her head slightly, and he noticed the calm slope of her ivory neck, unexpected, like a bathing bird. "That was kind of droll," she said. "I know a lot of fellows who tell jokes, but I don't think any of them has real wit."

"You go out with a lot of guys?"

"Well, I'm not burning my candle at both ends, if that's what you mean . . . but I haven't unearthed my Prince Charming, either."

A dish of ice cream appeared before him and took away the need for a reply. He was beginning to be disillusioned with her. That was the trouble with people. They all had private lives. Everybody was destined somewhere, storming right along. He was storming right along too, but he stormed alone. He wondered, just for the sake of wondering, how you got involved in somebody else's life. Everybody always had somebody. Not that he wanted anybody. He was a self-made man, and self-sufficient. All he needed was customers.

"Everything's just so good," she said. "That roast beef was as tender as a mother's love."

He smiled at her, a bit of ice cream clinging to his lower lip. She licked her lower lip, and he suddenly knew she was signaling for him to lick his. He did, and the ice cream went away. He had never before received a message in flesh. He felt himself stirring under the table. She was wearing silk stockings, and he could hear the whirr they made as she crossed her legs. He stirred again. It would be embarrassing if he had to get up. She was the same color as the peach ice cream. He took another mouthful and savored it.

"I am not cut out for marriage," he said. He might as well put his cards on the table.

He was just about the funniest thing she had ever seen. "Me neither. But I am a very good fiancée. I've had three rings, just like a circus."

"I certainly don't think it's a good practice to tell somebody you'll marry them and then break it off."

"Well, I would never, ever marry anybody just to be polite. Marrying somebody is a very big step. Just think, if

I'd married somebody I didn't get along with, well, I don't know how it would be, just too awful. That's all."

"I suppose you know what you're doing."

"About the only bad thing that's come of it is that my mama's been slightly scandalized and the Cedartown *Standard* has refused to print any more engagement announcements featuring my picture."

"All that engagement stuff is a lot of foolishness, if you ask me. When my sisters got married they went down to the courthouse and then got on with their business."

"Oh," she said. "I want a fabulous wedding with bridesmaids and flowers. I've been planning it since I was a little girl. I'm going to come down the center aisle of the First Methodist Church on my daddy's arm, carrying lilies of the valley, and Miss Emma Swinbourne's going to sing 'O, Promise Me.' It's going to be a night wedding, so there can be candles, and all my bridesmaids are going to carry gardenias and be dressed in peach satin with green velvet ribbons in their hair."

"If we left the world up to women all we'd have is ceremonies and tea parties."

It was as though he had poured ice on her fire, but she could burn through that. "And who do you think wants it that way? The men, that's who!"

"I don't want it that way."

"You and those like you. Let me tell you something. When I was coming along, I wanted to be a doctor, and you have never heard such a howl. 'That's a man's world,' they said. Well, there's not much I give in on, but I got it from all sides, so in I gave. Being a nurse is something, and that's what I am, and a damn finer one you'll never see, but I'm other things too, and if one of those is somebody who wants a little romance, then I'll fight for that and keep it alive. I gave in on one thing I wanted in this life. I'll be damned if I'll give in on another!"

He couldn't imagine what he'd done to upset her so. She had blazed out at him as though he were responsible for all the bad things that had ever happened to her. He was hurt, a bit scared, and more than a little peeved. He looked around to see if anyone had overheard. He certainly would have picked a more private place to launch into such a tirade. He heard the sound of her stockings again. He had had no idea that his hearing was so acute.

"I'm sorry. I didn't invite you down to fight. I just thought you might like to have lunch. You were very nice to me at the hospital. I hope I haven't hurt your feelings. I didn't mean to, if I did."

Her eyes were growing moist. "Oh, no," she said. "I'm the one who should apologize to you. The lunch was very nice. It couldn't have been better. And I just love your place. I never imagined there was anything like it in Atlanta. It's so sophisticated. It looks like a dream after a rich meal. I'm afraid I'll never get invited back."

"Any time. Any time at all. No charge. Just tell Miss Fan you're my nurse. She'll know."

"Oh, I'd never do that."

"I insist."

"Oh, I'd come here with you, but not alone. I just hate freeloaders."

There's something to this girl, he

thought. "Don't go," he said. She smiled, dipped her napkin into her water glass, and gently patted her lips. It was the daintiest thing he had ever seen, like a mama cat.

She winked at him, his first, and stayed. Another dish of peach ice cream found its way before him, and the golden autumn afternoon drifted into twilight while he told her of his growing up and things that he had felt, spoke haltingly at times, drank his way through four glasses of water, his throat drying up before the words did.

"My goodness," she said at last, "it's almost dark. It's the first time in my life I ever spent the whole day in a cafeteria." She reached for her purse and pulled out a cigarette, seeing the disapproval in his eyes but determined to have it. "Got to have my Luckies." She lit up and exhaled a phenomenal stream of smoke.

"I'd think a nurse would know all about what smoking can do to you," he said.

She smiled and continued smoking. "Wouldn't you, though," she said, and watched in rapt fascination as Preston absently toyed with his shiny blue tie, bringing it to his mouth and chewing on it. "I don't think I ever saw anybody chew on their tie."

He dropped it immediately, mortified. He hated his weakness more than he hated himself, and at this moment he hated himself enormously. "Yeah . . . well . . . uh . . ."

"I guess it beats biting your fingernails," she continued, "but aren't you ties full of tooth marks?"

"That's enough of that!" If she had been a man he would have hit her. She knew how to give the screw a final turn.

She picked her gloves up off her purse and held several frayed fingers toward him. "I chew my gloves," she said, and grinned with her confession.

He grinned back. The corners of his mouth gave little tremors at the unaccustomed exercise.

They sat there for while, just showing each other their grins.

"Are you going to New York to the World's Fair?" she asked.

"No indeed."

"I hear it's wonderful. A real glimpse of the future."

"Just another place to spend your money."

"That's where I think I'll spend my vacation. I want to see everything while I'm young. You have no idea of the people I see who worked all their lives so they'd have an easy time of being old, and now that they're old, they've got it but they can't do anything with it."

"Money's hard to come by, and so's a place of business. I'm a businessman through and through. That comes first with me, and always will."

"Well . . . As long as you're going to be married to a cafeteria, it's nice that it has a woman's name." She reached into the empty chair and picked up the sweetheart roses, limp after their long day. She rose. "It's been most enjoyable."

He was surprised. "You going?"

"Got to get these in water. My wedding bouquet." She looked at him evenly, no beaming smile this time.

He got up. They headed for the door.

"I . . . er . . . thank you for the day."

"It was my pleasure."

"You're a good nurse."

They stopped by the revolving door. Its brass fixtures gleamed with the setting sun, passing some of it along to her. "I like The Melba," she said.

He nodded in agreement, as though it were not his place at all, just some place special they had come upon. "What kinda pie you like?"

"Oh. I dunno. Any kind. Pumpkin."

"I'll send you one."

She looked straight at him, her lips moving in unspoken thanks. He knew she was telling him all kinds of things. He didn't know if he understood them at all. He was deaf and dumb in the land of other people. He shuffled nervously, moving around to hide his embarrassment, while his uncontrollable right hand stole down to grab the tie and bring it upward.

For an instant they were holding hands, the tie entwined. "Only bad boys eat their ties," she said, smiled, winked, and with casual magic stepped away from him, twirled through the revolving door, looked his way once through plate glass, then vanished.

Preston stood there a moment, looking at the place where she had been. It was his fractured skull, that's all it was, that made him feel so strange. He would go home early and get some rest. There was work to do, but he would take it easy. He didn't like this feeling at all. He shook his head to clear away the foolishness. He had never before heard of anyone named Palmetto. He decided he never would again. He walked back toward the kitchen with a vengeance.

Chapter 4

October was almost gone. Palmetto sat curled at the far end of the awful sofa, listening to Phil Spatalny and His All-Girl Orchestra Featuring Evelyn and Her Magic Violin. They were playing "Silver Threads Among the Gold." She had been crying softly and was beginning to sniffle now, the sounds of stopping. Mrs. Pitts, her black Scottie, named for a wrathful former landlady with no tolerance for puppies, stood impatiently wagging her tail, moving from one foot to another. Palmetto got up, put her feet into galoshes, pulled on a raincoat, and crushed the droopy khaki hat down over her head. No umbrella today. She felt like getting into it.

She let herself out the side door of the house that belonged to Babe and Bob

Shaw, a ruddy, energetic, childless couple in their fifties. They were good to her, a cross between parents who understood and a big sister and brother who didn't compete. She loved them dearly. She hoped they didn't see her and tap on the window, motioning for her to come in for a drink.

It was a big, lonesome brick house, "out in the sticks," as they said. There was an enormous well-trimmed yard that sloped down to a fishing pond. A rotting but still serviceable boat was tied to the end of the flecked green dock, where she stood leaning against a post, bobbing softly with the rest of the dock, watching Mrs. Pitts pee, then investigate the world in the rain. How wonderful girl dogs are, she thought. She had grown up raising male bird dogs and hounds, speckled short-haired things that always pointed away. Bitches were somewhere else, in heat behind fences, tongues hanging out, serviced for a fee.

She walked off the dock and started briskly around the pond, pulling off the hat and shaking her hair. Had she been a more poetic spirit, she might have run naked around the pond, but she was satisfied with wet hair, defying a cold. Perhaps if she had been with a boy the idea might have come. She always had her best thoughts when she was paired.

Mrs. Pitts ran ahead and behind. I wish I had your energy, she thought, then felt old inside, as though she'd passed her peak and missed it, been somewhere out in space and come home to find the party over, only dirty dishes and filled-up ashtrays left.

She had had her days, though, times that came back to her in rainbow colors, the yellows, blues, and greens of the cut-glass world she grew up in. She had had a wide tomboy streak, and dresses were the punishment of her childhood. She and Winnie Hill. My God! How long ago that was! The early twenties. They couldn't have been any more than ten or eleven.

* * *

It was summer, and they had sneaked

Mamie's prized crystal pitcher out from under Ludilla's nose while she stood facing the sink, singing about Jesus and washing butter beans. Palmetto had taken the silver ladle, too. Winnie had made the lemonade, a bucket of it, and they had sung "Down by the Old Mill Stream" in harmony all the way to the railroad tracks, the heavy bucket leaving a crisscross of red welts on their palms.

A group of chain-gang prisoners were working, overseen by a wiry, cadaverous guard who held a shotgun under one arm. The prisoners, chained together at three-foot intervals, were digging a trench along the track.

Winnie was scared and backed out at the last minute, which was what she could always be counted on to do. Palmetto was scared too, but she'd rather be scared and do what she had to do than back out of it and be a chicken along with Winnie.

"We brought some lemonade," she said to the guard.

The prisoners had stopped and stared at them. She felt silly, felt weighted down by the big blue ribbon that drooped among her dangling curls.

"Get on back to work," the guard had yelled.

It made her mad. The guard was just trash anyway. "They can have some lemonade," she said.

"Get on outta here!" he yelled at them.

Winnie was more than ready to make an exit, but Palmetto would have stood there if it had harelipped hell. "I'm Judge Alfred Russell's little girl, and if you don't let us give them some lemonade you are shortly going to be busting rocks yourself."

She stared him down. The prisoners stopped. Winnie and Palmetto had given them the lemonade right out of Mamie's silver ladle. They even gave the guard some, making him wait till last. "Here's a nickel," he had said.

"I don't want your money," Palmetto said, and walked away. Winnie hesitated, and when she caught up with Palmetto she was clutching the nickel in her hand. They were around the bend now, and frail Winnie was out of breath.

"Did you take that nickel?"

"I did."

"That's the rottenest thing I ever heard of."

"Palmetto Russell, your daddy's a judge and you get a nickel every time you hold your hand out. My daddy works at the mill."

"If you're going to be a slave to what your daddy does, then you can just stop tagging along with me."

"You little bitch!"

It was the worst thing Palmetto had ever been called to her face. Before she knew what she was doing, she had heaved the pitcher at Winnie, who ducked and let it smash against a rock. They were so stunned that they just looked at each other and burst into tears.

They were friends again by the time the town came back in sight, Palmetto knowing she was going to get it about the pitcher but calm. "All they can do is spank me," she said. "I'm not going to be killed or maimed. Mama knows that Daddy raises Cain when I get spanked."

"One of these days somebody's going to stand up to you, Palmetto Russell."

She didn't remember the spanking at all, though she did remember that Josephine, her older sister, had been nasty to her for a week, because Josephine had been scheduled to inherit Mamie's pitcher.

Everything had seemed possible in those days of childhood that stretched as wide and far as the limitless acres of corn and barley in back of the house, row after row, creaking in the wind that ended up blowing them into the Depression.

They kept the house but sold the car and got a cow named Beautiful, whose milk they drank. Mamie churned and made butter. Palmetto outgrew her girlhood gathering eggs.

Mamie finally let Palmetto bob her hair, after having seen it dragged through the soup too many times. Short hair was more a badge of womanhood than her burgeoning breasts, which were practically being stunted by the tight stays they made her wear.

She had fought her losing battle about medical school and was resigned to being the greatest nurse since Florence

Nightingale. It was June, and she was going to graduate from high school. It was the day of the Senior Class picnic at the Big Spring. Tomorrow she would graduate and be a member of the world. All her life seemed to have been a headlong rush for this moment, dreamed of, talked about, planned for, and now here. She was afraid.

Why had she ever wanted to outgrow her perfect life? How could she endure anything else? But she had planned on having a good time and that was what she would do. She had on a blue dress. It brought out her eyes.

Buzzy Shoemaker. Six foot three and coal-black hair. Seventeen, too. He wanted to be a flyer, was just crazy about airplanes, and she had told him what a fool he was, that he'd get killed and then what would she do? But boys were boys, and stubborn, and he went right on with his plans.

He walked beside her out the kitchen door, where she had taken the basket Ludilla had packed, the crusts neatly trimmed from all the sandwiches.

Mamie was in the chicken lot, gathering eggs, which she folded in her apron and held before her. "Hello, Buzzy."

" 'Lo, Miz Russell."

"Don't keep her out too late, you hear? Have her in by midnight."

"Yes, ma'am. I will."

"And don't drive too fast. Keep both hands on the wheel."

"Oh, mama! Why don't you just print up an instruction list?"

"Young lady, you're still living under this roof . . . But you do look pretty. Pretty as a picture. If you pass your daddy on the way home, get out of the car and show him how pretty you look."

"Oh, I'm a great beauty," Palmetto said, turning and laughing.

Mamie had laughed, too. "I wouldn't go that far," she said.

Suddenly Palmetto's eyes had filled with tears. She grabbed Mamie, hugging her hard, almost crushing the eggs.

"Mercy! We'll have scrambled eggs right here in the yard," Mamie said, but she saw the swimming eyes and traced her hand along the smooth young cheek.

They were the Class of 1927. A banner proclaiming this sagged over the picnic area. About twenty girls and some of the teachers set out the food. Palmetto and Winnie unwrapped sandwiches and laughed at funny old Miss Dukes, who had made it her mission to fan the flies away.

"Shoo, flies," she said. "Winnie, you and Palmetto better see how long those boys are going to play baseball."

They had fled. Winnie was no longer frail — if anything, she was larger than Palmetto, and wiser, as if she'd picked up extra information while Palmetto had spent her afternoons at the Red Cross rolling bandages and dreaming noble dreams.

"My goodness," said Winnie as they went toward the baseball field. "If Miss Dukes didn't have flies to shoo, what would she do?"

"That's kind of sad, you know."

"I mean that as a joke."

"We're going to have a lot of chances. Look at poor Miss Dukes and some of those others. The next major event in their lives is going to be death.''

''Palmetto, I don't want to listen to that.''

''I wonder what they did wrong. If I thought I was going to end up some shoo-fly old maid, I'd go jump in the deepest part of Big Spring.''

''What in the world has gotten into you?''

''I just feel reflective. That's all. Don't you ever?''

''Not if I can help it.''

They had climbed a grassy hill and looked down on an improvised baseball diamond, where a hectic game was in progress. From their vantage point the girls could see both the game and the picnic preparations. They were all tinted gold by the setting summer sun.

Palmetto's eyes were full again. ''I wish I could take this moment and freeze it in time.''

''Why?''

''Because everyone I love is well and close by and I am having a happy life and I don't want it to change. I had this terrible dream the other night. I dreamed that I was holding sand in my hands. I had cupped them together and I had all the sand I could hold, letting it slide between my fingers just the way an hourglass does, very smoothly and slowly, and then, just about the time it was all gone, I discovered it wasn't sand at all. It was my life, and I couldn't hold on to it." She began to cry, the tears resting on her cheeks, not flowing, glistening along with the rest of the earth as the sun fought to keep from going down.

Winnie took her hand and pressed it. "It was just a dream. It doesn't mean anything. Nothing bad is ever going to happen to you. You have a charmed life." Then she too began to cry. "I've got something to tell you."

Palmetto felt a breeze upon her drying tears. "What?"

"Leamon Biggers and I got married last night."

Palmetto was so stunned that she knew she let Winnie see it, and that was not the way it was supposed to be at all. She was supposed to be happy. "Why?" she asked, in spite of herself.

"Why do you suppose?"

They cried and hugged again. "You'll be so happy," Palmetto said. "I just love Leamon."

"We are happy," Winnie said defiantly. "We really do love each other. But don't tell a soul. We can't announce it till after tomorrow. They might not let him graduate otherwise."

"I won't say a word," she promised, and felt more alone than she had ever felt before. Her best friend had gone through all those things and she had never known it. She was still a child, had gotten left behind somehow like poor Miss Shoo-Fly Dukes.

The picnic ended. She and Buzzy walked by the stream. It was dark along the Big Spring. Only the katydids and rushing water made noises. They sat on a knoll above the stream and leaned against a patient oak that bore initials.

"This time next year, we'll be college freshmen," he said.

"This time next year you'll have

forgotten all about me,'' she said. ''You'll be stepping out with some coed and doing God knows what.''

''If I'm going to be doing God knows what, I want to be doing it with you.''

''You can get that idea right out of your head.''

He gave her a helpless, melting look. ''I've tried and I can't.''

Palmetto knew truth when it presented itself and always let it have its way, though this was the first time she had ever been faced with truth that needed more than mere acknowledgment.

''Oh, Buzzy.''

''I love you, Palmetto.''

''I love you too, and I don't want to lose you.''

''You couldn't lose me if you wanted to.''

''I feel like I'm losing everything.''

He took her in his arms and pulled her roughly with ignorance and urgently with need. ''You'll always have me,'' he said. ''You'll always have me.''

She always had that night. Nothing was

ever better or ever worse. Time went by, and so did Buzzy, and the others who came and went and said, "You couldn't lose me if you wanted to," only she did, but they lost her, too, and grieved as she did, and forgot except in moments when names no longer matched with faces and faces faded, turning into pangs and breathless waking moments in the night when they realized that something had slipped beyond them, lost and gone forever, but, like Palmetto, they went on with others and others and others, each one being the journey's end, and each one saying, "You'll always have me."

* * *

The rain had stopped around the pond where Palmetto and Mrs. Pitts walked. Palmetto decided she might live. She flung a stick, and Mrs. Pitts took off after it. Damn that Preston Vacalis, she thought. It had been three weeks, and she hadn't heard the first thing from him. The nerve! He had liked her a lot more than she had liked him. She hadn't even liked him that much, the more she thought about it. She couldn't imagine getting serious with anyone who chewed his tie. She laughed out loud at the memory of that. She would fix him good.

Mrs. Pitts stood wagging before her. Palmetto sighed. You flung the stick once, you had to fling it twenty times. "Go fetch," she said, and threw it.

Chapter 5

Preston knew the men meant trouble the first time he laid eyes on them. He was sitting in afternoon splendor in the booth nearest the door, as he had done almost every afternoon of The Melba's two years. He sat there promptly at three, when the lunch rush had faded and the lines were being closed and cleaned. Elvira always made him up a tray: four vegetables, meat, a piece of cornbread, iced tea with a little grape juice in it, and ice cream. He ate as he skated, with delicate precision. He prided himself on good table manners. He glanced down at his fingernails and smiled. He had begun having manicures, a gentleman's thing.

He had deftly finished his rutabaga and paused a moment, looking up, smiling hospitably in case anyone was looking his

176

way, searching for a salesman to come, as they usually did, beckoned to his table by a manicured motion. But today was Wednesday, and they came on Tuesday and Thursday. He inhaled deeply, preparing himself for ice cream. Then the revolving door revolved and in came the trouble.

Their names were Welsh and Greener, no "Mister" to either. They wore suits, dressed like educated men, but he could tell the kind they were from their manner. They seemed to know him, too, regarded him with thin, over-hearty smiles as they stood above him, waiting to be asked to sit down. He let them wait, sat spooning his ice cream, keeping his face blank and pleasant.

"What can I do for you gentlemen?" All the right words in discordant tones.

"We're from the Amalgamated Restaurant and Cafeteria Workers Union."

" 'Fraid that outfit got by without me hearing of it," Preston said. His eyes went small, everything within him, contracting into a nervous bullet. The ice cream lost its taste, was only cold. He continued spooning.

"Can we sit down?"

"Suit yourselves."

Scoe, standing by the cash register, saw them, knew something was wrong when Preston didn't signal for iced tea or coffee. He watched a moment while Miss Fan toted up some figures, using her fingers as well as the register; then he turned in time to catch Mattie and Sadie looking toward the table as though they knew what was going on. Mattie saw him watching and nudged Sadie, and they went back to work — slowly, though, keeping up a pretense.

"Unions have come of age, Mr. Vacalis. We're here in good faith."

"I've got no complaints against unions. My father was for 'em, got arrested and thrown in jail for fightin' for 'em. But what I wanta know is this — did Scooter Monohan have anything to do with this?"

"We're not at liberty to go into all that."

People used words like "faith" and "liberty" when they were up to no good.

"We're not trying to tell you how to run your business, but somebody's got to

178

protect the workers' rights."

"What about me?" Preston said. "Don't I have some rights? I'm not John D. Rockefeller. I'm a working man."

They looked at him smilingly, telling him with the upturned corners of their mouths that he wasn't fooling them a bit, looking at the lovely trappings that made him guilty.

"What about the other eating places?" Preston asked.

"They'll come around."

"When you get them, come back around to see me and we'll see what we can do. I want everybody to be fed from the same spoon."

His feet curled up in the highly shined tooled-leather shoes. He rocked them evenly back and forth from heel to toe. He chose to make them disappear, stared straight ahead as though they had.

Welsh and Greener looked at each other. They had been made to disappear before. They rose, still smiling. "You'll be hearing from us." Greener made the mistake of extending his hand. Preston refused to see it. They left, walking close together in their gabardine suits, Welsh stopping to get the Free Weight by the door.

Preston sat staring into the opaque space, the ice cream melting in his dish. Victor, the mailman, came in, his sagging pouch jerking him to one side. He smiled and called out to Preston, who was oblivious. He went on over to Miss Fan and Scoe. "The boss is out gathering wool today."

"Yes, suh. He is. Mattie, get a cuppa coffee for Mista Victor."

"Thank you, Scoe." He unloaded his mail. Miss Fan pulled her glasses down from her forehead and shuffled through it, passing it to Scoe along with an oblong box in brown wrapping paper.

Scoe hesitated, then walked over to Preston, standing in front of him until the eyelids opened a bit wider and let him into view.

"You know anything about this union business?"

"I heard some talk."

"Then why the hell didn't you come to me? Why am I the last one to

180

hear about something?"

"If I was to come to you with every little bit of talk I hear, we'd be seeing too much of each other."

Preston's anger had turned to hurt. He slammed the side of his palm against the table, rocking the dishes. "You can't have a damned thing! Every time you get a little something you got people lined up trying to take it away from you. Everybody up North is unionizing and putting up barricades. People trying to tell you how to do this, trying to tell you how to do that. Everybody's trying to get something for nothing."

He paused for breath. Scoe had seen him wind to a tirade before, repeating his little wounded phrases. Scoe used the pause as an escape.

"I know what you mean," he said, placed the mail on the table, and hurried away.

Preston sat brooding another moment, then looked up and saw himself in the mirrors across the room, saw The Melba in its glory, thought of the evening meal he was now serving and the fact that it seemed to be catching on. It might be paying for itself within the month. This was business. That was all. It was a man's game. The best man always won. Would win. He thought of Welsh and Greener and snorted, more in contempt than pity. This was Preston Vacalis's Melba Cafeteria, and nobody was going to tell him how to run it.

He looked down at the package, picked it up, turned it over, almost sniffed it. He got gifts of food from wholesalers. He didn't know what this was. He picked up his knife and slit the string. When he opened the box and saw what was inside, he was blank for a moment, not knowing what to make of it. He scowled, then let out a high-pitched cackle that caused the help and the few remaining customers to look at him.

Inside the box was a brand-new tie. The nipple from a baby bottle had been firmly stitched to it.

The Rex Club stood on the wooded banks of the Chattahoochee River. It had once been a private home with sculpted lawns terraced down to the water's edge.

Now strands of electric lanterns stretched where the gardens were trampled by couples come to dance and have cocktails and maybe some lucky further amusement among the overgrown hedges.

Preston didn't approve of it at all. He felt most uncomfortable among people his own age who were out simply to have a good time. He could still make no distinction between a good time and wasted time. He hadn't gotten where he was by going out at night and whooping till the sun came up. When he had called Palmetto and gruffly, anxiously invited her out, the first thing she had said was "Oh, let's go to The Rex. It's my favorite place, next to The Melba. Rex and Melba. If they were people instead of restaurants, we could marry them off."

"The Melba is a cafeteria," he had said.

She hadn't said anything at all to that, just as she wasn't saying anything now as they pulled into the drive-in area, where cars could get curb service from red-coated black men who weaved in and out among the parked and moving cars like

Martian fireflies, round steel trays held over their heads and a high-pitched, unfathomable jargon coming from their throats.

"What are they talking about?" he asked.

"They're just calling out orders."

He snorted, imagining what The Melba would be like if they called out their orders in vocal shorthand. But he was stunned at the business the place did. Amazing how people were so willing to throw their money away.

He slammed on the brakes in surprise as a wiry black man jumped out of a group of wiry black men and hopped onto the hood of the pickup truck he was driving. The man grinned a gummy grin at Preston and inserted a numbered card behind the windshield wiper. Palmetto laughed. "It's what they do. We're his car now. Nobody else can get us."

"I thought we were going inside."

"We are. He just opens the door and things. They all do it."

Preston shook his head and followed the man's frantic waving to a stall at the far end of the first aisle, facing a graded red-clay area where The Rex was obviously getting ready to expand.

He cut off the motor, then the lights, and sat still for an instant, wanting to turn to her and say, "I'm sorry. I made a mistake. I want to go home. I've got work to do." But his door was opened for him, and he had no time to say anything at all, just look at the grinning black man and get out. "Rudolph. Rudolph. At your service. That's me. Just ask for Rudolph. Call for Rudolph." He spoke in a high voice, as though all that yelling in the damp night air had stretched and thinned his vocal cords. He bounded around the pickup, limping slightly. One of his shoes had a high orthopedic heel. He opened Palmetto's door, and she got out.

She was wearing red tonight. Preston had some reservations about the color, but he had to admit she looked just fine. It was a warm night for November, and she wore only a cloth coat. She took his arm as though it were the most casual thing in the world. He started toward the building, but he could feel her holding back, see her glance going sideways. Rudolph was standing there, his grin at attention. "Hope you folks has a big night," he said.

Preston thrust his hand into his pocket and tossed him a nickel. "Always somebody with their hand out."

Palmetto started to say something, but held her tongue.

The music came over the lawn like the haze of smoke which followed it. It was a big band, and they were playing "The Way You Look Tonight." Palmetto hummed along with it, putting the music in her walk, scattering a few of the lyrics.

"You have a pretty voice," he said formally.

"Don't I," she responded. "It's one of my favorite things about myself, but I've done nothing with it, other than sing in a wedding or two. One summer I had the idea I'd be a singer, but where I come from if you're not singing opera or choir it's considered immoral. Of course, I don't know where Kate Smith fits in."

They arrived at the entrance. A striped canopy went down a flight of several steps, and the white swinging doors with brass plates swung busily. A red carpet stretched from an old carriage block all the way inside. There was a life-size blowup of a beaming, slick-looking man in tails. Some tipsy lady had left a lipstick print on his photographed cheek. A rainbow of glittery silver letters went over his head from shoulder to shoulder. BOOTSIE SHOE AND THE SATIN SLIPPERS. Preston looked at it and narrowed his eyes in suspicion at a man who'd get dressed up like that and have his picture taken.

"Come on, hotshot, let's cut a rug," Palmetto said, and pulled him through the double doors.

Once inside, the music caught him, surrounded him in a florid, imitation Paul Whiteman style, led him through the marbled foyer, where a floating staircase climbed to rooms where gambling was said to go on, that and other things for special guests who came out to sin rather than stay home and do it in the dark. There were oval niches in the walls, filled with fresh flowers in Chinese vases.

Fresh flowers in November, that must

have set 'em back something, Preston thought as Palmetto smiled at a man in the doorway. He smiled as though he knew her and led them down more steps into the main ballroom, enormous, with a domed ceiling and plaster ivy trailing the walls. There was a raised bandstand contrived to look like seashell. Artificial silver palm trees stood at either side of the stage and continued throughout the room, set at intervals by a line of French doors that opened into a terrace which ran the length of the house. Across from the doors was a leather-trimmed glass-topped bar. Behind the bar was an enormous aquarium. Preston's eyes were opened as wide as his mouth. He had never seen anything like it. Huge, multihued fish swam slowly, some of the smaller ones making it through a glass trough and swimming the distance of the bar, streaming silently under glasses, napkins, ashtrays, pocketbooks, and elbows.

The music changed to "Indian Summer." Palmetto closed her eyes and swayed her shoulders. It made her feel a part of civilized society, going places and doing things, always looking good and having money and never, never, never getting old. "Isn't it something?" she asked him.

"It's all right," he allowed, hating it, loving it.

A tuxedoed waiter with a white napkin over his arm stood at the table. Preston's mind went blank. All he could think of was iced tea and peach ice cream. They would laugh him out of the place.

"I'd like a French 'Seventy-five," Palmetto said. "What about you?"

"I'm not much of a drinker."

"Give him a French 'Seventy-five too. They're very mild."

Preston thought he saw some slight, eye-moving communication between her and the waiter, but he couldn't be sure. He couldn't be sure of anything, particularly the girl sitting across from him. She was too familiar with fast night places to suit him.

"Are you okay?" she asked.

"I'm having a good time."

"I'd hate to see you when you're feeling blue."

"I don't go out much."

"Well, you ought to start. You wouldn't want people thinking you're a stick-in-the-mud, would you?"

"I don't care what people think of me as long as I'm doing my work and not bothering anybody."

"Listen, I'm sorry I opened my mouth," she said, and turned in a tiny huff to watch Bootsie Shoe lead the band, his arms moving as energetically and predictably as a haymower.

The drinks arrived, tall and frosty, with mint and fruit sloshing over the top. He thought for an instant how much it must cost to have all that frothy, wasted liquid spilling by the year, but it was pretty to look at.

Palmetto turned, happy with the refreshment, deciding to give the evening another chance. "Bottoms up!" she said.

They drank, Preston thinking a moment, then smiling cautiously. "It's all right."

The French '75 left a slight, fluffy mustache on his top lip. She reached across the table and brushed it away with a gentle finger. He almost crossed his eyes looking down at the red-polished nail.

It's too much red, he thought. Red dress, red nails, red lips. And the red lips moved too much, not just talking, puckering slightly, the lower lip disappearing at moments as she nibbled at it; then her too-pink tongue would lick across the furrowed lipstick. Definitely too much red. He took another drink.

"Why didn't you ever call me? Was it my breath?"

"Why do you think a thing like that?"

"Well, I'm not scarred up or grossly overweight, and I thought we had . . . you know . . . a nice feeling between us. So I just wondered why you didn't call. Not, God forbid, that I have to sit home waiting for the phone to ring, but I did sort of wonder. I bet if I hadn't sent you that tie I'd never have heard from you again."

"I'm glad you sent it. I thought it was funny. I think you're funny."

"You're kind of a hoot and a holler yourself," she said, signaled to the waiter for more drinks, and reached into her red crushed-velvet purse for her cigarettes.

She put one in her mouth and waited an instant for a match to be struck before her. When nothing happened, she indicated a matchbook on the table.

"I'm not going to light it for you," he said. "I don't approve of it."

"You ever heard of manners?"

"I'll take morals."

She lit it herself, as angry as the orange flame, inhaled with a vengeance, and exhaled copiously, showing her vexation. "If I have to choose between being loose and a social retard, I will opt for looseness every time."

"I'm sorry," he said. "You've got me wrong. I think you're nice. You practically saved my life. I'd have to like you even if I didn't like you, but I do like you. I hope you know what I mean. I would have called you. I thought about you. I'm just not much of a ladies' man."

"That may be what I like about you."

Their new drinks came, and he had to guzzle the first one down.

"Why don't we dance?" she asked.

"The main reason is I don't know how."

"Want a lesson?"

"Too many people."

She picked up her drink and stood up. "Come on."

She started toward the French doors. It was going to get complicated. He knew it. It had been all right sitting at the table. He was getting used to it; now she wanted to do something else. Women were like cats. They never let anything alone. She wouldn't be content until she had done something to embarrass him. He picked up his glass and followed her.

The moonlight cut a path down through the shedding trees that bordered the river. Palmetto sat on a balustrade overlooking the lawn, where couples wandered. He stood in the doorway and saw her in profile. She was intent on something, her lips pursed with the effort of concentration. With the faint light on her, she looked like the subject of a dim, romantic oil painting. He was overtaken with the feeling that she needed to be saved from something, but it was a vague, frightening something that he needed to be rescued from himself. She was going to make trouble for him. He knew that much, knew it so certainly that he almost turned and ran back through the haughty, elegant Rex, into the well-loved, much-abused pickup truck and away to safety. But where was safety? Things had a way of finding you and spoiling other things. He had to fight so hard just to keep the little bit he had. There was no way he could see taking on anything new.

Preston stepped onto the terrace. "Somebody sure had a lot of money to throw away."

"They made something beautiful."

"Whenever anybody wants to waste money or be lazy, they say it's restful, it's fun, or it's beautiful. I don't buy that."

Palmetto's eyes flashed as though she were going to do battle for something small. He saw her feisty tilt of head and was prepared for her, but she fooled him. "I'm going to show you how to do the fox-trot," she said in a businesslike manner. "You'd better watch closely and get it right the first time, because if you don't, I'm going to hit you. And I mean really pole hell out of you."

He had to laugh. He couldn't help it. His smile beamed on her like the moon. She took his hand and led him toward a large, comfortable shadow that would obscure them. He felt clumsy and light and altogether foolish. "What was in that drink?" he asked.

"Oh, good things. Champagne and rum and a little gin. Oh, and oranges, too. Got to get that Vitamin C."

"I think you've gotten me drunk."

"I haven't even gotten myself drunk, and if you're that loaded you must have the capacity of a canary. Now, here, give me your arm. No, the other one. That's right. And the other arm goes here, around my waist. Not so close — you've got to look down and watch the feet."

"If I have to look down I may fall over."

"Lean on me. Now, it's very simple. Just count to yourself for a while, then it'll come naturally. We're going to start with the box step."

"I don't think I can do it."

"Don't be silly. They train dogs to do

this. Now follow me. Here we go. Turn. Touch. Side. Together. Got it?"

"I don't know. I'm sorry. Did I hurt you?"

"I'll live. Come on. Don't stop. You're about to get it. Turn, touch, side, together. Turn, touch, side, together. You're really very apt. What's that noise?"

"What noise? I don't hear anything."

"It's jingling."

"Oh."

"What is it?"

"It's my change. I have to make a lot of change, so I carry a lot." His ears were practically turning red in the dark.

She didn't want to laugh, pressed herself against him and left a smear of lipstick across the front of his white shirt, but it was no use. Out it came, in cascades that made her eyes water.

"I'm sorry. I'm sorry" was all she could say for a moment, still leaning against him, but sending her cool, sweet fingers up to caress his face. The fingers told him things his ears would never have believed. He laughed with her, holding her close and moving without counting.

"How much change do you carry?" she finally managed.

"About ten dollars' worth."

"Mercy, sugar, you'd better watch out for a rupture."

They laughed again, their tumbling voices blending with the lilt of "Sweet Leilani."

"Very good," she said at last.

"Good teacher . . . And a good nurse . . . Miss Palmy."

"I never had a nickname."

She was so small, so little. How she did survive? Her heart was beating against him like a tiny bird. A tiny bird. And winter was on the way. His arms went around her, forgetting the box-step formality. He suddenly wanted to do wonderful things, to be brilliant and bright and witty. He wanted to tell her the best thing that had ever been said. "Stick with me, kid," he told her, feeling debonair and graceful. Why did he need the fox-trot when he was about to fly? It was then that they heard the first yell.

The music continued and the others in

the shadows made no moves. The yell came again. There was desperation in it.

"Did you hear that?" Preston asked.

"If I didn't I'd check into the Home for the Deaf."

He took her hand and went down the steps toward it.

"Where are we going?"

"Sounds like somebody hurt. Maybe they'll need a nurse."

They pushed through the bushes that separated the terraced lawn from the drive-in area. They came out on a rise that overlooked the cleared dirt. A Buick was making crazy circles in the dirt, slowing, then speeding up, making hairpin turns that sent up a spray of clay clods. Several of the parked cars began to blow their horns, and some turned on their lights. The waiters had run to the edge of the clearing and stood huddled, watching the spectacle of Rudolph sitting above the headlight on the driver's side, hanging on to the hood ornament for all he was worth.

There were four men in the car, drunk and laughing, straw-haired bumpkins up from some place like Locust Grove or Stockbridge, raising hell, trying to create enough commotion so that they'd have something to talk about for the next six months over the factory roar.

People had gotten out of their cars. They didn't seem to know how to react. Some of them thought it was funny. They whistled and clapped. Others, just stood silently, feeling it was wrong to have some little old nigger scared half to death, but they didn't want to have to take a stand over something that didn't concern them. So they stood and watched, and the car drove on.

Preston was enraged. "Don't people have any sense at all?" He had known something like this would happen, had known it, known it, known it. He shook his head disgustedly. If Palmetto hadn't been there he would have spit on the ground. He started resolutely down the hill. She followed.

Preston walked through the line of cars, stopped, then stepped out onto the hard-packed clay. "Stop it! Stop it!"

The driver honked his horn, thinking he

was getting encouragement.

"Stop it!" Preston yelled. He had never seen anything so stupid. He and his family had escaped from being people like the ones who were doing this. They had done their best and held their heads up high, and here was nothing but a bunch of lowdown trash making themselves the center of attention. He didn't know who the little man on the hood was, but he knew his evening had been trod upon by men with unwiped feet. For a moment back there he had been far away from who he had always been, almost been in another world, like the life he had seen in the picture show.

He stalked the car, walked directly in its path, not flinching as the lights bore down on him and the horn blasted. He would stop that car. He would stop that car if it was the last thing he ever did.

Oh my God, thought Palmetto. I've gotten him drunk and he's going to get himself killed. Oh, please, Jesus, don't let him get killed. I'll be so good.

"Stop it! Stop it! Stop it!"

It stopped scant inches away from

where he stood. Three of the waiters rushed out and removed Rudolph from where he sat, frozen, on the hood.

The driver stuck his head out the window. "What the hell you trying to do? You some kind of a nigger-lover?"

Preston looked at the man. His teeth were as yellow as his hair. "If you want to fight, get out and do it like a man. I'm not riding on your hood."

"Lemme out," yelled a boy in the back seat.

He struggled to get out of the two-door car. Preston clenched his fists.

Then Palmetto came running up to the driver's window. "You better get outta here. Get outta here. They got the police coming." There was a conspiratorial urgency in her voice. She fixed the driver with an earnest smile.

"I don't care about any cops!" the boy yelled.

"I do," said the driver, nodded his thanks to Palmetto, and mashed the accelerator. They stood watching the path of headlights as it left the parking lot.

She stood beside him, her hands clasped

in front of her as she looked up at him. The moon was to his back like a crown.

"What did you do that for?" he demanded. "I didn't need any saving."

She looked at him head-on. "If I'm doing any saving, I'm saving you for myself."

He looked away. The glare of her truth was too much for him, but he stuck out his arm at the same time, and she came in close to him, a little bird again. He was pleased and proud and, as always, slightly embarrassed. He led her toward the pickup truck.

They could have gone back to Palmetto's apartment, but he never would have asked that, never would have let it happen even if he had seen her to her door and left her there with longing. He was the man. He had to find the place. And what if she said no? He didn't think she would, knew she wouldn't, but a belligerent, nagging voice that lived somewhere in the back folds of his mind kept saying, "What if? What if?"

He would have to do it casually,

offhand, spur-of-the-moment, as though it were only something to do that was no better or worse than anything else. A hotel was out of the question. That would require intent, would let her know. And home? He couldn't repress a snort at the thought of Sarah serving them breakfast in bed.

She leaned against his shoulder, a warm, gentle weight. He would have liked to put his arm around her, feel her tiny heart beating against his ribs, but he needed both hands for the wheel on the highway. The pickup had a tendency to pull to the left.

"I need to check by the place," he said. "You mind?"

"No." Only hurry, she thought.

He had a key ring that was almost bent out of shape with the weight of myriad keys. Oh God, she thought. He'll never find the right one, and we'll spend the night here in the street while he goes through each key trying it out. But miraculously he got the right key the first time. They pushed in through the revolving door.

The ferns swayed gently with the breeze they brought in with them, and Palmetto swayed too, the red taffeta rustling as she moved among the tables with chairs on top of them. Preston locked the door and turned to watch her. It was as though she were in tune with invisible music.

"Night falls on the cafeteria," she said.

He came toward her, not wanting her to get the idea that he had an idea, wanting to pick up on some kind of conversation they seemed to have lost the power to have. "You know what they charged us out there?"

She turned as he stopped before her, reached her hand up, and held his lips between the thumb and forefinger. "You know something? I think we like each other as long as we keep our mouths shut."

The fingers left him, but their touch remained. "I don't say much."

She was almost in his arms, and her red, beautiful, luminous, mysterious mouth was coming up to him as far as tiptoe would allow. She spoke, her voice sliding to a sigh. "But what you say is just so horrible."

The all-night light was burning behind the counter. It seemed to take forever for them to meet, but when they did, they seemed to dissolve together. They fit. For all the difference in their sizes, they gave each other balance.

The abrasive shadow that lined his chin cut roughly into her. For an instant she pulled away; then she could not get enough, tossing the smoothness of her neck and cheek against his roughness.

There was a zipper down the back of her dress. It opened effortlessly. She pulled back a moment, the all-night light making galaxies in her eyes. The dress crumpled to the floor. Without his help, she undid her brassiere. It, too, fell.

He put his hands protectively over her breasts, the roughness of his calluses making the nipples thrust forward. He had never touched anything like her, so smooth, so wondrous, like the answer he had had in dreams. This was real and moving against him. No, not against him, with him. Her hand was under his shirt, and his tiny, gravel nipples stood up for her, the muscles of his belly stretching taut as though he were lifting a great weight, only it was her he lifted, the tiny bird who needed to be kept warm.

He lay her down on the leather couch. Her arms remained held up to him as he dropped his clothes, standing over her, looking down.

She arched her back, ready to pull her pants away. "No," he said. "Let me." They came away so easily, such frail, delicate things to hold such another frail, delicate thing. He didn't want to hurt her, wanted to be so greatly tender with her, wanted his cock to slide into her, to give her the strength he was so sure she needed. He ran his hands over her smooth unblemished body, finally daring to touch the moist, open seam, watched her body rise and fall with locomotive passion. He leaned forward on top of her, her hips going up and her legs around him so that he was instantly in place. Then he hesitated. She opened her dark, mirrored eyes. Her lips parted. She lifted herself up, then fell back, and he followed her down,

down into a bottomless embrace. She was the night.

Then it was over and they were apart. It was still dark, but not as dark as it had been, and the cooks would come to stoke up the ovens by first light. He got dressed silently, keeping his back to her. She lay naked and contented, looking as though she was beyond ever being bothered again. That was the way with women. You gave them everything you had, used yourself up with them, and they just lay there afterward chewing idly on their fingers, not depleted at all.

"I'll bet that was a first for The Melba," she said.

Her voice grated on him, sobering him all the faster.

"You don't have to talk about it."

She had thought they were together in the same cocoon. His voice let her know she was still alone.

"Hadn't you better get dressed?" he said.

She got up and began to dress, coldly, efficiently. "There's a name for what you've got," she said. "It's called SPR — Soft Peter Remorse."

"I never saw anybody like you."

"Get a good look, sugar. You may not again. Seen my shoes?"

They were under a table. He slid them over to her. She put them on, stepped into her dress, stood tensely a moment, her back to him while he zipped her up, then walked without acknowledgment to the mirror, opened her purse, took out a comb and some lipstick, and began to mask herself.

"I know all about you prude types," she said. "You'll do anything the rest of us will, but first you've got to hide it, then you've got to feel guilty about it, and to top it all off, you've got to tell yourself it won't ever happen again, and as sure as it does, you don't blame yourselves, but whoever it was you did it with. I've been struggling out from under that kind of foolishness all my life, and I will be double-damned if I will put up with it from you or anybody else."

He had expected her to be contrite, to admit her baseness and wrongness. He was amazed that she had admitted his instead. He swallowed a few times. "I didn't mean to be a prude."

She slowed the furious combing of her hair. "I went a little overboard . . . but you did manage to spoil something that had been very nice."

She watched him in the mirror as he came up beside her. "I don't want to do that," he said. "I like you."

"I like you, too."

"If I can ever help you out in any way, just let me know."

She smiled. "And if I can ever help you out, just say the word."

"Come on now. You're making fun of me."

"And you were making bad of me."

"I didn't mean to. We're good friends."

"Friends indeed. And I'll take you up on your offer. You can give me a ride to work. I've got to go on duty in half an hour. The day shift is just about as much trouble as the night."

"Don't you need a uniform?"

"Oh, I keep one there just in case I need it." He looked at her askance. She caught the look and knocked it down. "And, no, I don't spend all my nights in wild debauch. Very few, in fact."

"I didn't say anything."

"But you were thinking mighty hard . . . My body may not be as pure as the driven snow, but my heart is. That ought to count for something."

He smiled at her and extended his hand. He liked her. She was sweet and funny and had so little idea about the world. There was so much that he could tell her that she needed to know. How had she gotten along before? She held his hand as they walked to the revolving door. They didn't need to talk. The sun was coming up. Its first beam struck the Free Weight scale.

Chapter 6

Waller, Rasnake, and Hildebrand sat around a table at The Melba. It was just after the dinner rush, or what was supposed to be the dinner rush. It had looked for a while as though it was going to catch on, but for no discernible reason it had begun to slack. He could run it another month before it started to hurt him. After that he could stand the pain a month, but then it would have to go. And the months were December and January, two of the worst. People were saving their money for Christmas instead of the evening buffet at The Melba. It was three days until Thanksgiving. It didn't pay to open on holidays, and, of course, all the help had their hands out.

Nobody got paid for a holiday. That was the way it was and always had been.

Everybody knew it, and it wasn't that way just at The Melba; it was everywhere. Everybody ought to have plenty of money anyway, if they'd held on to it, which he knew they hadn't. There had been four hours more work a day since he'd started the dinner hours. More work, more money. And nobody had had to work the fourteen hours a day, either. He had staggered it. They could come on every other day, and they could trade time with each other so long as he or Scoe knew about it. They had two hours off between the shifts, and the place was closed on Sundays. If they worked three meals, they got three meals to eat, and he knew that food went out of there unaccounted for all the time. Not that thieving was a big problem, but it was there like taxes. He kept his eyes open, knew what was in the stockroom and what they served. Elvira kept an eye on the girls. They knew it, too, though nothing was said about it, not to him at least, though he knew she had some things to put up with.

Now they were talking about Christmas bonuses. Mattie had cut her eyes around at him today, smiling out on the line just as the rush was slacking. ''I sho' am lookin' forward to my Christmas bonus, Mista Preston. I hopes we gets it time enough to do a little shoppin'.''

''You're running low on carrots,'' he had said, and stayed out on the line a minute, his hands on his lips and his brow furrowed. Nobody had said anything else, but he knew they had been talking about it. Nobody said anything to him unless it had been thoroughly discussed, and the one with the most nerve or influence got to say it. Everybody had kept on working, but he knew they were aware. He had pushed back into the kitchen and gone out into the alley, where Scoe and Fat Boy were unloading a produce truck.

His feelings were hurt. He would get to thinking that they were all one family; then somebody would say something and he knew they'd been talking and planning behind his back. They could dog a man to death. He yanked his tie out of his mouth, disgusted with that habit and disgusted with the memories it brought back. He had talked to Palmetto on the phone a time or two, but it had been over a week since he had seen her. That was another thing that galled him. He had a cafeteria to run. He didn't have the time, the money, or the patience to go running around at night courting or lollygagging or whatever it was. And whatever it was, he was about to be through with it. Was through with it, dammit! He hadn't even wanted to call her in the first place, just did it out of politeness, and she had sounded so sweet and gushy up until he had said he had to go; then she'd iced up, expecting he would ask her out and turning if off till she got her way. Women were interested in only one thing.

Scoe was inside the truck, handing out bushel baskets. He watched Preston and almost laughed. Whenever something was the matter, Preston debated it in his head, acting out all the parts, his lips moving silently and his head shaking with the emphasis of his mute arguments. Preston was a character, all right, but he had been getting stranger and stranger in the month since the unionizers had been around. Preston ought to come out more and try to accommodate instead of going back into himself as he did. He would have something to say to Preston in a while, but he would have to wait till the time came. If he said it now they'd do nothing but get mad at each other.

It was cold outside, and Preston wore no coat. He rubbed his big hands together and blew out a stream of foggy breath. He walked over to the truck and picked up a couple of baskets and went back inside. That was when Greener, the union man, stuck his head out the screen door.

Preston had gotten hold of Waller, who had called the others, and now they sat across from him at the table, drinking the end of their dinner coffee and smoking their cigars.

He was giving them a rundown of the union demands. "There's a five-cent-an-hour raise. Time and a half for overtime. Bigger restroom facilities. A safety grill by the coffee urns, because lotsa girls are gettin' burns on their arms. They want —"

"For God's sake!" Waller interrupted.

"How long does it go on? Ad nauseous?"

The others laughed.

"I'm almost through."

"And I am completely through listening," Waller said. "How about you gentlemen?"

"Any time is fine with me," Rasnake agreed. Hildebrand nodded.

They were looking at Preston as though he were a schoolboy bothering them for the fun of it. He smiled tightly. "I think they got some points. I don't like it any better than you, but we can't just say it's not here and refuse to acknowledge it. I read in the paper every day what they're doing in Detroit, and Pittsburgh, too. They used to have an anit-picket law in Alabama, and they just knocked that down."

"Whoever heard of niggers having a union?" Rasnake said.

"I'm not saying they got one," Preston said. "But I am saying they could get one. I checked with the labor board here, and with my lawyer. Everybody says, 'Don't worry. Don't worry. It'll blow over.' But they always add that they could do it and

216

cause a lot of trouble if they wanted to.''

Waller crushed his cigar into the saucer. ''Soft talk! I don't like to hear soft talk! Particularly from somebody I've got my hard-earned cash behind. First you get soft in your talk, then you get soft in your thinking, then it's only a matter of time — a matter of time! — before you get soft in what you do.''

He was talking loud, and some of the help were looking. This didn't do a bit of good. ''Mr. Waller —''

''I'll let you know when I'm finished. 'Cause I can tell you right now that no union or anybody else is going to come in here and bust up what I've built.''

Preston slammed his fist against the table. Dishes shook. Heads turned. ''Just a damn minute! I built this place up! It's your money, but it's my sweat!''

Maybe they had just wanted to get a rise out of him, because they smiled and chuckled and three hands patted his arm. They wanted him to be one of them. He was sure of it. This was just a bad part of the initiation. They wanted to be sure he wasn't weak.

Waller wiped some ashes off his tie. "Nobody's saying you didn't build the place up, son. Nobody wants to take away your accomplishment . . . nobody in this room, anyhow. But if you want to be the boss, you got to be the boss every minute. It's up to you to let 'em know that when you say 'Frog!' that you want 'em to by God jump!''

As Waller spoke, Hildebrand and Rasnake hunched forward, nodding their heads like penitents at a revival. They were strong, smart, successful men. Maybe they were right. They talked as though they were, but the union men talked as though they were too. Preston had always tried to stay in the middle, and now it looked as though he was going to be trapped there. He wanted to believe Waller. He wanted to be strong like that. He had thought he was that strong, and now he wasn't sure.

"Amen!" Hildebrand said.

"Amen!" added Rasnake.

They thought it was a contest, like football or King of the Mountain. Only it was his mountain, and he didn't want a fight on it. But if there was a fight, they had to back him up and he had to back them up. "Amen!" he said.

Christmas was on a Thursday that year, and this was the Sunday before it. So far as Preston was concerned, Christmas Spirit was only slightly less deadly than smallpox. They would have to be closed on Thursday, and most everyone he had talked to seemed to be making a long weekend of it, going out of town Wednesday night and not returning until Sunday. New Year's was the next week, and the whole thing would be repeated. A punch to the kidneys followed by a smash to the jaw. At least New Year's had a saving grace. Hildebrand had a party-giving friend who didn't want his house messed up. He had booked The Melba for New Year's Eve, and Hildebrand had said to hit him with the charges. The man had money, and he didn't mind paying. The man had even hired Bootsie Shoe and the Satin Slippers away from The Rex for the night. Preston hated to scalp anybody, but he contented himself with the knowledge that somebody else would have charged the man a lot more.

Hildebrand was going to be at the party. He had told Preston to bring a girl and party with them. He might just do that. It wouldn't be at all bad for him to be seen having a good time in public with a pretty girl on his arm. He liked the picture it made in his mind. The reality, however, was something else. He liked Palmetto, but the idea of her was easier to get along with than the actuality. In his mind she smiled, looked pretty, and did as she was told. He wanted to keep her that way.

He had breakfasted with Sarah that morning. It was the one habit away from work that he enjoyed. She had fixed waffles, a great favorite of his, and sat on the other side of the table in the yellow breakfast room overlooking the side of the large yard that sloped down to Peachtree Creek. It looked as though it might snow. The sky was milky, and the ground was bristled with frost. If it snowed it would stick, and that would cut more into business. Preston scowled. He had been reading the funnies, trying to work up some amusement over Maggie and Jiggs, but they left him as cold as the weather.

Sarah poured coffee. He put down the paper and decided to talk. They were so accustomed to each other that they rarely talked. Other than the fact that he knew everything about her, he knew very little. She took care of the house. In spring and summer there was gardening. Books came monthly from a club, and in half an hour she would be leaving for church, where everyone shook her hand and she was seated cordially in the same pew Sunday after Sunday next to deaf Mrs. Wiggins, who grunted audibly with the sermon and wore a mouse-colored necklace and dead foxes that were slowly molting on her dun-colored crêpe-de-Chine suit.

Sarah wore spectacles now, had for the last several years. They were thin steel things that she wore far forward, because she was afraid that the bridge would cut into her nose, leaving the deep indentations that some of her weak-eyed friends bore. Most of Sarah's friends were much older than she was: old maids, widow ladies, and nervous, overstuffed women embedded in stopped-up marriages. They were the ones with problems the others clucked and shook their heads over. "Poor things," Sarah and her friends would say, for a moment feeling glad, as though their states in life were chosen rather than randomly reached, their destinies having persisted over their wants.

Preston watched Sarah as she spread butter over her waffle. She did it as she did everything else, precisely and thoroughly. Each of the griddle holes received a drop of butter. She was racing toward the goal line of forty. It was as though she needed a mantle of years about her to protect her from the things she was afraid to know.

"I wish you'd come to church with me today," she ventured. "Everyone's always asking about you."

"I've got to go down to the place."

"It seems like you could take a Sunday off."

"If I don't do nobody else will."

"I read somewhere that anybody who was his own boss deserved it."

They smiled. There was a knock at the front door.

"Now who in the world can that be on a Sunday morning?" She wiped her mouth on a cotton napkin, rose, and left the room. Preston tried to read Brenda Starr. She had orange lips. He didn't like Brenda Starr, and he didn't like orange lips, but something about her reminded him of Palmetto. The lips were very full — that was it. He wondered if they trembled when she kissed, the way Palmetto's did, then shook his head in disgust, because she was a cartoon character and didn't kiss anything. She also had a Mystery Man, someone in the background of her life with power over her, the power of love. He wondered if Palmetto had a Mystery Man somewhere, a secret sorrow. She must. Other people's lives were full of things.

Sarah came back to the breakfast-room door. She was beginning to wear rouge, so he couldn't see that she had gone pale, but her hands were trembling "Royal's come back," she said. "He's out front. He says it's your house and he won't come in unless you ask him."

Royal had grown a bit thicker with the years, but at twenty-eight he had held on to the finger-snapping jauntiness that recalled Doc in the drunken happier moments that sometimes came back to Preston in spite of his wish to remember his father only as gaunt with failure. He had liked to think of Royal in the same terms. Here he was back, no coat on a frigid day, and no tie either, the collar button of his shirt yanking it tightly around his neck. He swayed on his heels, rubbing his palms together in the cold. Preston stood in the door, looking at him for a moment before either of them said a word. He didn't know if he was glad to see his brother or not, but he couldn't turn his back on flesh and blood.

Royal grinned and shrugged. "Us bad pennies always come home to roost."

"At least you got a home to come to."

Preston stepped stiffly out the door. They shook hands. "Come on in here where it's warm."

They sat in the breakfast room. Sarah's

voice went an octave higher with emotion and stayed there despite her attempts to bring it down and instantly smooth Royal into the neat, well-made bed of her life. She made more waffle batter and boiled more coffee, then furtively returned her Bible and kid gloves to a desk drawer in the hall. She didn't want him to think anyone had changed their plans because of him.

Royal, it seemed, had been wrong all along, had been wandering here and there, unfulfilled, wanting to be back home practicing the things Preston had preached.

It was no news to Preston that he had been right all along. He was soft-spoken in victory, just nodding his head at Royal's elaboration of his misspent life.

"Preston's got a cafeteria," Sarah called from the kitchen. "It's such a wonderful place. A grand success. He named it after Mama."

"Congratulations, brother. Things must be going pretty well. I always knew you'd go somewhere."

"It's a rough life.," Preston said. "Not easy at all." He didn't want Royal to think all he had to do was stretch out and relax.

"Yeah, but you've done real well. This beats where we used to live." They laughed for a moment, suddenly close in the things they had survived.

"Maybe I can find a place for you."

"I'd appreciate that, Presto-chango, I really would."

"Nothing fancy, but it'll put money in your pocket."

"I been wrong about a lotta things."

Preston checked a smile and nodded gravely.

Sarah entered with waffles. "Now, Royal, we're not going to do the first thing except be glad to see each other. Nobody was right and nobody was wrong. We're glad you're back, and no questions are ever going to be asked, but in a few minutes I'm going to have to get on the telephone and let the others know you're back."

"Mama died," Preston said. He said it abruptly, and it hung in the air.

"She died for me when I left. I knew I wouldn't see her again. That's when I did my mourning.''

Sarah touched his hand. ''She went quietly. There was no pain.''

Preston stared out unblinking at the silver day.

''But everybody else is just fine,'' Sarah said. ''The girls are married. All of them! And they're just doing so well. You've got nieces and nephews. And Jimmy! Well, you wouldn't believe how well he's doing. He's at the University of Georgia, and he's made the Dean's List every term. He's going to study law. We're just so proud of him!''

''That's what you wanted to do, ain't it, Presto?''

''I thought about it.''

''I'm glad somebody's getting to do it,'' Royal said.

Then there was another knock at the door. Sarah rose. ''Mercy. This has turned into Grand Central Station.''

Preston and Royal remained seated across from each other. Each met the other's gaze for a moment; then Royal smiled and shook his head. ''It's been a long time since I've had anything that smelled this good." He went at the waffles with such force that Preston knew it had been a while since he had had anything to eat. He felt proud that he could feed his brother, proud that he had made something of himself. He had done well, though he hated to admit it, afraid that the admission would make his accomplishment disappear, afraid like superstitious Oriental farmers who never celebrated big harvests but bemoaned them publicly so that the gods would not be jealous over their prosperity and send them famine. But he was rising. He had to admit that much. And if there were any obstacles in his way, well, they'd just have to go. That union wasn't going to hurt him. He blew on his coffee and took a sip, gazing at his handsome black-haired brother over the top of the cup. He could use somebody at The Melba to help him out, somebody like him, somebody he could trust. In spite of all his thoughts to the contrary, things did work out. Life was falling into place. Then Sarah stood in the doorway, shaking her head and laughing.

"Royal, you haven't changed one iota!

Introduce your wife."

Her name was Joan. She was quite attractive, blonde. She laughed a lot and had graceful hands, which she used when she talked. She was from Nebraska and couldn't get over the South, charmed by everything. She carried a large, gift-wrapped package and had the coat to Royal's suit over one arm. She had a well-proportioned smile, and her voice carried a touch of wryness. "I sometimes think I'm married to an escapee from an asylum. But that's Roy Al for you."

"It certainly is," said Sarah. "It doesn't look as though Royal's as bad off as he let on."

"Glad to hear it," replied Preston. And he was and he wasn't and he wasn't and he was.

Royal had done well himself, had gotten involved in insurance in Omaha and was starting up an office in town for Reliable Fidelity. Insurance companies always had such four-square names. Royal had a foursquare name himself these days, Roy Al. He claimed Royal Vacalis was a bit exotic for insurance and Roy Al placed him closer to the ground.

He had laughed and pounded Preston on the back, apologizing for his joke, but his eyes didn't beg anyone's pardon. The eyes were as cold as Preston's could be when his mind was made up and all the doors were closed. The eyes had knives in them and gave tiny turns that brought their points home.

Sarah had laughed and laughed, taking it only as a joke, refusing to see the meanness. She fixed Joan a plate and sat down at the table. She said a little too much, laughed a little too loud, and felt a little too good to suit Preston. He felt betrayed when she said, "Well, that just goes to show there's more than one way to skin a cat."

Preston had been very polite to Joan, though he knew that Roy Al had told her of their conflict and felt that she looked at him as if gauging the enemy.

"This is for you two." Roy Al was saying, pushing the package toward Sarah. "Open it up."

"Oh, Royal. I mean Roy Al. You

shouldn't have done it. What a surprise. It's just too pretty to open. I want to save the ribbon.''

She opened the box with studied carefulness, saying, ''Ooh!'' and ''Aah!,'' meaning it and saying it because it was supposed to be said. Women were regular jugglers. They kept a lot of things in the air. They were strange, unfathomable creatures who had to be kept at a distance.

''My word!'' Sarah exclaimed. ''I never dreamed of anything so grand.'' It was a clock with German writing on the face and parts that moved beneath crystal so they could be seen.

''It's nice,'' Preston said, hating it at once.

Sarah set in on the mantel, where he had to see it every day. It was Roy Al rubbing Preston's nose in his success. Preston willed the clock to stop, but it kept maddeningly on. He never told the time by it.

Chapter 7

New Year's Eve — the last night of 1939 — arrived. Business had been a bit better than he had expected, but they shut down the lines an hour early so the help could go home for a while before coming back to serve the party. It was Preston's first catering job, and he found himself elated by it. He paced nervously through the kitchen, looking over shoulders and sniffing into pots. He was having to do Scoe's work, too. June Bug and Fat Boy had both laid out. He knew they'd be back on Monday, hobbled by excuses and no telephones. Elvira had brought in a twelve-year-old cousin to help, but Scoe had to be out there on the floor, showing him what to do. He planned on firing June Bug and Fat Boy, planned on it as soon as he could get somebody to take their places, but he surprised himself with the knowledge that it wasn't going to be easy.

His people were like that damned clock of Royal's. When they were all there and working, they were like a smooth piece of machinery. Precision. That's all he wanted. How wonderful it would be if they could all be machines who didn't talk back, had no sick relatives or angry creditors who had nothing better to do than ring the phone. They had automats in New York City. He titillated himself with that thought for a moment, then found that he was listening to the music of the voices of his people. They had all had plans of their own, now set aside to serve the party. Most of them had pooched out their lips and grumbled when he told them of it, but now they were laughing, putting the place together as though they were going to be the guests themselves. They were wearing their white-and-black uniforms, but they had their own finery on beneath them. Their low-heeled, shuffle-worn work shoes were replaced by high heels and wing tips. Everybody's hair was fixed a little differently, and he caught the flash of several pair of dangling ear-rings. He thought for a moment to put a stop to it, then realized that he liked it, was smiling with them, was waiting as if it were his party.

Elvira and Sadie exclaimed, "Oh, chile!" as a florist's truck pulled up and three delivery boys began to carry in table arrangements. Three of the boys were pumping up helium balloons in the corner. Miss Fan, Mattie, and three of the girls were draping white linen cloths over the tables and were handling with exaggerated care the crystal champagne glasses and silver trays that had been sent down by the hostess. Scoe yelled that the man with the champagne was in the alley. They all laughed deliriously at the mention of champagne. Preston would have smiled himself, except that somebody needed to retain a firm, sober hand. He gave them all a good scowl and hurried toward the kitchen door, angry with himself for being almost hypnotized by the siren song of their good spirits. He had given them each a twenty-five-dollar bonus, and it had come directly out of his own pocket, to the tune of fifteen hundred dollars. It looked as though they had spent it all on costume jewelry, lipstick, and brilliantine. None of them has a lick of sense, he thought. Not a lick.

As he pushed out through the door, Sadie did a swaggering, pompous imitation of him, and the others went breathless with hilarity.

It was 7 P.M. The party didn't begin until eight, a sophisticated hour. The place was set up. Everybody was downstairs, taking a last-minute rest before the work began. Preston made a final inspection tour, paused by the fountain, and looked at the shiny paper hats in boxes by the door. He had never been to a New York's Eve party, had heard New Year's Eve celebrated once or twice over the radio, had smiled and nodded his head over the screaming, horn-blowing foolishness of the broadcast multitudes in Times Square. Now he was actually attending a New Year's Eve party. He was a man of the world. He thought of Palmetto. He would outdo The Rex tonight, and he had The Rex's band.

He went to the pay phone near the scale and called her. He should have called her before now, he supposed, but he hadn't really wanted to, but now that he wanted to, he wanted to more than anything he could remember. There was something that he very badly wanted to show her. He thought it was a good time.

"Hello," he said when she answered. "Guess who this is."

"I do not indulge in telephone games."

"This is Preston . . . Vacalis . . ."

A pause. A burst of recognition. "Oh!" Another pause. A cordial tone. Too cordial. A stranger's voice. "How nice to hear from you. Are you in town?"

"Of course I'm in town. Where else would I be?"

"I really don't know."

"We're having a little party at the place tonight. Little party? It's the biggest thing in town. You want to come?"

"Why, how nice of you to remember me. And I'd just love to come. The only thing is, we're going to another party earlier. And somebody else is having a breakfast. One of those all-night things. But we'll try. We'll try very hard to drop by for just a sip of champagne."

"Who is 'we'?"

"But I have a date, of course. I mean, you weren't asking me for a date at the eleventh hour, were you?"

"No. Not at all. It's an open house. Everybody I know."

"I'd just love to meet your friends. I know they'd be absolutely fascinating. Let's just say we'll try very, very hard to make it, but if we don't I want you to promise not to hold it against me."

"Oh, nothing like that. Don't want to put you to any trouble."

Bonne année," she said. "That's French for 'Happy New Year.' "

"Happy New Year to you, too."

He hung up the phone and looked expressionlessly at the cafeteria. He was very tired. His energy seemed to have been sucked right into the telephone. He didn't know why he had called her in the first place. All she was interested in was gadding about. Among other things. He felt as rundown as the old year.

Palmetto was doing night duty in the maternity wing. She had sworn she would only work days from now on, but Agnes Ritter's boy friend was in town from Charleston, and they wanted to celebrate New Year's together. She couldn't be any more than twenty-three, Palmetto thought. So young and pretty. The boy was still in law school. New Year's was for lovers, anyway, with all its plans and hopes and drunken kisses.

She caught a glimpse of her reflection in the nursery mirror, then willed herself to look beyond it at the six cribbed babies. Two were crying. Three were sleeping. One was lying silently with open eyes. What must he think of the world? she wondered. Wish I could tell him something good about it. She wasn't going to cry, dammit! She seemed to be turning into tears lately. She wondered briefly if she were losing her mind. Mamie's mother had lost her mind going through the change. Things like that ran in families. Usually skipped a generation. But she was only twenty-nine. She couldn't be going through the change at twenty-nine. Though things like that had happened. She knew it from medical books. She knew too much.

If she hadn't had a child by the time she was thirty, she would never have one. Would have her tubes tied. If you didn't have your first baby before you were thirty, the odds were high that you would have something retarded or deformed. That was her horror, more than getting old or being alone.

She had just come out of training and assisted Dr. Dunbar in a delivery. It had been a little boy. A Mongoloid with a big, droopy, purple-veined head. She thought she had screamed, but maybe she hadn't, because nobody looked at her. Maybe it had only been the sound of her own gasp against the white mask she wore. Maybe it had just gone back into her and was echoing. And it took it so long to cry. Why did he have to spank it and make it cry?

It had been quiet in the room. They had given the poor mother a quick hypo. She could sleep another few hours before knowing what she would have to know for the rest of her life. She remembered when it was over, scrubbing again with Dr. Dunbar. "Don't ever bring your first child into the world if you are over thirty," he told her. "Many do it and get away with it, but it's a risk. My mama did it. She almost got away with it." Sweet, harelipped Dr. Dunbar. His funny, twanging voice made everything he said sound so funny. He was a very funny man. She wondered if he had to be funny so that the people who would have laughed anyway had an excuse for the laughter.

She went back to the chart room. Some interns and orderlies were having a party. They had mixed grape juice and grain alcohol to make Purple Jesuses. A couple of interns were wearing nurse's caps to be festive.

The phone rang. It was a man from the *Constitution* wanting to know if they had anyone in labor who might have the first baby of the New Year. They had two in labor, but Dr. Dunbar said that neither of them had dilated a nickel's worth. "Try Crawford Long," she told them. "We've got two we don't expect before sunup."

The women had gone into labor just as she started her shift. By the time she went off they would have brought life into the world. Her life was being measured from shift to shift. She would have been very depressed if she hadn't hated Preston Vacalis so much. One good thing about hate, it gave you energy.

She smiled, winked, and refused a sip of a Purple Jesus. Somebody had to be alert if they were all going to tie one on. She needed her wits about her. She wanted to go into the new decade with a clear head.

It was 1940, and the bells rang out. The dark decade was gone. Newspapers were already speaking of the new decade as the Fabulous Forties. "Life begins at forty" was an old saying. It had to be true even if it was a cliché. Everybody knew that all the clichés were true. Terrible things were going on in Europe and there were starving children in Armenia, but it was so far away and they were foreign people. Some people said there was going to be a war and some people said there was not going to be a war. You could believe what you pleased. Everybody who had been to New York to the World's Fair said you just wouldn't believe the future. It was all there and it was going to be wonderful. All you had to do was wait.

Down at The Melba, Bootsie Shoe and the Satin Slippers played "Auld Lang Syne" while Scoe and Elvira clasped hands briefly behind the coffee urn and Sadie and Mattie opened the revolving door a notch and let the balloons float into the room, looking at each other with pride as though they had performed magic. Preston stood in a corner with his arms folded, waiting for the party to be over so he could get home. He nibbled sadly at his tie.

Palmetto could hear the muffled sounds of church bells and horns as she walked back down to look at the babies. *"Bonne année,* babies," she whispered. "That's French for 'Happy New Year.' "

Chapter 8

Roy Al's green DeSoto raced down Spring Street and screeched into the train-station parking lot. A car backed out of a place near the entrance. "Somebody's been living right," said Roy Al as he guided the car into it. All four doors opened, and he, Joan, Preston, and Sarah made a dash for the terminal, the winds threatening to steal Sarah's flowered hat. Sarah was on her way to see Jimmy get his degree at Little Commencement in Athens.

Sarah had nice legs, but they weren't used to running. She laughed nervously in her flyaway voice, clutching Preston's arm with her right hand and bringing the purse in her left hand up in front of her breasts. She thought it vulgar for a woman to run. They always jiggled in the wrong places, calling attention to themselves. She never went anywhere, and she was going somewhere in a whirl of rush and last-minute delays that had them certain she would miss the train. First Roy Al had been late, and then Preston; then she had put her handbag down and couldn't find it until Joan spotted it on the seat next to her. They had been so tense and angry getting underway that she had almost cried and cancelled the trip; then Roy Al started laughing as he roared through yellow lights over Preston's protests. Joan laughed. She had a nice, warm laugh. Then Preston laughed, too, and she had joined in. Now that they had started they were having trouble stopping. Everyone was making witty remarks that meant nothing, setting one another off again. I must remember all this, Sarah thought. I have to tell Jimmy.

Roy Al got the ticket. Preston carried her bags. Joan held her gloved hand to stop her from wringing them together. "I just know I forgot something," she said.

"You didn't forget a thing," Joan assured her.

"But what if I did?"

"Then you'll either have to buy new or do without."

They ran down the flight of concrete stairs. People and steam swirled past them, men in hats and women with fur collars. Redcaps and conductors shouted in competing choruses. Vendors with peanuts and Cracker Jacks and candy hawked up and down the endless ramps between the trains which moved in and out like Chinese dragons, hissing and fuming. Everybody in the world seemed to be going some place. Sarah had never been on a train, had only waved at them as a little girl. Now she was going off on one. The bobbing terror within her was about to surface.

Preston was handing the luggage to the porter, and Roy Al was slipping her two twenty-dollar bills and a plain envelope. "The money's for you. The envelope's for Jimmy."

"Oh, Roy Al, I couldn't."

"Could and are." He smiled and winked.

Preston turned to them, anxious to get

her on board. They smiled at each other for an instant. They had made it. Then his smile changed; a longing came into his eyes, as though he'd had a vision.

Sarah turned to follow his gaze and saw a pretty girl in a light-gray suit with a purple scarf. She was kissing a handsome young man who was boarding another train. A baggage cart clattered through their line of vision, and when it had passed the young man was gone and the pretty girl was walking toward them. A cluster of violets was pinned on her shoulder. What a lovely girl, Sarah thought.

She walked right up to them, smiling brightly.

"Why, Preston Vacalis! You scoundrel!"

They all looked at her. Preston squirmed.

"Off to see the wide, wide world?" she continued.

"Seeing my sister off on a trip. This is my sister, Sarah, Palmetto Russell . . . Miss Russell."

"Palmetto."

Sarah couldn't get over how pretty she was, charming and slightly sassy, with traveling eyes that didn't miss a thing.

"Royal Vacalis," she said, looking at the surprised Roy Al. "I'll bet you don't remember me."

Roy Al looked at her hard, couldn't place her, then roared with laughter when he did. "I do! Good God! How you been? You're looking fine."

"I'm glad one member of this family knows how to pay a compliment."

"How do you know Preston?"

"That's obviously a well-kept secret."

Preston wished that she would go away. No. He wished that she hadn't been there in the first place, because now that he had seen her, he wished that she would not go away.

The conductor walked the length of the train, yelling, "Board!"

Sarah looked as though she'd been shot. She jerked her head around as if she were seeing them for the last time. "I feel like the countriest kind of a bumpkin. People will look right at me and tell I've never been anywhere."

Palmetto took her hand and looked straight into her eyes "They'll think nothing of the kind. You look very glamorous. Like Myrna Loy. She wore a hat like that in a movie I saw last week."

"Aren't you sweet," Sarah said.

"That's a matter of debate," Palmetto replied. She reached up and took the violets off her jacket. "Here. A girl who's going on a trip needs plenty of flowers."

Joan and Roy Al kissed Sarah good-bye. She looked at Preston, not knowing whether to kiss him or shake hands. Palmetto gave him a shove toward her. "You silly thing. Kiss your sister good-bye."

Preston kissed her dryly on the cheek, and suddenly Palmetto threw her arms around her and gave her a big hug. "And one from Palmetto," she said. "Have a wonderful time."

"Oh, I will. I will," she said. She was about to cry, and it was showing in her voice. She turned and lurched up the metal steps, overcoming her fright as she went, met by a smiling porter who knew that traveling ladies were sometimes upset and needed a little ginger ale.

The four of them stood on the platform, waiting until Sarah had taken a seat and waved excitedly. Preston and Palmetto had not had to speak to each other. Roy Al was a good talker, and Joan had proved friendly. "You busy tonight?" Roy Al asked.

"As a matter of fact, I'm not."

"Hey, Preston, you know something? We've never had a double date."

Leave it to Roy Al to make some kind of halfwit remark like that. "Yeah . . . well . . . I mean . . . that is . . ." He reached for his tie, but Palmetto distracted his hand with hers. She was laughing. "You old smooth talker. You've twisted my arm."

Roy Al nudged Joan, and they took a step toward the train window, carrying out an exaggerated pantomime with Sarah.

Preston and Palmetto looked at each other for a long moment, then simply stood together, glad for the distraction of the crowd, but sending their feelings into the air, above and around them, setting them apart. They began to breathe in unison, though they weren't conscious of it.

"I didn't think you'd care anything about hearing from me," Preston said. "You sounded pretty put out."

"Oh, my bark's worse than my bite. In fact, my bite's pretty nice."

For the second time in a day, Preston was laughing for no discernible reason. What a treat she was to look at. What a lovely girl she was. He didn't even look up when the train pulled out.

They were back at The Rex. Everybody raved over the French '75s. Palmetto thought it was desperately chic to be there in a short dress. It was as though life was too busy and exciting to have time to go home and change. She and Joan got to know each other in the powder room. They sat on tufted velvet stools in front of a mirrored wall, their purses resting on the counter in front of them. They put on lipstick and checked for too much rouge, striking up an instant intimacy while never taking their eyes off themselves.

Preston and Roy Al peed side by side, making the obligatory shaking show as they finished. "Good to the very last drop," Roy Al said.

Preston took a downward look and glimpsed his brother's cock as he flipped it back inside his shorts and zipped his pants up over it. He couldn't help wondering where it had been.

They walked toward the white porcelain lavatories while porters armed with towels stood to the side. "Palmetto," Roy Al said. "How about that? Why didn't you tell me?"

"Nothing to tell." He began to wash his hands. He looked at Roy Al. He had to ask. "You got anything to tell?"

"About what?"

"Her."

Roy Al had known a few jealous men. Their voices were always strained and their eyes evasive. He wiped his hands on an outheld towel and looked at his brother. "She's a nice girl, Presto. That's all you need to know."

"She's not shy."

Roy Al sighed and shook his head. He took his brother's arm, flexing his grip in and out as if trying to get through to him. "Take my word for it. That's no sin." He guided him back to the main room.

They were at the table with another round of drinks. They had toasted and toasted and toasted. "I love toasts," Palmetto said. "They make me feel like café society." She grinned at Preston. "Or I should say cafeteria society."

Preston was lost in admiration for her. He drank and licked the foam off his mouth.

"When did you get to be a drinking man?" Roy Al asked.

"Just being sociable," Preston said. The words jumped out. He felt he was indulging in repartee.

Palmetto laughed. "Just give him a French 'Seventy-five and he's so sociable you practically have to call the police."

Joan pretended to be shocked. "Why, Preston!"

Preston went beet red. Palmetto slid her hand off the table and gave his leg a squeeze. "Nice talk," he said. He couldn't stop grinning. He ought to feel foolish, but he just felt fine. A French '75 was ice cold in your mouth, but it was nice and warm all the way down.

Roy Al looked at Palmetto, then at Preston. "I wonder if I can steal your lady for a dance . . . if she's willing."

Palmetto was ready. "Sure she's willing."

Roy Al was up and standing behind her chair. "Now just a minute," Preston said. "I don't know if I'm willing."

"Then you'd better be willing to do a little dancing yourself," she said.

He dazzled himself with footwork, twirled out of his chair, took her hand, led her onto the floor, took her in his arms, and began to dance. He didn't content himself with the box step, either. He pumped right along. It was like the magic night he discovered skating.

"You certainly must have been gadding about," she said.

"I haven't been gadding anywhere."

"Everybody who believes that can stand on their head."

"Honest."

"Then where did all this dancing come from?"

"That happens to me. Sometimes I can just do things."

"You sure can!"

"Who was that you were with at the train?"

"Just somebody."

"Somebody who?"

"Somebody who means absolutely nothing to me."

He had to settle for that. He danced her by the bandstand.

Bootsie Shoe gazed benignly down from his baton. Palmetto caught his eye. She smiled vivaciously. He nodded and spoke. "Evening, Preston . . . Miss."

"How's it going there, Bootsie? Sounding real good tonight." He had to think about death and the union to keep from smiling, but he didn't crack and whirled her away, dancing her along the line of French doors.

She was so amazed she didn't say

anything for several moments. She would die before she would — or maybe she would die if she didn't. "I thought you hadn't been gadding about."

"I never lie."

"You never do anything but. You and every other thing in pants. How did he know you?"

He was offhand about it and whirled her onto the terrace as he answered. "He's working for me now."

She stopped dead still and looked up at him. She let her hand drop from around his neck and let the other go limp in his hand.

Of all her many horrors, there was one that galled her in particular. Whenever she broke up with someone, she liked to think of him as being helpless without her, consigned to live the rest of his life in afterglow. But in her many-chambered heart, there was an icy dread that one of her old boy friends would go off and get rich and famous without her. That would kill her. It surely would. She had never had that fear about Preston Vacalis, and the logic of it almost knocked her over.

He was the very one who'd do so well and get right along without her. He had seemed so attainable; now he was unattainable.

"Oh?" she said coolly, and turned to face the gardens.

He wanted to bring himself to tease her, but he couldn't. She was too hurt and fragile.

"They played at the party down at the place on New Year's Eve. I thought I'd surprise you with that. Bootsie's a nice fellow, from right here in town. I think I told you, I've been trying to build up the dinner trade. They come in three nights a week, and I give 'em dinner and they play for half an hour. Dinner's picked up a bit. I'm breaking even."

She continued to look away from him until her eyes had stopped glistening with relief. "Alabaster balustrade," she said.

"Huh?"

"When I was growing up and very romantic, I read something about an alabaster balustrade. I thought it was the most wonderful thing I'd ever heard of. All I ever wanted was to grow up and have a house with an alabaster balustrade. And here I am sitting on a balustrade, and I don't know if it's alabaster at all. And you know something? I couldn't care less. Why is that you're already tired of some things by the time you get them?"

"I'm afraid you lost me."

"For good?"

"No, just on that one."

"Why don't you come and sit beside me?"

"I don't know if this is alabaster or not, but it sure is cold."

"Cold butt, warm heart."

"I don't think that's any way for you to talk."

"That is just the way for me to talk, and if you don't like it you can lump it. Oh, Preston, why do we always have to fight about things that are so unimportant? I want to fight about big things."

"I don't want to fight at all."

"Oh, yes you do. You're worse than I am about that. And you get mean and indifferent. You really do know how to hurt, you know."

"I don't know how to hurt anyone. It's

other people who know how to hurt me.''

He was every helpless boy she had ever loved and fought with and hurt and been hurt by. ''Dear God, Preston, I hate to admit it, but I missed you. Now put your arms around me and give me some sugar. I am just parched for a kiss.''

There was never anything like her, he thought. He almost hoped there would never be anything like her again, but so long as she was there with him in the garden on a night when spring was almost there, well, what could he say to that? He could only open his mouth to let her into it. He closed his eyes, the way she did, and felt as though he was off in space. For a moment he was. Then they landed with a thud, having fallen the five feet from the balustrade to the soft ground behind the blossoming azalea bushes.

He opened his eyes. ''Are you all right?''

She didn't acknowledge him, and when his lips were away from hers she kissed the air, moving her mouth the way fishes did when they needed something more than air to live. He could never get over her.

Never, never. She was soft where he was hard and went inside where he protruded. If he could have thought more clearly at that moment he could have solved the mysteries of the universe, but answers like that always came at inopportune moments, and her mysteries were far more appealing.

Chapter 9

When he looked back on it, Preston still found it hard to believe that such a little thing could have started at all. It was ludicrous. But it was never funny, and the wisdom of time never made it any easier for him. It remained an omnipresent hurt.

It had been over six months since the union had first revealed itself to him, like a bad report from the doctor. And even though he hadn't heard from them every day, their presence was still with him. He had checked with a couple of restaurants, short-order joints, and two other cafeterias. They had all been close-mouthed about it, as if their voices would summon it back up. Contacts had been made though, polite insinuations that would later turn to something else. The union needed a target, and they were biding their time about selecting one. When one had been selected, the others could breathe a sigh of relief, going their way a little longer, watching out of the corners of their eyes the agony of a skirmish. The time was coming when something would break. Preston hoped he wouldn't be the one, but it wasn't a coward's hope. He was a man of destiny, of confidence. His country had never backed away from a fight, and neither would he.

It was Friday, the first hot day of spring. There was always a day in April as if someone had opened a door to peek in on summer and received its furnace blast. Most people had still not shed their winter woolens, and they went down the streets scratching and pulling at themselves. The Melba was scorching.

Both lines were long today, but there was not the usual cheery murmur. The customers were restless, moving from one foot to the other, each impatient for his turn, but once they got to the counter they took their time, the power of decision seeming to have been sucked up by the heat. They were passing up the stew and the chicken à la king and heading for the tuna and chicken salads, everybody asking for a lot of ice in the tea and buying icecream cards so the girls would bring the homemade icecream to their tables.

As Scoe said, "Don't need to turn the ovens on today, just set the food out on the stove. It'll cook itself."

The kitchen was stifling. The three cooks had sweated through their big white hats, the stacks of which toppled listlessly. Elvira, Mattie, and Romona worked on salads. They were just barely keeping the counter supplied. June Bug clambered up from the basement, lugging a trash can of shaved ice.

"Mista Preston, we ain't got but 'bout two mo' cans of this ice."

"Mista Preston, this the last of the chicken. What we gon' do, just make plain salads?"

"Mista Preston, I am wo' out turnin' this ice-cream handle. You gots to get me some relief."

"Mista Preston, we low on glasses.

Everybody takin' two today. We gon' run out.''

He had to send Scoe in the truck down to the ice house. He put three extra girls on the floor just to scavenge glasses. He had Mattie cut up several hams, and had to laugh a moment when Elvira said, ''It's time I invented a roast-beef salad.'' She proceeded to hack up a roast, and the customers proceeded to buy it. It was only twelve thirty. They had two more hours to go.

Then it looked as though they would make it. Drew began to play some sprightly tunes on the organ: ''Row, Row, Row Your Boat,'' ''Paddlin' Madeline Home,'' ''Toot, Toot, Tootsie, Goodbye.'' Everyone seemed to pick up on the melodies, seemed to revive, coasting along on the tune, working the way he liked to see them work, like a team. Preston's clothes were sticking to him, but he had to step into the freezer locker to grab some eggs. The chill went through him, and he was breathless for an instant, his heart pounding as though he'd run a mile. He stopped, stunned by the flash of his own mortality. He put his hand to his heart. Suppose he just keeled over right there. But there was no pain, just the flutter. He took a couple of deep, cold breaths and picked up the eggs. He didn't have time for anybody's foolishness, much less his own.

"Beat the heat!" he called, walking through the kitchen. "Beat the heat!" He glanced at the stove clock. It was just after two. He set the eggs on the counter and looked around for Sadie. She wasn't there. He stuck his head out the kitchen door. The line still stretched almost to the scale. "Where's Sadie?"

The workers on the line shifted their gazes to him. No one answered, but he could tell they knew, because they had all looked at him. They had been waiting for him to ask. They went back to their work, and he returned to the kitchen. He was about to call out for her when she appeared at the top of the steps. She had on her feathered street hat, a coat over one arm and her shopping bag on the other. Mattie was with her.

"Where do you two think you're going?"

"We quits at three."

"It ain't but two."

"This is Daylight Savings Time day. You getting an extra hour outta us that we ain't gettin' paid for."

"You get that hour back in the fall!"

"That ain't doin' nobody no good in April."

That was niggers for you. When they got mad they retreated into their own blackness. They went expressionless, and he couldn't tell what they were thinking. They reminded him of Palmetto in the way they had of refusing to be dealt with.

"What are you trying to pull?" he yelled.

"We ain't trying to pull nothin' 'cept what we entitled to."

Entitled. Entitled. Would he never hear the end of that word?

"I pay you for that extra hour in October."

"That ain't no way to do."

Preston was not about to tell them the sad state of The Melba's finances, but things were still running too close to give him any leeway. He had not made back

265

the money he had put out for their Christmas bonuses. "I've got no truck with sorriness, not a damn bit!"

"Mista Preston, you got no cause calling me or Mattie neither one sorry. And don't neither one of us 'preciate that cussin'. We church women. You don't know how to treat people."

"That's the truth," Mattie echoed.

They had made him feel mad and ashamed. They were good women. He liked them. He liked to sit across the counter from Sadie when she chopped vegetables, the paring knife going with machine-gun precision while she told some of the funniest stories he had ever heard. He liked it when somebody would sing, not any Deep South cotton-picker sing-a-long, just somebody in the kitchen singing in the middle of washing a pot or peeling a potato. If they were good, the others would stop their talk and listen, sometimes shaking a head or tapping a foot if a mood was caught. He could never express himself like that. It was one of their ways he envied. Sometimes he felt close to them. Sometimes he felt as if there were no barriers at all. But, of course, there were. There always were.

"I treat you as well as you've ever been treated, and you know that as well as I do."

"You ain't treatin' us right now."

"What about last year when you had to be off three days? You didn't get docked. Not a red cent. And what about all those times I went outta my way to take you home? Both of you."

"Them ain't things we owe you for. Them just things you done."

"Well, if you two are in such an all-fired hurry to get out of here go on and go, but stop by Miss Fan and see what we owe you, 'cause you ain't gon' have a job to come back to."

They hadn't expected that. They might have been told to; it might have been what they were supposed to make happen; but they hadn't expected it. Preston looked intently at Mattie and Sadie and they at him. The cords of his neck had been standing out; now they had subsided, but his face was still a hateful red. His heart was racing again, but he didn't let it bother him.

"What is this? Some kinda union conspiracy going on?" He saw no point in waiting for an answer. "Sure it is! You're just acting on orders like dumb sheep. Well, let me tell you something, the only orders you're ever going to follow at The Melba will come from me. Now if you want to follow some damn low-class, pipsqueak bunch of Yankee unionizers, go ahead and follow them, but I'll tell you something, you chose the wrong ones!"

Sadie nodded gravely, looking at the floor. Mattie looked at her. Sadie was clearly the leader. "Well," Sadie said, "if that's the way it is, that's the way it is. Come on, Mattie." They walked slowly across the kitchen and pushed out through the door to the main room.

Work in the kitchen had stopped. Eyes had been on him, but when he looked up the eyes went down. Still, there was a silence that was more piercing than the muffled roar of customers. Preston felt ridiculous. He had lost his temper, just flown off the hook, when what he should have been was cool, calm, and collected.

He hadn't been the boss. He had just been one of them. ''Y'all runnin' out of something to do?'' He swooped up a rack of clean, dripping glasses and headed for the counter.

The kitchen workers looked at one another. He had done it to Scooter, but Scooter had asked for it. Now it was Sadie and Mattie. That was something else. Slowly, they went back to work.

For the next week Preston felt like a stranger in his own place of business. The heat wave broke, and customers crowded into The Melba with increased appetites from the bracing air. The dinner trade was at last edging into profit. Waller, Rasnake, and Hildebrand had complimented him on it. They were there for dinner nearly every night. ''Dining delighted and free,'' as Waller continued to say. He told them about the Sadie-Mattie incident, and they were more upset over the fact that it had happened than why. ''Uppity, that's the key word,'' said Hildebrand. The others nodded. Preston thought they were getting to be a regular choir of affirmation for one another, but perhaps they always had been. Perhaps that's what had drawn him toward them in the first place. There were times when you had to know you were not alone, that there were others like you. Being boss was not easy. But now he was not easy with them either. He felt they were always judging him, making comments when he wasn't there and letting criticism slip slyly into their compliments. He knew the help talked about him. Hell! That was the way with help. He had done the same when he was help.

He didn't hire anybody to replace Sadie and Mattie, just transferred two of the floor girls under Elvira's supervision. They were slower, and sometimes he had to add a third girl and bus a few tables himself, but he had to show that they could get along without anybody. At the end of the first week he began to tell himself that things were back to normal, but there was no more singing in the kitchen.

It was the first day of May. All day

270

Preston had felt there was something he should be doing, but he couldn't remember what it was. It nagged him several times an hour. Finally, at the end of the day, he checked through the books to make sure he hadn't overlooked a bill. It was a matter of honor to him to be paid up on everything before the due dates. He got up from the table and went downstairs. Maybe he had left something off the order sheet.

As he went through the kitchen he tried to joke with Fred, the baker. He always got a rolling baritone laugh out of Fred, but today all he got was a smile as he looked briefly up from the rising dough. They were making it as tough on him as they possibly could.

Downstairs, he picked up the order sheet and went into the stockroom. Scoe was there. "Getting low on squash and eggplant," he said.

"I want to talk to you about this union thing," said Preston.

"What about it?"

"If you're in with it, say so and let's know where we stand."

"I don't know yet, but I'm like you. I'm gon' stand where it does me the most good."

"You and me have known each other a long time. I don't want that coming between us."

"You know better than that."

"Just so you know . . . And you make sure Elvira knows."

"She knows . . . What about Mattie and Sadie?"

"They walked off the job. I can't put up with that. Sometimes you take a chance and get away with it, and sometimes you get your nose chopped off."

"There are two sides to every story," Scoe said.

"What's been going around?"

"Ain't nothin' been goin' 'round but what went on up there in the kitchen and what you know. People just think you flew off the handle. That's all."

"This is my place! I can fly off the handle in it if I please."

"You soundin' like a child."

"Don't you go tellin' me what

I sound like!''

Scoe regarded him silently for a moment with infinite but outraged patience. Then he shifted his gaze over his shoulder, bent, surveyed a few bushels of cantaloupe, and made a mark on the pad he was carrying. That's the way an argument with a white man was. It always came down to a matter of rights: what you had a right to do and not to do. It had to do with places. ''I put him in his place'' was what they always said. Scoe didn't mind places. Everybody had to have one. He just didn't like the difference in where they thought his place was and where he wanted it. He had been thinking about going to Detroit or Washington or New York City, but Elvira had kept him close to home and told him tales of folks who had come back from the North and kissed the red-clay Georgia ground. ''The grass is always greener,'' she had told him, in words he hadn't wanted to hear and turned away from. She used examples too — people who had been slaves and now had servants of their own. But it was just so damn hard to try to get ahead when you could hardly see the way to get along in the present, much less the day after tomorrow. His life was piling up around him in crates and bushel baskets.

Preston stuck his hand inside his pocket and came up with wadded money. He handed it to Scoe. "Next time you see Sadie or Mattie, let 'em have this. I hated to let 'em go, but you know I can't go takin' 'em back. Everybody'd get the idea all they have to do is walk out when they get good and ready. I can't have that. Don't tell 'em where it came from, either. And for God's sake don't say anything to anybody else."

Scoe stuffed the money into his back pocket. Preston looked around nervously. He hated to be seen doing things like that. It was like being caught on the toilet. There just ought to be privacy for some things. It was a damn shame you had to reveal yourself to other people.

He went back upstairs, sat down, and had Romona get him some ice cream. He sat listlessly spooning it, not calmed at all. Most of the help were gone. The place was closed for the afternoon. He looked up.

Some of the ferns were turning brown on the ends. It was the first time that had happened. He would have to get somebody in here to take a look at them. And that would cost money. If Melba were still alive she would have known just what to do. There were always ferns in the back of their house.

Then what he had forgotten came to him. Melba had always loved fresh flowers. It was part of the scent she carried in his memory. When he had been a little boy she had given him an idea. She told him that on May Day the children in Holland would go out and pick flowers to make May baskets for their mothers. They would put them outside the front doors, knock loudly, and hide, watching the mothers find the flowers and wonder who had sent them. The mothers never knew, it seemed, were totally, willingly fooled. He had done it for a long, long time until the others had caught on and stolen the idea. He had stopped then. It was a child's game. Funny how the things came back like debris in Peachtree Creek. He remained a moment watching the ice cream melt, then called out to Elvira, "I got to make some calls. I'll be back after a while."

Roses were six dollars. He had cringed at the price. They were not in season. There were red and white and yellow. He had taken the white. Red was for the living. He felt foolish standing over the grave. He had forgotten to buy a vase, had taken them in the box. If he put them on top of the tombstone, they would probably blow off. He lay them at its base, pushed them firmly against it, a thorn breaking through the green tissue paper and sticking him — sharp and sudden, piercing some sleeping instinct in his marrow. How long it had been since he had cried in the comforting folds of Melba's skirts? He wanted to do that now, wanted to go back into lived-through time and catch his breath and be told everything was going to be all right. But the moment of his childhood had been so brief, he found scant comfort there. He needed to be comforted by something warm and sweet and soft and gentle. He thought of Palmetto.

* * *

He had seen her twice since the night at
The Rex. Once she had cooked dinner at
her place. Babe and Bob Shaw had come
down, gotten drunk early, had a quick
mean fight, made up, gotten maudlin,
taken each of them aside and said, "Be
happy while you're young," had a
nightcap, endured a silence, nudged each
other and blamed each other for staying
on too long, hugged them good night long
and earnestly, and departed, climbing the
wooden steps, knocking against the
railing, beginning another argument.
Palmetto had decided to let the dishes
wait. She had nestled down beside him in
front of the fire.

"You've got a nice place here," he had
said.

"Oh, it's all right for now. But it isn't
mine, you know. It's not a home. It's just
some place to live."

"I know what you mean. We always
rented until I bought."

"I'd like to see it sometime."

"My sister Sarah knows how to run a house."

"I liked her."

"She's a fine woman. I don't think we've ever had a cross word between us. I think when you're brought up the same way, you have the same ideas."

"Too bad there's such a thing as incest; if it wasn't you could marry her."

"There really is nothing you won't discuss, is there?"

"Incest is in the Bible."

"Skip it! Just skip it! I am not cut out for marriage, and if you're lookin' to get that way, then you had better go and look some place else, because you are barking up the wrong tree with me."

"If you are calling me a bitch in heat, thank you very much."

"What?"

"When I invite somebody to dinner, it doesn't mean I want to share my life with him. It means I want to serve him dinner."

"I didn't call you any bitch in heat."

"You certainly implied it."

"I did no such a thing!"

"I suppose everybody blames your bad manners on your tragic childhood, but you aren't going to get away with that with me."

"It's getting late and I've got to get up early."

"I'm sure your big sister's waiting to tuck you in."

He wanted to hit her. She was the most aggravating human who ever drew breath. He didn't like dogs, either, and the Scottie she had was shedding. He'd probably have to have his suit cleaned. He turned and walked toward the door.

"Come back here," she called.

He turned.

"I was addressing the dog," she said, scooping Mrs. Pitts up in one arm and opening the door for him. "Good night," she said crisply.

"Good night," he said. "I enjoyed the dinner." The dew had fallen, and the grass was tall. He had to walk through it to get to the car. By the time he got there, the cuffs of his pants were soaking.

They had made up in a way. He had
sent her a pie. She had called to thank
him, and to inform him that there were
two "t's" in Palmetto. But she had been
very sweet. She had a way of doing that.
He had asked her if she would like to go
somewhere. He found out she was going
to die if she didn't get to see *Gone With
the Wind*. They had stood in line for an
hour and sat in the show for four. She
cried so much that he had been
embarrassed when the lights went up.
Then he saw that all the other women
were tear-stained. The Loew's Grand was
making a fortune on that picture.

He had taken her home. They had
stayed outside, making love in the pickup
truck. She was sure that Scarlett O'Hara
had been all about her. He didn't think
Rhett Butler was about him, though,
especially when he got his arm into the
steering wheel and honked the horn,
setting off a chorus of barking dogs. The
night seemed to be full of them. Palmetto
laughed, but he didn't think it was funny,
which naturally made it funnier for her.
He had pulled his pants up. "You have

the sense of humor of a sore toe,'' she told him, and got out of the car on her own and went into the house. That was three weeks ago. He hadn't seen her since.

* * *

It was just after three o'clock. She would just be getting off duty. The cemetery wasn't too far from Piedmont Hospital. He might be able to catch her. He ran from the cemetery.

He made all the lights on Memorial Drive, found a parking place right in front, and bounded up the steps, catching her just as she came out the front door. She looked tired. Must have a hard case, he thought. ''Hey!'' he called.

She looked up, surprise in her eyes. Then it faded. ''Hello,'' she said, as though it were the most ordinary thing in the world to run into him there.

''I didn't even know if you'd be here or not. I just took a chance. You could have gone out another door.''

''No,'' she said wanly. ''I always come out this way.'' She smiled briefly and walked away.

She must be still mad. Women always wanted to make up. Why couldn't they just pass over things, the way he did?

He ran down the steps and stopped beside her at the bottom. "Why'd you walk off?"

"I had a hard day. I'm tired."

There was a low wall that ran along the sidewalk. "Why don't you sit down?"

She walked over to it and sat down docilely, as though it might be the answer to her problems. He walked over and sat beside her. "I guess you wonder what I'm doing here."

"No."

He had never received so little encouragement. "Oh! . . . Well . . . I thought I'd just drop by . . . see how you were getting along."

"As well as can be expected." She looked out the passing traffic.

"I'm glad somebody's all right," he said. "That damn union's still trying to come in and organize my help. They're making headway, too."

"Why, that's wonderful. It's about time

people started to get a little control over their destinies."

"You don't know the first thing about it."

"Then why are you trying to make conversation with a fool?"

"Let's talk about something else."

"I'm willing."

"I mean, you just can't let a bunch of outsiders come in and tell you how to run your business."

"You're right."

"Huh?"

"I'm agreeing with you. I thought that's what you wanted."

"You don't mean it, though."

"At least I'm saying it. You can't have everything."

"You are impossible."

"No. I'm very, very possible."

He was sorry he had come. She was giving him a headache. This had been a bad day from the start. He ought to just get up and walk off and leave her sitting there. It was exactly what she deserved. "How's Babe and Bob?"

"Fine."

"And that dog. What's her name?"

"Mrs. Pitts."

"Yeah. How's she?"

"Just fine. Going to have a litter."

"What did she do? Get out?"

"Yeah . . . Just like me."

It almost passed over him — did for a minute, then came back and got him in the back of the head like a boomerang. She had really told him something this time. The knowledge seeped into him like setting concrete. He went dry, had to clear his throat, felt he had to spit, but couldn't come up with a drop of moisture. They sat together in silence on the wall, Palmetto looking ahead serenely and Preston clearing his throat and occasionally exhaling with great force.

"Put your head between your legs," she said. "I think you're going into shock."

"Don't go telling me what to do."

"I'm not telling you what to do or what you have to do, because as far as I'm concerned you have to do nothing."

"Well, that's something. That's certainly something. How much?"

"A couple of months . . . For God's

sake, don't make a meal out of your tie!''

He dropped the tie, got off the wall, and began to pace. He looked at her intently, trying as hard as he had ever tried anything to look into her head.

Palmetto met his look and began to come to life with indignation. ''You're just dying to ask me, aren't you?'' she said. ''Dying to! Well . . . I will tell you whose baby it is. Mine! I don't need you or anybody else to give my child a name. I'm proud enough of my own.''

People were passing by close enough to hear. ''Let's go some place else.'' He took her arm.

''I can get anywhere I want to go under my own steam.''

He had had enough. He grabbed her arm again, yanked her off the wall, and guided her firmly along the sidewalk to the pickup truck. He opened the door, put her in, went around to the other side, and got in. They sat there for a moment.

''I just don't know what to say,'' he said.

''Why don't you not say anything until we get to my house and then say 'Good-bye.' "

"I can't do that."

"I can."

He turned to her and grabbed her by the shoulders. "Go ahead and do it, dammit! You're not doing me any favor, you know. I got my own troubles. I'm gon' have a strike on my hands if I don't watch out. I don't know who's for me and who's not. My backers won't back me. I came to see you 'cause I thought it would take my mind off my troubles. My God, what a thought that was!"

"I am not now nor ever will be a trouble of yours, Preston Vacalis!"

"You have been a trouble of mine since I met you."

"Then consider that your troubles have ended."

He clamped his hand over her mouth. "I know women can be ornery, but there was never one such as you. If you are having my child, then you are going to have it like it's supposed to be had. And that's with my name on it."

She tried to bite the flesh of his palm. He took his hand away. "My child does not need any stamp of approval!''

''I have never hit any woman, much less a pregnant one, but I suddenly feel that I am not above it.''

''I don't want to have a deformed child,'' she said. ''It'll be the easiest thing in the world for me to have an abortion.''

''Hush up about that!''

''It would. I could have it done this afternoon and go back to work tomorrow. That's one of the advantages of being a nurse. And it's not all that serious. But this is my last chance to give birth before I'm past thirty, and you don't know how high the statistics are when you get past thirty. And I want a baby that's normal . . . that'll be all right . . . And nobody's ever going to *have* to marry Palmetto Russell.''

She began to cry, and he folded her to him, the shoulder of his shirt going wet with her tears. ''Come on now . . . don't cry.'' He patted her back, trying to be gentle. All he ever wanted to be with her was gentle, except when she made him want to be otherwise.

Her tears stopped, but a sobbing catch

lingered in her voice. "I have no intention of interrupting the calm and orderly flow of anybody's scheduled existence."

He couldn't think with her sniffling against him. "Sshhh . . . sshhh . . . Miss Palmy . . . Miss Palmy . . ."

She turned her streaked face up to him. Some strands of hair were stuck against her cheek. He pulled them away. There was such a peaceful, truthful look in her eyes, like the calmness that overcomes a lake after a violent storm. He smiled at her. He didn't know why. He certainly didn't feel like smiling. Then he heard himself say, "I don't know if I'm what you're looking for, but if I am, you got me."

The sob had left her voice softer. "I don't know if I'm in love with you or not," she said. "But I have this idea that you'll be absolutely lost without me."

He felt like crying too, but he couldn't do that, so he began to laugh, and pulled her toward him. People were passing right by the truck, but he couldn't stop laughing and hugging her.

Chapter 10

Preston always took his time about making conscious decisions, and if he'd ever had to make a decision about getting married, it would never have happened at all. But once it became an obligation, there was never any question about it. He was going to marry Palmetto, the same as he was going to make his bakery order for the week on Tuesday. It was part of the schedule.

It was Sunday night. He sat on the big back porch, looking down toward Peachtree Creek. Sarah was in the kitchen, fixing supper. Sunday was her cooking day, and she spent all week preparing for it. One Sunday a month they had the family over. At least one night a week she went out to dinner at the homes of the various sisters. Preston was always invited and always busy, and saw their houses once a year on the excuse of a holiday. He sent them turkeys for Christmas, hams for Easter, and a bushel of peaches during the course of the summer. The sisters and their families showed up at The Melba for a Saturday lunch once a season. It was free, and they protested and surrendered with smiles. They kept the free lunches to a minimum. None of the Vacalis family liked to overdo.

They would be getting some early peaches in a couple of weeks. He decided to send Araminthia the first bushel. She was his favorite sister, yet he saw her no more than the others. She was quiet and didn't call attention to herself. He liked that. He would have liked to have asked her about married life. She would answer him with what she knew. She was not a giggler. She was a serious woman. She worked hard to help her husband and raise children who sat with their hands folded and said ''Sir.'' He had almost called her that afternoon, but had stopped with his hand on the receiver. What could she have told him? What could anybody tell anybody else about love and marriage?

No, it wasn't love exactly. He hadn't had time to think about that, but it wasn't love. Love was what people wasted their time with in magazines and movies. It was for people who didn't have anything better to do. People wrote songs about it as though it were the only thing in life worth writing songs about. How come nobody had ever written of the thrill of serving fifteen hundred people at lunch in a three-hour span in a beautiful room with ferns and mirrors and fountains?

When Palmetto had admitted that they didn't have the time to prepare for her long-planned church wedding in Cedartown, she had suggested a candle-lit cafeteria wedding, with the help serving as attendants and Bootsie Shoe and the Satin Slippers playing ''The Wedding March.'' He hadn't known if she was serious or not, but he had slapped that idea down.

''We'll go down to the courthouse, like my sisters did.''

''You've got another think coming if you think I'm going to be any courthouse bride.''

''What in God's name is the matter with that?''

''If you don't know, there is no point in telling you.''

They had settled on a justice of the peace. They would do it Monday night, after the cafeteria closed. They would have had more time on Sunday, but Monday was payday, and he always made up the payroll early that morning. She said that Babe and Bob would have a little wedding supper for them, but he had to get his orders in on Monday night and didn't have the time. If she was going to be hungry, he'd have Elvira pack a box with egg salad and chicken. She had liked the idea.

''A wedding picnic,'' she had said. ''I'll get some champagne.''

He had started to tell her that he wasn't going to start his married life with hard drinking, but sometimes he had to do her like he did a child, just not say anything and let her think you agree until the time comes and then put your foot down.

He had spoken to her once on the

phone today. They had both sounded formal. It had been like making an appointment. They were very polite. He would see her tomorrow night at eight.

He looked at his watch. It was almost eight. Twenty-four more hours. A day. A complete day. He had never thought of himself as single. He had always been surrounded by too many people with claims on him for that. Now, suddenly for a dying moment, he was free. Free. He had never been before and never would be again. He suddenly ached for the life he had never led. He had meant to be a charming young man about town. Of course he had. He had just been so busy he had forgotten it. He had remembered it too late. It was being taken away from him. People were always taking things from him. He closed his eyes, rocking in the creaking chair.

"Supper in five minutes," Sarah called from the kitchen window.

"Jimmy back yet?" he answered, as though life was going on for him and not ending.

"Oh, we're not going to wait for him.

No telling when he'll come dragging in."

Jimmy was another problem. He did as he pleased and kept his own hours. He made his own money and was of age, but Preston thought he had a definite lack of respect. He lived free under their roof, but obligations came with that. He would have to speak to him. But what would he say? He was just his older brother, not his father. But he had been more of a father than Doc had ever been. Doc. He hadn't thought of him in a long time. He was dead now, more than likely, lying in some potter's field or maybe sunk somewhere in the sea. He sometimes thought of Doc as having taken to the sea, lost to land, spending his life on foreign horizons that disappeared behind the rise and fall of constant waves. Preston had vowed never to be a father. He was afraid he would be like Doc. Now he was following in his father's footsteps.

The screen door closed softly. Sarah came onto the porch, wiping at her neck with a handkerchief. Her hair was up, and stray wisps of it were curled from the stove heat. "It's a roast. Will you carve?"

He prided himself on carving. He had a fine sharp knife and gleaming fork that had been given to him by a meat wholesaler. The name was stamped on the handle. Sarah had stuffed orange rinds with sweet-potato soufflé. She put them in a muffin tin and embedded marshmallows in them, then bent to run them under the broiler.

The hymn had been running through her head all night. They had sung "Beulahland" in church. It was the kind of revival song that made you want to nod your head and tap your foot. She liked to sing, and in church she could do it. Her voice got lost with the others, and she lost her self-consciousness. Without the hymnal she could only remember one line. "We are feasting from the manna from a bountiful supply, for we are dwelling in Beulahland."

Sometimes she felt sorry for herself, but today in church she had known what she had to be thankful about. She had looked around at the little old ladies and genteel old maids who sat clustered in navy and white and occasional daring pastel down front and to the right of the pulpit. They were the ladies who had their Sunday dinners alone or shared them with a cat, going in groups to Mary Mac's Tea Room on Friday nights and looking at the world through sad, frightened eyes. She could have been one of them, but she was the sister of Preston Vacalis. She had a place. She was alone, but she had a place. She cherished her solitude, but she had seen how that could eat you up. She had two things. She had herself and she had her life with Preston. She hummed softly as she closed the door to the broiler.

"I think we ought to start having people in," she said. "Not that we're hermits, but we have been a bit anti-social."

He was going to have to tell her sooner or later. He had been putting if off all day. "Uh . . . Sarah . . . I haven't been as antisocial as I should have been."

"How's that?"

"I'm thinking about getting married. In fact, I am . . . tomorrow."

She didn't say anything, but he could see the contractions of her throat as she swallowed repeatedly.

"There's no call for you to get upset."

"But who?"

"Palmetto Russell. You met her at the train."

There was some leftover mixture of sweet potatoes. She tore off some waxed paper and began to crumple it around the edge of a blue bowl.

"I see no reason for things to change. This is a big house, and I don't see that one more will hurt."

She had always exempted Preston from the fact that he was a man. Preston was always so busy and good. Now he was just a man, giving orders about how things would stay the same.

"Oh, Preston. Don't you know anything?"

"Huh?"

"Go and sit on the porch. I'll call you when it's ready."

He touched her shoulder. She stiffened.

"Are you sure you're all right? There's no call to get upset."

"I'm fine. I think I heard Jimmy's car. Tell him to get washed up."

Preston left the kitchen. Sarah put the

serving dishes on a tray to carry into the dining room. There was too much room. Then she remembered the sweet-potato soufflé. She burned her hand opening the broiler. The marshmallows had turned to ashes, and the orange rinds were dry.

The first Monday in May was a long one. Preston was up an hour before dawn, bathed, dressed, and ready to leave the house when Sarah appeared in her flannel wrapper, her eyes circled in sleeplessness. "What shall I do?" she had asked.

"About what?"

"About me and you and that girl?"

"Her name's Palmetto."

"What shall I do about us?"

"There is nothing to do. Things will stay the same."

"How can you stand there and tell me things won't change when it is most evident that they will?"

He started shaking his head, a thing he did when he was cornered. Women seemed to love nothing better than backing you into a position you couldn't get out of. "Well, if they do change, they don't change today . . . or tomorrow . . . or the day after. Now go back to bed and get some sleep. We won't be back till late tonight.''

"You mean you're not going to have a proper ceremony?''

"We're going to get married the same as the others did. What was proper about that?''

"Because we all went to the courthouse together and then had lunch, and if you remember correctly we all had corsages and you all had carnations in your lapels.''

"Well, there'll be none of that tonight!''

"That is no way to welcome someone into the family.''

"I didn't think you even wanted her.''

"She is not mine to want, but I can tell you this much, you're not showing any consideration for her or for me.''

"What about me?''

"You're a very good provider, Preston . . . in some areas, but there is a lot more to providing for people than just putting food on the table and a roof over their heads. I hate to say this to my own brother, but you've been turning into a very selfish person, and it's not getting any better."

He couldn't believe his ears. She had never said a word against him, and now this. He opened his mouth and nothing came out. He looked beyond her to the door and headed for it leaving her standing against the rising light.

He was too busy to notice the rise and fall of tempers around the place. Spirits seemed to be up, but then they always were on payday. Finally the last envelope had been handed out, the place closed and mopped in the afternoon; then the chairs were put back under the clean tables and the steam table was reheated for the dinner hour. Bootsie and the band got there at six. They were nice boys. He liked them. He had thought they'd be heavy-drinking, high-life types, but most of them had day jobs. Bootsie ran a showroom for ladies' shoes, and his real name was Purvis Blye and he was from Prattville, Alabama. Preston had thought people like that were just born sophisticated. He and

Bootsie weren't so different at all.

They had big, farmboy appetites, but he didn't begrudge the food. They played well, and the customers liked it. He had even moved a few tables so they could dance if they wanted to. He figured that The Melba was the only cafeteria in the world that featured a band and dancing. He thought about putting up a billboard out on the highway into town. He would advertise it as "Dancing under the Ferns."

Preston sat in his booth, waiting for seven o'clock to come. He didn't have any appetite, but had managed some succotash. They were playing "The Song of India." He liked that one. It painted pictures in his head. He had seen photographs of the Taj Mahal.

For his next cafeteria he thought he'd do a place like the Taj Mahal. Wouldn't that be something! The Taj Mahal Cafeteria! He didn't know what it looked like on the inside, but he imagined men in white with turbans. He'd have the cooks wear turbans instead of hats, and all the floor girls would wear those floating things with veils. And plumes. He'd have plumes instead of ferns. There was a place he'd seen in Cascade Heights. That area was going to boom. He'd put it there and shuttle the help back and forth where they were needed.

Then the song ended and he came to from his dream. How could he get another place when he didn't even have this one yet free and clear? His head was always in front of what was going on on the ground. He had to get The Melba. He couldn't go waiting all five years to buy his partners out. And he could do it, too. The bank would lend him money. He wasn't making as much as he had hoped he would, but things were picking up. They were putting up an office building down the street, and that would nearly double lunch. He had been in business three years now. He was hit with another idea: open a place and call it The Confederacy. He guessed he got that idea from being under union fire for the last eight months.

He got up and went to check the coffee urns. He enjoyed making the coffee from time to time. It made it seem as though he had his hand in everything. He didn't have any idea about how to cook, but he knew if it was done right. Besides, he was the owner. He didn't need to know all those things.

He was thinking how much he did know and how well he was doing when he looked up and saw Waller sliding his tray in front of the urns. Preston poured him a cup of coffee and followed him to a table.

Waller was a concentrated eater. He said nothing and looked up only once before finishing his meal; then he wiped his napkin lovingly across his face in a circular motion. His lips were shining from gravy. He sipped his coffee.

"This hits the spot. The Melba has a good cuppa coffee."

"Secret to that is a clean pot."

Waller would always be his friend. He had given him his first decent job and had backed him on his first venture in the world of competition. Waller understood him, would know that he had to buy them out. He had to tell Waller what he wanted. He couldn't stop himself.

"I want to be my own man," he said.

"I want to buy you and the others out."

Waller looked up. He gave a distant, thoughtful smile, like something out of a painting. "It's an old story," he said.

Preston didn't like the tone. It was something he had heard before. He had used it himself. On the help.

"A feller learns from an older feller, comes to him for help when he needs it, gets the help, makes use of it, does well, gets ambitious, and forgets the older feller altogether. Where do you propose to get the wherewithal?"

"I can raise it."

Waller surveyed The Melba. "This is a nice, profitable business we've got here. I like being in the cafeteria business. So do Rasnake and Hildebrand . . . And we're going to stay in it. We're getting along in years. But you, you're a young man. Footloose. Fancy-free. If you're unhappy with something . . . why . . . you can just go off and do something you really like. You got all the time in the world."

"I didn't mean it that way. I didn't mean it the way it sounded. I'm not trying to get rid of anybody."

"Let's just forget about it, then. It's been a long day. You're tired. I'm tired. And I've been a young man myself. There's things I've said I'm glad others forgot."

Waller stood up. He looked bigger tonight than he usually did, stood straighter, too. He wasn't fading away, the way Preston kept thinking he was. Preston rose and walked him to the revolving door. Waller shook hands with him formally, the way he almost never did. "Yes, sir," Waller said. "I do like the cafeteria business." He tipped his hat toward Miss Fan and spun through to the street.

It was time to go. Preston went through the cafeteria, told Scoe to lock up, and went down the steps to the alley. He cringed all the way, wanting to kick himself for having tipped his hand. Now they would be harder to deal with. He should have waited till he had the bank's money, then overwhelmed them with cash. There was nothing like money in the hand. He had been a fool. Goddammit, he couldn't think of anything bad enough to call himself. His cheeks were puffed out, swollen with the rage he felt against himself. What a fool he was. What a goddamn fool. He slammed into the cab of the pickup truck and went screeching out of the alley. He could certainly think of better things to do tonight than getting married.

Chapter 11

They drove along a narrow two-lane road with shoulders that dropped directly downward from the asphalt. Preston felt as though he were driving down a plank. He hunched forward over the steering wheel, peering into the yellow darkness the head-lights made. They were going to McDonough, a distance of thirty miles.

"I don't know why we had to come this far."

"It was the closest one I could find."

She hadn't said much the whole way, just sat there looking straight ahead, a large suitcase propped on the seat between them. He was in no mood for marriage, but he had at least tried to be civil. She wasn't trying at all, had only given a distant "Hi" to him and pointed to the suitcase. Women were always in search of people to help them load and unload. She had had more conversation for the dog. "Oh, Mrs. Pitts, Mama's going to be back directly. There's food and there's water, and here, here's Mama's pretty pink bedroom slipper that you've always wanted. I'm sure it's delicious."

"That dog will chew that shoe right up."

"I'm giving it to her."

"That beats anything I ever saw. It's a perfectly good shoe."

"I wouldn't give it to her if it were all torn up."

"I can't understand that."

"Well, if you don't understand it, there is no point in trying to explain it to you."

How many times would he have to hear that?

They saw some signs pointing to a roadside park.

"Pull over by that park," she said.

"What for?"

She looked at him as though he had just fallen to earth from a distant, uncivilized planet. "You don't think I'm going to get married in a street dress, do you?"

It was the highway department's excuse for a park: two wooden picnic tables and a huge rusted tin trash can that was jagged on the top. He sat on a bench, looking away from her toward the woods, munching on a chicken wing from the box Elvira had put together. What had he gotten himself into?

"You bought a dress just to get married in?"

"It's called a wedding dress."

"I'm not made out of money."

"I've been trying to figure out what you are made of. I rejected flesh and blood."

She was standing on the far side of the pickup truck in her slip. There were pins in the dress, and enough hooks and eyes to blind a sewing nun. She would do them herself. She wouldn't ask him for anything. She caught a glimpse of herself in the rear-view mirror. She didn't look like any bride she'd ever seen. Nothing had ever turned out the way she thought it would. Now she was getting married to a man she hardly knew, and she knew he didn't want her. If it hadn't been so awful, so downright tacky, she'd have cried. But how could you cry with your butt shining in the moonlight in some roadside park when you were trying to get into a wedding dress so you could get married by a justice of the peace with a drooping mustache and tobacco-stained teeth?

Then she saw him standing on the other side of the hood.

"I don't think it's right if we fight on our way to get married," he said. The moonlight struck the ridge of his nose. Half of him was light and the other half was darkness. But the light side was so unexpectedly dear and tender that she drew in her breath and just stared.

"Are you all right?" he asked.

She reached inside the window on the driver's side and pulled out the headlights, then stepped in front of them, her long cream-satin dress rustling about her.

"Am I?"

She was beautiful. He had never imagined anything so beautiful. She wore petticoats under the dress, and looked as though any moment she might fly away.

There were beaded butterflies and curlicues around the skirt. He wouldn't have been surprised if she had turned and shown him wings. Melba had told him about fairy princesses, and he had forgotten. He wondered why.

"You look fine," he said. "Just fine . . . pretty . . ."

"I didn't want you to be ashamed of me."

"Why do you want to say a thing like that? I would never be ashamed of you."

She smiled. This would all be over soon and they could live a normal life. She was waiting to be kissed.

"I got a ring," he said. He reached into his coat pocket and pulled it out. It was wrapped in a napkin. "It's not gonna knock your eyes out, but it'll do. It was my mama's. She left it to Sarah. Sarah brought it down to me this afternoon. She wanted you to have it. So do I."

Sarah had come with eyes too dry and a face too bright and put it in his hands. Then Araminthia had called, laughing and crying and saying not to worry about a thing. There were no such things as secrets any more.

Palmetto had taken off her red polish and wore clear. The ring sparkled against the finish as he slipped it on her finger. She kissed the ring, then clasped her hands and brought them to her breasts. He bent and kissed the ring as it rose and fell with her breath.

Well, they couldn't stand in the park all night listening to the crickets. "You ready?"

"As I'll ever be," she replied.

They walked around the pickup, and he opened her door. She had her foot on the running board when she stopped and looked at him through the rolled-down window. "I hope I can make an easy life for you, Preston. I've got a mind of my own, and it gets me into trouble from time to time. I've been told my tongue is sharp, but I don't mean for it to be. That's just the way I see the world. I hope I can show it to you my way and you can show it to me yours and that we can learn to adjust our ways and visions. Not change totally, just make room for each other in our hearts and lives."

He wished that he could talk like she did. He could listen to her all day when she was saying something nice. He wanted to tell her something nice, too. "This is all kinda sudden to me, you know . . ."

"If you don't want it to happen . . ."

He grabbed her shoulders. "Don't you ever say that again!"

Maybe he did care after all. Anyway, he certainly knew how to shut her up in a way she liked. "Last chance to kiss me before I'm your wife," she said, and leaned through the window to touch his lips.

People went to bed early in McDonough. Preston's pickup rolled down the empty streets. The only lights were around the courthouse. They didn't expect people to need them. Palmetto looked out the window. She had always thought of Cedartown as the only small town in the world. It was perfect. All the others had things wrong with them, but by night she had to admit that they were pretty much the same. People out that time of night were up to no good, and here she was getting married. And pregnant to boot. She had been warned against things all her life, and one by one she had tried them all. This was where they had gotten her.

They left the low line of buildings and turned onto a wide street where oaks and elms lived in harmony and the big white houses sat back a ways. "I don't think this is it," he said.

"Yes, it is. Keep on going. It's the right street."

She saw the sign. It gleamed like cats' eyes in the night. JUSTICE OF THE PEACE. It was printed in stick-on letters attached to a board nailed to a tree.

It was an antebellum house that looked better by night. Paint was chipped from the columns, and there was a weary sag to the roof. They were halfway up the cobbled walk, where grass grew out between the stones. Palmetto stopped and turned.

"What's the matter?"

"I forgot my Kodak."

"What?"

"The camera. It's in the suitcase."

"What in the world?"

314

"I have no intention of getting married without having a few pictures of it."

She lifted the front of her dress and ran back to the pickup. He watched her. Her mind was a labyrinth containing no straight lines. To get from one point to the other, you had to go round and round. He shook his head and looked to the moon for understanding.

The door was opened by a wizened black woman who clutched a robe to her throat and carried a kerosene lamp.

"Is the justice of the peace in?" Preston asked.

"Who wants to know?"

"We've come to get married."

"Hang on."

The door was closed in their faces. "Maybe it's too late," he said.

"Of course it's not too late."

"I think they've gone to bed."

"Then they can just get right up. I'm a judge's daughter, and I know the law. We've even had them come to our house at all hours. The idea!" She raised her hand to knock again.

"Hold your horses. Give 'em time." He

liked her spirit so long as it wasn't used against him.

The door was opened by an elderly but robust woman. She wore a scarf over her bunned hair and a cheerily quilted robe that ladies were calling housecoats. "Come in. Come in."

They felt as if they were walking into a world that had ceased to exist. The hall was hung with dark oils of grave-eyed people who seemed to be beckoning from back in time. A staircase led up at an incredible angle. They walked past darkened rooms where Palmetto saw furniture shrouded beneath sheets. She reached out and clung to Preston's arm.

The old lady led them to a room at the side of the house. The lights were on. Palmetto was relieved to find they had some electricity. Cleota, the black woman, was pulling sheets off the furniture. It was old and fine, covered in threadbare velvet.

"It's just lovely," Palmetto said.

"I keep this room for the weddings. There are so few one wants to entertain these days. You didn't bring witnesses?"

"No, ma'am."

"Cleota, you had better get Dink."

"What about me, Gran-gran?"

Bobby, a little boy of nine or ten wearing pajamas, stood in the doorway. He was wide awake and excited.

"You may ask them if you can watch, but you can't be a proper witness till you're eighteen."

"Can I?" he asked.

Palmetto knelt to him, her dress billowing out around her and her flawless pale neck catching the glow from the chandelier, where every third light burned. She touched the little boys's cheek. "You can be the ring bearer," she said.

"He'll be thrilled to death. Go brush your hair," the old lady said.

"Your husband wasn't asleep, I hope," Preston said.

"Oh, he's been asleep for fifteen years." She walked across the room to a desk, opened a drawer, and took out a Bible. Preston stood with his mouth open while she pointed to a portrait that held a commanding view from between dusty damask swags that clung loftily to the wooden casement windows.

The old lady seemed to have remembered something. Preston hoped she remembered to call whoever was in charge.

"My goodness," she said. "What do you know? I've been as blue as indigo all day and I couldn't figure why. It was sixteen years ago today that we put him in the ground. He died on the twenty-sixth and was buried on the twenty-seventh. Mercy me! The mind forgets, but the heart never does." She walked over and touched the portrait on the cheek. "I love you, Precious," She blew away the dust that remained on her finger, then turned to them with a smile. "He's always with me. Life goes on."

Preston was growing fidgety. "Well . . . uh . . . who's the justice of the peace?"

"Why, I am! I'm the only woman justice of the peace in the South. There was an article about me in the Atlanta *Constitution.* I'm Mrs. Inez Remus."

"I never heard of a woman marrying folks."

"Legally empowered by the Sovereign State of Georgia."

Palmetto had given a delighted shriek

and hugged her. Preston had shaken his head and held his tongue, though he practically had to bite it to do it. Good God! What had he gotten into? Here he was, in the middle of the night, marrying a girl who seemed sworn to love everything he was against. They were being married by a senile old lady who carried on conversations with a dead man. Their witnesses were two old darkies who wanted to get back in bed and would probably expect a tip, and a child who chewed gum. What was the world coming to? He curled his toes up in his shoes.

They were still curled when it was over. Palmetto took pictures of them all. She had also brought in a bottle of warm champagne. Mrs. Remus produced some glasses from a sideboard. Preston was sure they needed washing, but she only blew them out. Nobody seemed to think anything about it except him, and he once again decided to keep still. They toasted several times. Everybody said the bubbles tickled their nose. Then he was standing with his arm around Palmetto and they were raising their glasses for the camera as

Mrs. Remus, Cleota, and Dink stood behind Bobby and made sure he did it right, though they hadn't the slightest idea of what he was doing. Then everybody got a hug and they were back outside again, holding hands and running down the walk while the denizens of the house stood on the porch and tossed grits — they were out of rice. Mrs. Remus called out, "God Bless."

They were headed back toward Atlanta. She sat close to him, the suitcase on the floor and her head on his shoulder. She looked up at him. He was intent on the road, both hands on the wheel. She loved his intensity. She kissed his cheek. "Isn't it strange that just a few words can bind you together for life?"

He didn't take his eyes of the road. "I don't know how binding that was. I'll check it with my lawyer tomorrow."

She thought he was teasing. She nibbled at his ear. "What about tonight?"

"What about it?"

"Where are we going?"

"I got to get back down to The Melba.

We're serving a Chamber of Commerce breakfast in the morning. This is the first time we've had 'em, and I want to keep 'em. Today was payday, and I can't be sure who'll show up."

He *had* to be teasing. "But this is our wedding night!"

"You got an obligation, you carry it out. I've done one. Now I've got to get on to the next one."

It knocked the breath out of her. She sat up and moved to her side of the seat. He didn't seem to notice. She looked out at the blurred lights. They were becoming more numerous. They were back in Atlanta.

She sat on the sofa near the scale while Preston checked the orders and lined up tables. He didn't have to do that. She knew he didn't have to do it. It was just busywork. Anybody could have done it. But she was not going to get mad. They could burn her with irons or lash her to moving wagons, she was not going to get mad on her wedding night. Wedding night. She must be the only bride in history who had spent her wedding night in a cafeteria. She got up and smoothed out the wedding dress.

Preston watched her. He could barely think. There she is. There she is. It kept going through his mind like a stuck record. What was he going to do with her? She kept staring at him like a cat, trying to get behind his eyes. She had succeeded. Then she stood up and smoothed herself out. She used to be a little bird; now she was a cat.

"How much did you pay for that dress?" he asked.

"It was paid for out of my pocket in cash."

"Waste of money to buy something you're only gonna wear once."

Preston Vacalis was the meanest thing who ever drew breath. How in the world had she gotten married to him? "At the start we're getting off to, I'd say my chances of getting to use it again are getting better all the time."

"What the hell kind of remark is that?"

"A truly felt one."

She continued to sit there, watching

him. He wished she would turn the power of her gaze in another direction. "I got work to do. Somebody's got to keep a roof over our heads and food on the table."

She picked up a sugar dish and flung it at him. It whizzed by his head and shattered against the coffee urns. He was amazed to see that tears were running down her cheeks.

"This is our wedding night," she screamed, "and you have denied me any semblance of love! You are so cold and heartless you can't have anything — and you sure as hell can't have me!"

She picked up her suitcase in one hand and her skirts in the other and headed for the revolving door.

"If you go out that door, you can damn well stay out!"

"Happy to oblige," she called, and pressed herself into the door, setting the suitcase down and pulling the dress inside with both hands. She had to hop to get the door to move.

It was almost dawn. A dingy light streaked the buildings. He kicked a table and winced. He pushed out the door and stood on the sidewalk. She was almost to the corner.

"Stop right there!"

She wanted to keep going, but she couldn't resist turning in the middle of the street. "Who do you think you are, giving me orders?"

"I'm your damn husband, that's who!"

"Is that what you think a husband is? Somebody who goes around giving orders?"

"When I see somebody running around like a chicken with its head cut off, I think they need a few orders."

"I am perfectly capable of taking care of myself."

"If you are so high and mighty independent, why did you think you had to marry me?"

"I didn't *have* to marry anybody!"

"I didn't mean to say it that way."

"The things you say you don't mean are the ones you really do mean."

He had reached the curb. She had put her suitcase down in the middle of the street, but still held her skirts up. They circled each other warily. The big Coca-

Cola sign across from the Loew's Grand glowed brightly in back of them.

"You see," he said. "That's the way you are. You take little slips that don't mean a thing and you turn 'em until nobody knows what anybody means, including you. You've got to come back to earth once in a while."

"All I've done lately is hit the earth with repeated thuds."

"Are you ready to come to your senses and come back?"

"I am ready to come to my senses, but that in no way involves coming back with you."

She picked up her suitcase and turned away.

"I'm not coming after you again!"

"Thank God for small favors."

It was the last thing she said. She went sailing off down the street toward the bus station, where the neon greyhound galloped eternally without destination.

"To hell with her," he said under his breath. He had been taken to his limits. He was exhausted. He looked up and down the street, hoping fervently they hadn't been seen.

"You're the early bird." It was Elvira. She and Scoe came around the corner, their brown faces glowing. They must have had a good time getting up, he thought.

"Morning," he said.

"I thought we'd beat you here," said Scoe.

"Yeah . . . well . . . we got a big day. I wanted to get an early start. Come on."

They preceded him in through the revolving door. He was about to push inside when he stopped and walked to the top of the hill, looking down at the bus station. Palmetto was not in sight. He stiffened. "Good riddance," he said. But he stood there in the windy dawn, looking down the hill. He was free again. He had been rubbing the nubby fabric of his tie. He brought it slowly upward.

Chapter 12

He went to the bank. They were as heartless as Palmetto. He had done all that work and gone all that far and he was still not far enough. The bankers had crinkly smiles and gleaming watch chains. They always looked just beyond or to the left of you. He decided that if he lived long enough and worked hard enough and made enough money, he would try a test. He supposed that for every ten thousand dollars he had in the bank they would look at him a little closer, perhaps focus on an ear and work their way toward his eyes.

Banker's eyes were dull and full of false goodwill when they spoke to him, but he had seen them dart and fill with light when men with money passed by. He had worked so hard and pulled himself up just to see the next plateau he had to pull himself to. He wondered if his reach would ever catch up with his vision.

It was over a month since he had married and lost Palmetto. He had decided he would never call her until she called him, but Roy Al and Sarah had made him go back on that.

Sarah had called a few hours after Palmetto's departure. She had asked if they were coming home that night. He had told her yes and not elaborated. When he got home that night the entire family was there. There was a wedding cake and flowers. There were presents and champagne. There were embarrassed faces and no bride to kiss. "How awful," they had said. "What happened?" they had meant. They gave each other telegraphic looks, changed the subject, and stayed anyway. Families were families at funerals and weddings, and if one turned to the other, their ways of coping and commiserating was part of what made them families. "Well, all I can say is she's a fool to have missed this party," Maybelle said. Maybelle was the pretty one. She had just turned twenty-five and was two years married. She had newly conceived, but the men didn't know it yet. Her stomach was still flat, and she took sideways glances at it in the gold-leaf mirror. She wore a red knit dress, and her breasts were so full that they threatened to burst through the material. She only had a little morning sickness, and she told Araminthia that women should always be six weeks pregnant. She had never looked so good. People couldn't take their eyes off her.

Maybelle was filled with love for everybody that night. She caught Preston alone in the kitchen, sitting on the edge of the table. "Is she just the meanest thing in the world?" she asked.

"No," Preston answered. "She's very nice. This never occurred to me before, but she kinda reminds me of you."

"I like her already," Maybelle said. "Do you love her very much?"

"I don't know."

"Well, no wonder she left you. Women have to be loved."

"I don't know what to do."

Maybelle couldn't believe it. Her brother had always known what to do. She had always been afraid of him, but his fierceness had been parted like the Red Sea, and someone had marched over him where he had never thought to be touched. She loved him suddenly, though it had never occurred to her to do so. He had never seemed to need it. Now he did.

"It'll come to you what to do," she said, and bent to kiss his cheek. Her breasts grazed his arm. She was wearing red, Palmetto's color. He almost embraced her, then caught himself and sat blinking after she had left the room. Something bad was wrong with him. She was his sister.

"You've got to call her family," Sarah had said when everyone was gone.

"I won't do it."

"Roy Al and I discussed it."

"It's nobody's business."

"It's everybody's business now, and we're not going to have her family think that we are common. Now, she has been gone almost twelve hours, and if you are not concerned about her welfare, we are.

If you don't go to that telephone and call her, Roy Al will do it."

People were speaking to him in a way that they had never dared before. What had happened to him? He was afraid to look in the mirror. He was afraid he would see what everybody else was seeing.

But he had called, had spoken to her father. His toes curled up as he asked about her, getting no consolation from the man's gruff manner. He tried to think how he would feel had they changed places. He was an intruder there, had done them wrong though they had never met. Then a woman, Mamie, got on the line. She was brisk and informative. Palmetto was home and fine but resting and thank you for calling. "Tell her I called," he had said. "Don't worry, I will," she had replied, and hung up.

He called twice more and each time talked to Mamie. He detected a note of warmth. Each time he called just before noon, when he was sure the father would be out. He had prided himself on being a straightforward man. Now he was sneaking around on the telephone. The first Friday after she had gone, he had Scoe put a bushel of peaches on the train to Cedartown. He repeated it every Friday for a month, until he got a one-line letter from Palmetto: "Peaches are running out our ears. Please stop or send something else." It was signed "P." It gave him hope. He changed to hams and turkeys.

He was waiting for his heart to harden, but it was slow.

It got to be July. He was working harder than ever. He was sitting out front one afternoon when Welsh and Greener, the union men, arrived as they had done before. They had acquired a veneer or ease in the place, nodding to several of the floor girls, who nodded shyly and dashed away, not wanting to be branded on the job. "Like to talk to you," Greener had said, sliding into a chair.

Preston got up. "See my lawyer."

"You got to face us sometime," Welsh said.

"I'm facing you now," Preston said clenching his fist. "If I catch you around here again, I'm gonna de-face you."

He had caught them around there

enough — standing at the end of the alley at the end of a Saturday shift, talking earnestly to the women who looked at them with wide, doubting eyes, shifting the weight of their shopping bags while making up their minds. And he had said nothing. What was there to say? Everybody said it was a free country, but it didn't seem so free for him these days.

And it had gone on so long. One by one they were trying to win over his employees; then they'd come to him with a full slate of things. He'd like to catch one of them in the alley sometime when he was in the truck. He had to stop this. He couldn't think like this. He was a man. He would fight them a man's way, without trucks in an alley.

Greener had given him a smug smile. "I hate to hear that. You are gonna be seeing us again whether you want to or not. Everybody down here is ready to go but you."

"Anybody wants to go can go."

"That ain't the case. This is the last roundup, friend. You are going to have the union in here or no cafeteria to have a union or anybody else in."

It was an effort for Preston not to hit the man. He had a face that needed it, sharp features and soft cheeks like mortar that hadn't quite dried. Preston pointed toward the door, and after a moment the men left, making sure they paused near the scale and looked around the room, giving a general nod to anyone who might be watching. Everybody was.

He had checked them out. They had some hangnail affiliation with a union in Cincinnati. He had gone back to his lawyer with his worries. "A strike'll put me out of business."

"I don't think you're going to have any trouble finding coons who need to work."

"But they're my people."

"Don't let Eleanor Roosevelt hear that. She thinks slavery has been abolished."

"You know what I mean."

"Yes, I know what you mean, and if you got anybody there with a grain of sense they're going to know that no white man's union is going to come in there and change the world for them. The union's asking for a checkoff system, and you know what that means: You deduct from salaries and give it to the union. Those poor fools won't be making a dime more. They might be making less. They could get one or two concessions and feel like they've won something, but in the long run they're gonna get nothing at all. The country's got union fever now, and we got 'em springing up like crabgrass. In a coupla years all but the big ones will have died out.''

"What am I supposed to do till then?''

"Stall 'em. They don't have any money. You got more than they do.''

Preston managed a laugh. "I feel sorry for 'em, then.''

It was August. He kept thinking he felt better. The union hadn't lived up to their threats; maybe they were just bluffing. Waller, Hildebrand, and Rasnake seemed to think things were hunky-dory, laughing heartily through the steaming summer days. He didn't notice anybody sweating . . . except him. And he had never sweated so much. He was beginning to think that they knew something he didn't know. He hoped they did. Anyway, he was smiling and going along. There was no place else to go. There was once a pressman at Elmo Flagg's who was dying of diabetes. Everybody knew it but him, right up till the day he died.

Preston had dream after dream. He had dreamed of Palmetto three nights running. Every night he dreamed she was there, and in the morning the knowledge was as heavy to him as the damp, humid air that baked all day under the spiteful sun. He felt that everybody knew about him. His family knew about his marriage that wasn't a marriage. Scoe and Elvira knew, too. He admired their grace in letting him know without ever mentioning it. That was the way with smart colored folks. They could say things without weighing them down with words. He knew the rest of the help had gotten wind of it. They must be laughing.

Down at the bank they knew that Preston Vacalis wanted more than he could have. That knowledge must have gone around.

And Waller. Despite his protestations to

the contrary, Preston was sure he had told Rasnake and Hildebrand about his wanting to buy them out. Preston had always been a close man, keeping his secrets like quarters in a piggy bank. Now everybody knew everything.

He woke up one morning out of breath. He had dreamed of Palmetto again. She had come revolving in the door during the lunch rush. She was looking for him. He had tried to get to her, but there were people in the way, shrilly laughing customers with loaded trays. They were both fighting to get through them, but the customers wouldn't have an inch. Then suddenly they parted and began to point and laugh at Preston. He was horrified to find himself naked. He tried to find Palmetto, but she had disappeared. He turned to run for the kitchen, but the doors had swung open and all the help had marched out in their white uniforms, carrying picket signs. Doc was leading them. He turned around. There was a ringing. He had to make it stop. He went toward the sound of ringing, but he was on skates and he was falling, falling,

falling . . . until he hit his head against the bedside table.

He sat up and opened his eyes, out of breath and frightened from the dream. It had been so real. He was sure they were all in the closet, ready to march out. The ringing continued. It was the doorbell.

He pulled his pants on and came down the hall buttoning his shirt, but Sarah had answered the door. She admitted two big men who wore gray shirts with lettering on them. He rushed toward her and knocked her out of the way. He thought they were union men. He had read about burly union thugs.

Beyond the screen door he saw a moving van. He looked at Sarah. She smiled evasively. She pointed the men toward the breakfast room.

"Good morning," she said. "I didn't think they'd be here so early."

"What are they doing?"

"Preston, I've been meaning to tell you. I've found the cutest little apartment."

"Now cut that out. Just cut it out."

"And I've gotten a job. A good job. I'm going to be selling perfume at Rich's."

"I'm not going to stand for that."

"It may not sound like much to you, but I'm thirty-five years old and I've never held a job. I'm very proud of it, and those women make good money. I start off on salary, but I get to go on commission from the perfume companies in six months."

"You don't have to do that. I told you. Nothing is going to change."

"Of course things are going to change. Things have always changed for us. Where would we be if they hadn't? Mercy! I shudder to think. You and I had just gotten set in our ways. Why, when you told me you were getting married, I almost died of shock, but I suppose I'd rather die of shock than boredom, and we would have, you know, in time. Just turned to dust. You know something? They call me Miss Vacalis at the store. Nobody has ever called me anything but Sarah. I feel like a woman of the world. I'm going to have a whole new life."

"What am I suppose to do?"

She stopped and stared at him for a moment, touched by the child's earnestness in his voice. "You've never asked anybody what to do. You've just always gone ahead and done it."

"I think I did something wrong."

"So do I. You're the only person I've ever heard of who's been married for almost four months and has no bride to show for it. You've got to go over to Cedartown and get her."

"She's the one who did the leaving."

"Preston, nobody thinks you were abandoned. If you chased her away, go and try to bring her back."

She looked toward the breakfast room. "Be careful of that table," she called to the movers. "One of the legs is loose."

Chapter 13

August went blistering by. It hadn't rained for five weeks. Farmers were in hysterics. The papers were full of it. Business fell off a bit. Produce prices climbed sharply. He forgot to water the lawn, and it parched, sending dry cracks where thick grass had been. Peachtree Creek was a trickle of itself. Tempers grew short. When Preston came home from work he felt as though he were under a layer of dirt. Then one Sunday at the end of August it rained. It seemed as if it were trying to make up for the entire summer. It rained so long and hard that the ground couldn't absorb it all. Puddles and little rivers formed. Sewers backed up, and gutters ran over. There were pictures in the paper of cars stalled in the rain. Preston didn't go out of the house all day, just sat in the rocking chair and stared at Roy Al's clock, which Sarah had left to him. That night the rain had calmed enough for him to drive over to Scoe and Elvira's. He told them to take care of the place tomorrow. He had to take a trip.

It was sixty-eight miles to Cedartown through Austell, Dallas, and Rockmart, past the quarries and over Fish Creek. "I'm a Cedartown Gully Jumper," Palmetto had told him once, "and don't you forget it."

"How could I forget it?" He had laughed.

"You can't. I won't let you."

"Why don't you still live there?"

"I would if I could, but I can't. That was my childhood, and once you make the mistake of leaving that blessed state you can't get back in. I tried once, but the things I thought were so wonderful turned out to be absolutely ordinary. I can go back for visits, like Scarlett went back to Tara, but it's just to catch my breath."

He drove past a graveyard, over Wimberly Hill, by feed and tractor stores, beyond mortuary and department-store billboards, by the Dancing Mule, a ramshackle drive-in barbecue place where Palmetto had said there was bootleg whiskey available if they recognized you. He stopped at a light on the approach to a viaduct that arched over the railroad tracks. The street sign said COLLARD VALLEY ROAD. He took a right.

The road was gravelly, the stones ricocheting against the underside of the pickup reminding him of the noise the grits had made falling against Mrs. Inez Remus's walkway. "My God," Palmetto had said as they ran for the street. "It's supposed to be rice and I get grits. It's the story of my whole life, very makeshift and just a little bit off."

It looked as though it was going to be the story of his life, too.

It was the last lush moment of summer. Birds flew from far, bobbing trees and swung on the wires between telephone poles, the limitless decoration of the road. Fields of corn were yellowing, and Queen Anne's lace grew wildly out from them, dotting the red gullies and swaying under the weight of butterflies. He was driving down the road to Palmetto's childhood.

Nobody knew he was coming. He was afraid they would have told him not to, so he had just come ahead, with five dozen eggs as a gift, feeling foolish now as he passed rows of henhouses.

He knew the house when he saw it, she had described it so well. It sloped up and back from the road, the front of it shaded by benevolent elms. It was a two-story house — three if you counted the tin-roofed cupola crowned with a weathervane rooster that spun in the breeze that set the trees to shaking. He parked the pickup and got out. It was three in the afternoon, and hot. The wind was welcome.

Preston put his coat on, pulling nervously at it, thinking of wrinkles and wanting to be smooth. Ludilla, her head in a rag and a dust mop in her hand, met him on the porch. She regarded him from top to bottom. He smiled. She gave no indication of her approval, but evidently he had passed. She spoke as she began mopping the porch. "You looking for Miss Mamie, she around the side."

"Thank you," he said, but she ignored it.

There was an old covered stone well on the side of the house. A honeysuckle vine wrapped around it. There were six cushioned wicker chairs that looked embedded in the grass. A child's rocking horse, attached on springs to wooden mounts, was near a crumbling plaster birdbath. Preston walked under the windows, wondering if Palmetto was inside, watching him. It was hard to walk with curled-up toes.

There was a large vegetable garden in back of the house. A scarecrow in an old straw hat waved to him in the wind. He had never seen the sky so blue and cloudless.

Mamie Russell didn't see him. She sat at the edge of the garden in a print housedress that was as faded as the large pink-white towel that stretched beside her; it was laden with brushes and combs, each gleaming wetly in the sun. Beside the towel was a white enamel basin of water and several squeezed lemons on the ground. Mamie's hair was white, and it hung down to the middle of her back. She brushed it, her back to him. He stopped, couldn't speak, feeling more an intruder than ever. He cleared his throat.

Mamie turned, a hand to the throat of her unbuttoned dress. He felt as though he'd caught her at her bath.

"Mrs. Russell?"

She knew him instantly. He was pale and worn and nervous, but Palmetto had gotten herself a handsome one. She lost her worry about how the child would look.

"I'm Preston Vacalis."

She stood up, making no fuss about the casual buttoning of her dress over the white slip. "How do you do," she said, and extended her hand. It was a large, rough hand, a man's hand with big bones and lines in it. She had been rubbing her hands with Jergen's Lotion, and they were slick. She withdrew the hand, but let the smile remain.

"I came to see Palmetto, though I don't know if she'll see me."

"Neither do I. She's off with her daddy now, though. They've gone to Cave

Spring to look at horses."

"If you want me to leave, I will."

She laughed gently, sounding like Palmetto. "I'd have no patience with you if you left after all that drive. I've just washed my hair. You've got to let me put it up. And change my dress. This one's for nobody's eyes but mine and Ludilla's."

"I think you look just fine."

"I think you'd better get your eyes checked." She almost laughed. "But I'm sure you can see well enough to help me gather my combs and brushes."

"Yes, ma'am."

He squatted over the towel and handed them up to her. "I always dry them in the sun," she said. "I think it makes them cleaner. So many people don't ever think to wash a comb or brush. You would simply be amazed. All my children have lovely hair." She paused, looking distantly into the profusion of blazing-red canna lilies. "My son A.J. had the prettiest hair you ever saw. It was so blond and thick and curly. Josephine and Palmetto were jealous of it. They had to have theirs curled. And he spent so much time on it. It had to be combed exactly right before he would leave the house. Then he started using that old Vitalis hair tonic on it. Stay away from that stuff, whatever you do. It made it look all matted, but you know girls. They liked the way it looked and smelled, and you know boys, anything to please a girl. And it was so pretty, like a blond pasture, if you can imagine such a thing." She looked back to the cannas. A.J.'s pasture was now a barren field of skin. "It all fell out," she continued. "By the time he was eighteen he was bald. I blame it on Vitalis." She held the combs and brushes clasped to her. The memory of his hair always gave her pain, but it was now a family joke, turned that way by A.J. himself.

Preston still stood there with his wide blue eyes. She touched his arm. "Don't be nervous, son."

"I'm trying not to be."

"Are you a lemonade drinker?"

"I sure am."

They started for the back of the house. "You'll have to see my husband for anything stronger. Or my children, for that matter. I forbid it under my roof, but that does not extend to the barn, where they all have their little nip among the flies. I suppose it is silly, but when you've been against something for so long you have to keep it up. Nothing hurts the loyal opposition more than to have the opponent suddenly give in.''

''I have taken drinks, but I have never enjoyed them.''

''Wouldn't you know!'' She laughed and shook her head, the white hair falling from her shoulders. ''The one on my side has to be on the outs with Palmetto.''

Mamie had put on a navy-and-white polka-dot dress and wore tortoiseshell combs in her bunned hair. She and Preston sat across from each other in the wicker chairs, angel-food cake and lemonade between them.

''Do you love her?'' she asked.

''I've never done much loving.''

''Prior experience doesn't matter.''

''I miss her. We've had a strange relationship.''

"Hers have always tended in that direction."

"Not that she's to blame all the way. But I've thought about it, and I don't know how to be any different. I'm ready to give it a try. Do you think she is?"

"She's bullheaded . . . But I am well versed in my daughter's faults. What about yours?"

He leaned forward, rubbing his palms together. He put his fingers to his face and exhaled between them. "I've got 'em. No mistake about that. I never knew how many I had till she started pointing them out. I never planned on getting married, you know. I've always had so much to do. I've got my own business now. Almost my own. Only I'm having trouble with it now. This damn union . . . Pardon my French."

"She never mentioned that."

"She didn't know how dangerous it is."

"Don't you think she should?"

"That's my trouble."

"You have to share them, too." How sad and sweet and lost he was. She wanted to hug him and tell him everything would be all right. But she could always be swayed by a man with a fine head of hair, and she knew it. "You're more concerned with what's on the head than what's in it," Judge Russell had told her once. "You stay to supper," she said now.

Mamie rounded up the whole family for supper. It didn't sit well with Palmetto at all. She could tell that Mamie had taken a stand, and was annoyed that her mother had turned what should have been an abrupt encounter into a celebration. She was determined not to give in.

She had given a little gasp when she and Alfred drove up to the house and she saw Preston's pickup. She had looked and looked for it before, but now that it was here, actually in the yard, she could think of nothing to say, felt only leaden with the baby, feet swollen and eyes puffy with dust.

"Are you all right, Palmetto?"

"Yes, Daddy, I'm fine. Looks like we've got company."

She had said hello, and not touched him or held his eye for very long, had stood at the foot of the stairs, one hand on the banister, spoken of weather and horses and her tiredness, had seen Ludilla setting the rosewood dining table with the extra leaf. Damn Mama, she thought. That's just like her. Meddling. "Ludilla, call me in time for supper," she had said, smiled wanly at Preston, and climbed the stairs.

They were all there when she came down, bathed and feeling better in the new maternity dress she and Josephine had gotten in Rome, the one Mamie had been asking her why she hadn't worn. There were Josephine and Bertram, her hearty husband, who laughed the loudest and longest at parties and cried the most at funerals. He was laughing now at one of A.J.'s jokes. A.J. made all the men laugh and all the women blush and shake their heads, till they got to the kitchen, where they laughed with one another. Lorraine was A.J.'s wife. She was a beauty, though she didn't seem to notice it the way others did. It was as though beauty were too rich for her blood and she wanted only to blend in. She had been an orphan, and took such loving care of Ray, her little six-year-old boy. Everybody took loving care of Ray. He was the family's only child, and spoiled rotten, as they proudly said.

They were making an effort with Preston, who kept smiling and nodding his head. Palmetto took a survey of the room. He stood up for her. She wished he hadn't, but was thrilled that he did. Mamie was out of sight. Her daddy regarded the proceedings with a dour face. He looked like a judge with his white hair and dignity. He sat in his rocking chair near the big radio. She crossed to him and stood beside the chair, rubbing his neck and holding his hand. Preston stared across the room at her as though they were the only two in it. She turned her attention to the window that overlooked the front yard, but she knew that his gaze was on her still.

"Y'all come eat," Ludilla said.

Everyone ate too much and laughed too much, told their best stories that got the same laughs in the same places, the others sometimes jumping the punch lines. What simpletons they are, Palmetto thought, but laughed where she had always laughed, because the things were funny still. Then, just as suddenly, she loved them all and hated herself for having felt anything but love for them, even Preston.

"Mama, sit down and eat," they all said. Mamie paid them no attention, and they let her serve them seconds. Mamie was like Palmetto. She did as she pleased whether she wanted to or not.

Palmetto and Preston sat together, guided there by Mamie. Mamie's face was blank with hospitality.

"You suppose your café could handle a bunch like this?" Judge Russell asked.

"Glad to see them," Preston said.

"It's not a café, Alfred, it's a cafeteria," Mamie said as she spooned more dumplings on his plate.

"Same difference."

"There's no such thing as the same difference unless you're talking about arithmetic," Josephine said.

"One and one is three," said Ray.

"Sounds like you're raising a banker," Bertram told A.J.

There was a silence. Palmetto caught Lorraine's eyes. "Daddy bought the most beautiful horse today. A sorrel. As soon as I have the baby I think I'm going to take up riding again."

Preston wanted to object, his mouth opened with the words, but he turned them into something else. "Are there any more pickled peaches?" Then he saw the dish. It was empty. He cringed.

"I'll get it," Josephine said.

Mamie swooped the dish off the table. "Keep your seat."

"Mama, your food is getting cold as ice," Palmetto said.

"I don't like it too hot," she said as she left the room.

"Mama is bullheaded."

"Leave your mama alone. She's all right," said Alfred. He took up for Mamie at the oddest times.

"I didn't mean to put anybody to any trouble," Preston said.

"Well, you did," said Palmetto.

"He did nothing of the kind!" said Josephine. "The idea!"

"We got plenty of pickled peaches,"

said Alfred. "My God. You sent us a freight car full."

A.J. started to laugh, and the rest of them joined in.

Preston blushed till his ears turned crimson. Palmetto smiled in spite of herself. Then Mamie returned with a dish full of pickled peaches. Everybody laughed again.

They sat in the living room. Dinner lay heavy on them. It was getting to be dark. A.J. and Lorraine had to leave to get Ray to bed. No one had bothered to turn on a light. They thought it drew mosquitoes.

Alfred was smoking a cigar, and Mamie walked through the room fanning the air, her sign of disapproval. "I hope you don't mind Judge Russell's nasty cigar smoke, Preston. It makes some people sick."

"No, ma'am. It's all right."

"You want one?" asked Alfred hopefully.

"No, sir. But thank you just the same."

"You're the first person I've met by the name of Vacalis. The first time I heard it I thought they were saying Vitalis."

Mamie did not stifle the sharpness in her voice. "No, Alfred. It is most definitely not Vitalis."

Judge Russell rocked a moment in agitated silence, then got up. "I got to go back there in the back and see if I can't take a hockey-doodleum." He walked through the room a slight bend in his shoulders.

Preston watched with his mouth agape. Palmetto blushed. Her daddy was obsessed with his bowels. It was nothing new to the family, but if you were new to the family it came as something of a shock. She wanted Preston to think her life was as perfect as a painting. She felt he had glimpsed behind the frame.

"Why don't you take Preston out and show him our little town?" Mamie suggested.

"I don't think he's interested."

"Yes, I am."

"Show him the Big Spring."

Palmetto got up. She felt as though she were as big as the side of a house. "Come on then."

They parked the truck on College Street and walked by the Methodist Church down toward the Big Spring. "That's where we go to church," she said.

He looked at it and knew it was where she had meant to be married. "This is a nice town."

"I love it. I wouldn't want to raise a child in Atlanta. It's too big."

"It's not where you raise it, it's how."

"I'll do just fine."

"Well, you know, I've had plenty of experience along those lines."

"You're being very nice, but you don't have to worry. I'm not going to ask for alimony or child support."

"What?"

"We can't expect to stay married, can we?"

"I'm hoping you'll come back with me."

"We're too entirely different to make each other anything but miserable. I want a happy life for me and my child."

"I want that, too. And I want to try and give it to you . . . I love you."

He had said it to her before in many

words, but he had never boiled it down to three.

She held her breath so she wouldn't cry. "Love is just the meanest thing that ever happened," she said.

They cut through the shrubbery at the Big Spring, walked over the crew-cut grass down to the single, pebble-strewn canal that marked its flow toward the reservoir. The lights were on at the picnic pavilion, and people were cleaning up. Preston brushed the willow fronds out of her way as she led him toward a bridge that crossed the spring where it got wider and the concrete canal gave way to a dirt bottom. They stood on the top of the bridge, with the moon reflected in the rushing water. The Taj Mahal occurred again to Preston. He wanted to tell her about it, but it wasn't the time. It was time for them to be sad for a while. He supposed that would be all right if something good came out of it.

"I'm sorry I can't be the kind of person you want me to be, but I am what I am, and every time you remind me of all the changes I need to make it seems so impossible and I just get more like I was to begin with. I know I got some faults, but I'm not all bad. Don't you think I'd like to be some Prince Charming for you?''

"Oh, Preston, let's just not talk about it. All my energy is going into this baby."

"Can I touch it?"

She couldn't deny him that. It was his life beating there too.

"Let's go over to the playground," she said.

It was a caked-dirt playground with a slide, a set of swings, and a jungle gym. She had been too old to play here when it was put up, and she had missed it.

He took her arm on the excuse of giving her support. He held her just under the elbow. "Are you all right?"

"I'm fine. They baby moves so much. And I've gained all this weight. All summer long I've been craving watermelon."

"Why didn't you tell me?"

"Craving is a common phenomenon among pregnant and non-pregnant alike."

"I could have sent you plenty

of watermelon."

"Dear Fathers, Preston, Cedartown is practically one big watermelon patch."

"I'd have sent you some anyway. I just want to do something for you."

"What you can do for me now is help me get seated in this swing."

"Do you think you ought to?"

"Yes, I do."

He sat here in the swing, then stood above her. The sky was clear and the stars were out.

"Can I touch it now?"

"Yes, but you better put on boxing gloves. He's been raising Cain tonight."

"He? How do you know?"

"Oh, we nurses know."

Her face was newly round, and she had never been more beautiful. He believed her. There were times when no secrets could be kept from her.

He knelt in the dirt by the gently swaying swing and put his hand on her stomach. She had to stop herself from putting her hand over his.

He felt the tiny convulsions and looked up to her in wonder. "It's like a bird fluttering."

"It feels like a bull in a china shop to me."

He looked up at her. She let him take her hand. He rubbed it against his cheek, then lay his face against her, listening for the hearts he hoped were his.

But she grabbed the chain of the swing and gripped it hard. That was men for you. They thought they could just come around and be sweet for an afternoon and expect it to last a lifetime. Nobody was ever going to make a fool out of Palmetto Russell again.

"I'm not going to raise him like a child at all," she said. "I'm going to raise him like a friend, and that's what you and I will have to be."

He got up. "If I have a son I want it to be a son and nothing else."

"Maybe it'll be a daughter and you won't have any interest in her at all."

That was a woman for you, tender as could be until the mood left, like a cloud that passed over the moon. They never had reasons for hurting people. They just hurt for the sake of hurting.

"You say I don't have any heart. You must think I don't have any feelings either. I got problems that you don't know the first thing about. I always thought that sooner or later things would get easier, but just when Easy Street gets in sight something goes wrong and it's as far away as it was before. I always thought I wanted money and success and that would make me happy, and then you came along. I didn't want to want you, but I did and I do. Maybe I drove you away, but I couldn't help it. If I have hurt you I am heartily sorry, and I would like to make it up to you if you would let me and show me how, but I am not going to come down here and let you stick needles into me."

He was out of breath when he finished, and she was ashamed. She wanted to take him in her arms, but she was afraid to let go now. She pulled herself out of the swing. "I'm sorry," she said. "I wish there had been more between us . . . or less."

He didn't bother to take her arm as they went back to the pickup. When they got to the house she let herself out and looked at him a moment through the window. "I'm glad you came. It was nice to see you."

"It was good to see you, too. Tell your mama and daddy I said 'bye."

"Drive carefully."

"Take care of yourself."

He pulled out of the driveway and onto the road. She watched until the taillights disappeared and all that was left was the dust that the wind carried off the same way it did the whistle from the railroad tracks that came across the graveyard and the fields, like something calling to her for comfort in the night.

She climbed to the porch and sat in a big old rocking chair and rocked and cried until the rooster crowed.

* * *

In the middle of September Preston received the message from the union. It had been almost a month since he had heard from them, and he had had this hopeful wish they had disappeared with the dog days, but they had only gone north to Cincinnati for consultation. He had never heard of anything good coming from the North. They gave him three weeks to let The Melba go union. If not, they'd pull his help out.

Preston ground his teeth and clenched his fist, but he kept his peace. That same day Scoe let him know he was with the union.

"Why?"

"I don't see how I got much of a choice. Everybody down here has gone over to 'em. These folks wants a union and they gon' get it. There been some rocks through windows and some people gettin' shoved when they didn't speak up for the union fast enough."

"You're scared. Is that what it is?"

"You know better than that. I ain't scared of anybody down here."

"Then why? You know as well as I do that this is a bunch of chiselers who got the law on their side for once. They can tell you they are your friends, but you know and I know that they ain't. Can't you see what they're after? The most they're asking for is a nickel an hour up. That's less than fifteen dollars a month, and they want seven fifty of that in dues, and they want me to give it to 'em 'cause they know they ain't gon' get it any other way. And they gon' turn right around, right around, and sell you out. I don't know what to say. I been as fair with everybody down here as I been with myself.''

''But you the owner. We ain't got none of this.''

''I'm the owner because, dammit, I earned it. I put this place together!''

''You always think you're doin' things by yourself that other folks is workin' just as hard as you to get done. You ain't never hired anybody new to replace Scooter, Mattie, and Sadie. I ain't saying we wanted you to hire anybody else, but you had three folks gone for nearly six months and the same work has been getting done and ain't nobody got extra for it.''

They were sitting in the stockroom across from the meat scale, on which was a box of roasts wrapped in brown paper and tied with wire. Preston stared at the weight lever. It was swaying, a little underweight. He would have to balance it. Things were all coming down on him. Down, down, down. He had thought it would get better in the fall. He should have remembered. Fall was when things went away, grew beautiful and vanished.

He looked at Scoe, sitting five feet away from him, his white apron stained with dirt, dried blood, and greenish prints from lettuce. The fronts of his shoes were slit open. He claimed it let the air in and calmed his arches, which were falling. He always did his work, knew what to do better than Preston. "The smartest nigger I ever saw," Preston said to Waller once. But as soon as he had said it, he was ready to take it back. Scoe wasn't a nigger. Scoe was just somebody else. He was special. And Elvira, too. She comforted him in her passing way. They had shared some things, like looks and hidden messages that lived in the air. He didn't need to explain himself to her. She knew.

But when they had had to choose, they

hadn't chosen him.

"We just looking for a little security," Scoe said. "I don't know whether we gon' get it or not. Don't know if there's any such thing in this life. But we gots to try. Colored been free too long just to be free and nothing else. We got a step coming."

"Why do you have to try and take it here?"

" 'Cause this is where we're at."

"Everybody's gon' lose something because of this."

"Well, I know it, and I'm sorry. It hurts me, too. You and me got feelings between us we ain't never said nothin' 'bout. They there for me the same as you, but sometimes you just have to do what comes along . . . if it looks good."

"What do y'all plan on doing? Walking out?"

"That's what they told us, but they'll be meetin' with you first."

Preston got up. "If that's the way it is, that's the way it is." He looked around the room. "We're running low on squash and eggplant."

"I already put it on the list."

Preston met with Welsh and Greener in a hole-in-the-wall office down on Luckie Street. It was late afternoon, and the neon was blazing from the restaurants that lined both sides of the street. He didn't have too much to do with the other restaurant owners. He was a cafeteria man. He thought that was a big difference. He did high volume. They did what they called cuisine. But he'd put his food up to theirs any day. *The Grapes of Wrath* was on at the Rialto. He didn't want to see that. He had problems enough.

He could tell what their operation was like from the dirty steps that led up to it. My God, he thought as he stepped around some broken glass, they ought to have more pride than this. It don't take much to operate a broom. No matter how far down he and his family had been, they were clean about it. You didn't have to live in filth.

If their office was little cleaner, at least it was bare, and some light came in across the fire escape. They had been sitting without jackets, but put them on when he came in. They were as nervous as he was, knocking papers out of a straight-back chair and pulling it up for him. He didn't want to sit down, but things were bad enough. He sat, folded his hands, and resisted the lure of his shiny silk tie. They were just the kind of men who made their living from blacks, he thought. The pasty whiteness made the downtrodden think they were speaking from the world of light, but when they had to deal with someone whose color should have made them equal, they fell back on unctuous smiles and oily phrases. Preston would rather have fought with them in an alley than this. He hated a man who fawned.

"You're keeping most of what you earn at the workers' expense," Greener was saying. "The days of the big moneymakers are over. There won't be any more Rockefellers."

"I don't want to be any Rockefeller. I just want what's mine."

"You got no retirement benefits. You got no sick leave. You got no insurance for them. If anything happens to them that's their tough luck."

"Nobody ever gave me any fringe benefits. I came up the hard way. But I take care of all my people. I even sent that Mattie and Sadie some money."

"But you wouldn't put them back to work."

"That's right. I can't have my help tellin' me what to do."

"People have got a right to be taken care of without depending on the whims of the master."

"I told you to get everybody else, then come back to me."

"We're not in business to do what you tell us to do. You're the flashy big boy in this trade."

"If you knew how small that 'big' was, you'd be kicking yourselves for wasting your time."

"You up-and-comers do know how to poor-mouth."

They were getting nowhere. They had heard what he had to say before. All they were doing was clenching their fists.

Greener got up. He was the amiable one. "The next step is to present you with a formal list of grievances," he said. "We can talk about philosophies all day."

Preston nodded and left. He had been holding on to the hope that he could do something, but nothing had been done at all. He headed down toward Five Points as the wind whipped through the gutter, sliding trash along and sending a mist of dirt over him. Some of it lodged in his right eye. It began to water. He wondered if people would think he was crying.

He hesitated a moment outside Waller's Haberdashery, then exhaled mournfully and went in. The eye was still running.

Waller was just closing up. After all these years, he had never changed his habits. He was always there before it opened and always there after it closed. Preston saw the slight frown as he came in, then saw it erased by the professional smile. Waller saw everyone as a customer.

"Got something in my eye," Preston said.

"Sit down in the light and let me take a look."

Preston did as he was told. He didn't seem to have the energy for anything else.

Waller rolled a handkerchief to a point, held Preston's lid open with one hand, and dabbed into the eye. Preston gave several jerks before Waller drew back. A tiny cinder was black against the whiteness of the cloth.

"Just a cinder," Waller said. "They ain't big, but they do hurt."

They had gone up to his office, which overlooked the store. Waller had a call to make, then listened while Preston recounted his day.

"I put in everything I own down there," Preston said.

"You shoulda let me know before you did that."

"What did you want me to do? Nothing?"

Waller reached over the desk and patted Preston on the shoulder. "I hate to see you so upset. But you'll get over it. I don't know anybody who ever really made it without getting something and losing it first. You ought to consider yourself halfway there."

"I can't lose this. This is mine!"

"I can tell you this much, son. The eyes

of the business community are on you. These unions are a coming thing. They knocked down laws in Alabama. Those steel mills are just breeding grounds. Look North. They've taken over everything up there. Now I don't mean they'll take over here tomorrow or next year or the next decade. I may live to see it, but not to deal with it. I'll be on custard and bedpans by that time. But you'll have to see it and handle it, and it's a good thing you're getting a taste of it so early."

"You just want The Melba to go out of business?"

"Better that than give 'em a foothold. That's an old battle strategy. The retreating army blows up anything that might give comfort to the enemy. You've got to reconcile yourself to it, Preston. The Melba is going to be a casualty."

Preston stood up. He slammed his fist against the desk. "I ain't going down without a fight!"

Waller looked at him calmly. "Oh, there'll be a fight. There's always a last stand and a fight. We'll see to that. But it's just to show that unions bring violence. That's all. Now don't look so down and out. There'll be other things. You'll come out of this with enough to tide you over till you can put something else together. We're all watching you, boy. This is a test. Some people can't pass a test, they just slowly recede into wherever it was they came from. I think you'll do better than that. I hope you will."

Preston left and walked all the way home. It was five miles. People were talking round and round, their conversations becoming tiny orbits they were compelled to follow. Why couldn't the orbits take each other in instead of colliding?

He got to the house. The lawn was overgrown, and there was a for-sale sign in front. It had just been put on the market. He would have to send one of the boys from the place to clean it before the buyers came.

He unlocked the door and went inside. It was an unfamiliar place. His home had been The Melba. He poured himself a glass of milk in the kitchen, but it had turned sour. He spat it into the sink and washed his mouth out. He went to his bedroom and lay on the bed in his clothes, staring at the ceiling until it turned to a plain white dream.

Chapter 14

Palmetto was sitting in front of the dresser in her bedroom. She was chewing calcium tablets and making a face at herself. There was an icy glass of Coca-Cola nearby to take away the taste once she had finished. She could see the rest of the room in the mirror. All summer long she had felt like a stranger here. This was a young girl's room, with pennants on the walls and stuffed animals drooped in chairs. In the far corner near the closet was a hope chest she had started when she was nine. The pieces of her silver pattern were stored in the chest. Her Aunt Evelyn had started her on that when she was only three years old, a piece of silver on her birthday, one at Christmas, and two on special occasions like graduations and tonsillectomies. Her pattern was called

Spanish Moss, and she polished it twice a year. She had always thought of the china and crystal that would go with it.

China and silver and crystal. They were brides' things. She began to cry as she chewed the calcium. She had never been a bride or a wife. All she had been was married and yelled at. Preston hadn't even carried her across the revolving threshold of The Melba. What she had was wedlock, with emphasis on the lock.

She cradled her burgeoning belly in her arms and bent her head, her hair falling over her face. She was ruining her complexion with tears. She just knew it. She had cried so much all summer that by fall her face would look like a creek bottom in dry weather. Whatever happened to what used to be me? she wondered. Then she swallowed the last of the calcium and reached for the Coke. If it hadn't been for watermelons and Coca-Colas she didn't know how she would have survived the summer.

Oh, Baby, she thought, what am I to do? Though she had made long lists of names, she hadn't chosen one, thought only of the baby as Baby. A few weeks ago she had thought about becoming a nun, but nuns with children had so much trouble finding work. And she would have to go back to work once the baby came. She wasn't going to live at home or on charity. If we got in the war she was going to enlist as a nurse in the Red Cross. Mama and Daddy could take care of the baby. They were just dying to get their hands on another grandchild. She would miss the baby so much. She grieved about it now as she drank her Coca-Cola and tried to stop crying. Beautiful, tender young men would die in her arms, showing her pictures of pretty girls back home and asking her to write. Then she would be hit herself, a shell fragment lodging in her throat. The last thing she would do would be to open her locket and look at her baby's picture. But in her mind all the dying young men looked just like Preston.

"If you don't stop crying and thinking morbid thoughts, you are going to mark that child." It was Mamie.

"Couldn't you have knocked?"

"You wouldn't have heard me above the misery."

"Anyway, you can't mark children. That's just an old wives' tale."

"I'm an old wife myself, Missy, and I know that there are things denied by science that are nonetheless true. Now stop that crying."

"I can't. I tried and I can't."

Mamie walked around the room straightening things that didn't need straightening. "I have never been as disappointed in a human as I am in you. The summer of 1940 will have to go down as the summer of Palmetto's tears."

"I am unloved and mistreated."

"I will give you some credit for perhaps having had a little mistreatment, but you are not unloved. That boy loves you, too. He drove all the way down here to show you, and you didn't give him a chance."

"Thank you very much, Mamie darling, but I don't call a sixty-eight-mile drive proof of undying love."

"If I were you, Palmetto, I would take what I could get."

Palmetto flung her hairbrush across the

room, though she took great care to make sure that Mamie was out of the way. "Get out of here and leave me alone!"

"I am still your mother, young lady, and you are not too big to have a switch taken to you, which is probably what you need."

She turned back to the dresser, put her face down on her arms, and continued to cry. "Nobody loves me."

"Everybody loves you, but nobody will if you keep on feeling sorry for yourself. Self-pity is a fool's pastime. Now straighten up from there and turn around. Winnie's downstairs. She wants to take you to lunch at the Wayside Inn."

"I can't go anywhere. I'm all blotchy." She sat up and sniffled. She looked at herself in the mirror. She almost cried again, but Mamie was beside her, meddling through the cosmetics on the dresser.

"You've got enough paint and creams up here to disguise yourself as Marie of Romania. Where's the cold cream?"

"It's there."

Palmetto let herself be turned around. Mamie knelt beside her, opened the jar, and began to smear cold cream all over her face. "You have the prettiest face in the world when you're smiling, which you haven't done all summer. Your daddy has been wanting a smile. I have been wanting a smile. And all we have gotten is the opposite. Now give a smile to your mama who loves you."

"Oh, Mama, I . . ."

"No, ma'am. No tears. I won't stand for it."

"I won't cry."

"And you see? Why, this cold cream is just doing wonders."

"Oh, Mama, I don't know what to do."

"Of course you do."

"But he was so mean to me."

"My darling, love has a lot of meanness in it."

"Not true love."

"True love. Your daddy and I have been together for almost forty years, and if that is not true love, then I have missed my chance at it."

"But you've always been so perfect."

"In front of you we have. And I trust

that you and Preston will be that way in front of this baby and any others you might have. Children have enough problems of their own without getting involved in the parents.' "

"And I suppose that parents have enough problems of their own not to be involved in the children's."

"Well, after a while you do expect the children to be able to handle them. But you know we're always here when you need us."

"I know it. And I love you. And Daddy."

"And Preston?"

"I don't know about him. I think about him all the time. But I have been trying very hard to hate him."

"How could you hate a nice boy like that?"

"Oh, Mama, you're not qualified to judge. He's got pretty hair. You'd have him crowned king."

"Be that as it may," Mamie said. "You've got to go and see him and try."

"I couldn't."

"Can and will."

"Mama, I can't go anywhere looking like this. I'm as big as a tent meeting."

"We'll go to Rome tomorrow and get you something lovely to wear. And you can wear my fur coat."

"The fox one?"

"But I make no allowances for pregnancy. If you spill anything on it you'll get Hail Columbia from me."

"But when?"

"Georgia Tech is playing Auburn this weekend. I think that would be the perfect time. Josephine and Bertram are going, and they'd just love to take you and Preston with them."

"But those are your tickets. Daddy's been talking about that game all summer."

"We've already talked about that. It's a long drive, and court's in session, and I'm going to be doing some canning. And we've got a radio sitting right there in the living room. It's just as good as being there."

"Oh, Mama." Palmetto pulled Mamie close and hugged her. Then they both had a little cry and called for Winnie —

married twice, and this one on the rocks — who climbed the stairs and had a little cry herself. Thank God for Pond's cold cream, they all said, and made themselves presentable and laughed and picked out dresses for one another, told one another how good they looked, and went off to the Wayside Inn, where chicken à la king had never tasted so divine.

Chapter 15

The union gave Preston their ultimatum on a Monday and gave him until Saturday to answer; if not, a strike would be called. He took the badly typed list of demands and put it inside one of the ledgers he usually carried with him. Monday night he passed the paper along to Waller down at the haberdashery. Waller read it, shrugged, and said little. Nobody had much to say to Preston these days. They had all seen through him, he supposed. He wondered what they saw.

Roy Al and Sarah knew about his trouble. Roy Al offered to lend money, and Sarah offered to come down and cook if he was going to try and keep the place open. "Why, I know ladies at the church who'd love to have something to do," she had said.

"It's not like that any more, Sarah. Folks just can't pitch in and help us get something done. This is an issue."

"I hate it when things get so complicated."

"Me too."

Roy Al offered his hand and a look in the eye. Preston had never been much for looks in the eye, but he met this one and was proud of it. He and his brother had come a long way to be able to speak and touch. "If you need me, Presto, just say the word."

"I wish I knew a magic word to make this all go away."

"Just lemme know what you want me to do and I'll do it."

"Thanks, Royal." He never could remember to call him Roy Al.

Everyone kept right on working just as they had, only they were quieter, neater, and worked faster. The last week of The Melba was like the Indian-summer weather outside. It was reaching the peak of its beauty before it went away for good.

Oddly enough, Scoe and Elvira were

hopeful. Preston talked to them that Monday night after the dinner meal. They were rearranging the bandstand, where Bootsie and the boys played. Elvira had come out of the kitchen in her gray cloth coat, carrying a tray with three dishes on it.

"There was just this little bit of ice cream left. I didn't suppose nobody'd mind if we ate it up."

Scoe had not known what to make of this. He wanted to be gone. It was hard for him to be with Preston, working together but on the verge of not working that way.

"Looks good," Preston had said.

Elvira put his plate on the table and set the tray containing theirs on an adjacent table. Preston picked up his dish, took a bite, hesitated, then walked to the table bearing their tray. He sat down. Elvira sat down. Scoe came around the side of the table, looked down at them, then looked at the street. Elvira handed him his dish, and he ate it standing up.

Preston looked up at the ferns. The leaves had been steadily turning brown.

"It don't look like we're gonna be able to save those ferns," he said.

"What they needs is to have tea leaves put in the bottoms of 'em," Elvira said. "Plus, they needs to be took down every night and sprayed with just plain water."

"It's about to be too late for that."

"What do you mean too late?"

"Y'all gon' be walkin' outta here and The Melba is gonna close up."

"Chile, you ain't thinking that!"

"Elvira, I know it."

"Mista Preston, we loves this place 'bout much as you do. We just wants to get some assurances. That's all. Tell him, Scoe."

"That's right," Scoe said. He poked sullenly at his ice cream. "They ain't gon' let us close this place up. You watch and see. This is an investment. It's doin' business and makin' money. They gon' come around."

"Yeah, well, if they are they've sure kept me out of it."

"You gon' have this place one of these days, but they got it now and they don't want nothin' to change. They gon' hang on to the bitter end, but they ain't gon' let it just go."

"That's what they tell me."

"Oh, Mista Preston," Elvira said. "They tellin' you that same as us 'cause they know we tells each other things and they don't want nothin' gettin' out. You'll see. Things is gon' be fine. Eat up that ice cream, Scoe. We gon' miss the bus."

They left him sitting there, looking out the window. The whole time there had been The Melba, he had not belonged to anyone except himself. The help had identified him with the owners and the owners had identified him with the help. Waller, Hildebrand, and Rasnake: He had wanted to be one of them, had patterned his every move to gain favor in their eyes. But Elvira had put her finger on it so effortlessly. He was merely the help, like everybody else.

He had thought he was independent. He was merely alone. He thought of himself and The Melba being on a raft. And there they were — Waller, Hildebrand, Rasnake — standing on the banks, smiling and waving, fat and full with food from The

Melba. They all wished him so well, and he was headed for the falls.

Were his backers letting him go over because they knew he wanted the place for himself? Or were they afraid for their own businesses? Did unions ever go after roller rinks? He could almost hear the sound of the falls. You couldn't go over and stay in one piece.

Preston looked around the room. When he thought of The Melba he didn't think of the men who had backed him. He thought of the people who worked there. They were The Melba. They were what he loved. Oh God, he thought. I'm turning out to be a fool. All his life he had tried to get away from what he was to get to what he wanted to be. He had never been happy with what he was. He always wanted to get somewhere. He had never considered that he was "here"; he had only been passing through. And he hadn't gone anywhere at all; everything that had meant anything had passed right by. He shook his head. No use thinking about done things.

Wednesday night Waller, Rasnake, and Hildebrand showed up, came in together just as Bootsie and the band were winding up with "Japanese Sandman." The band had changed its style somewhat. Paul Whiteman seemed to be on the way out, and others were coming in.

The men sat in a circular booth near the scale and had Elvira get them plates of roast beef with mashed potatoes, corn, and turnip greens. They ate slowly and sent back for cornbread once. Preston stopped by their table. He didn't know how to act. Whatever he did would be wrong. He crunched his toes up in his shoes, put his hand on the back of the booth, and leaned over with a smile. "Everything all right?"

"Just fine. Just fine."

"Anything I can get for you?"

"Not a thing."

"Don't bother 'bout us."

"We'd like to see you when they close down the line."

"Sure thing."

He walked down the line behind the counter. They had closed it and were scrubbing the steam table. This had always been his favorite time, when the place was his again. Now it would be his only three more nights. He stuck his head into the kitchen and saw that the cleaning was underway. He knew the routine so well that he could tell in the sweep of an eye what needed to be done. When it came to supervising, he was tops.

He waited thirty minutes before going back to the booth. It was a long thirty.

They moved to make room for him on the leather seat, but he was too quick for them. He pulled up a chair from an adjoining table. Usually he would have jumped at a chance to share a seat with them, but tonight he wanted to be separate. He wasn't kidding himself any more.

They had a plan, they said. They had decided to save The Melba. "You've just done too good a job here." The best." "No sense punishing you when we're after them." "You just got caught in the middle." "Making a nice little profit."

They wanted him to let them strike on Saturday night. The Melba was closed

Sundays anyway. They would plan right now to do without the dinner meal on Saturday. Let them picket on Sunday. Nobody would be downtown anyway.

Then they'd reopen on Monday with an all-new crew. Rasnake knew a cook who would be available on two hours' notice. There'd be no trouble getting waitresses and busboys.

"Hell," Hildebrand said. "We'll work white. We can get them as cheap as we can black. And those niggers out on the sidewalk ain't gon' start anything with a white. They're too scared of the Klan for that."

"We can even get more niggers, for that matter," Waller said. "There are too many people hungry to worry about twenty folks who have had it too good and don't know how to appreciate it."

"Amen," said Rasnake.

They looked at Preston. He licked his lips. "You mean fire them all?"

"That's right."

They were all smiling. It was the same thing he had heard from his lawyer. It seemed as though everybody was plugged into the same socket but him. He was supposed to be saved at the last minute. They lived his life like a football game.

Elvira had served them dessert and coffee. They all had apple cobbler with raisins. Rasnake picked up a chunk of leftover cornbread and pushed it around the lip of the bowl, picking up the last of the juice. He shoved it all into his mouth, then sucked the tip of his finger.

"I can't do it," Preston said.

They couldn't believe it. "You're not going to lay this business down over a bunch of dime-a-dozen niggers."

"They work for me."

The three men looked at each other in mute shared rage. There were no words, only looks and nods.

Well, Preston thought. I've really done it. This time I've really done it. He didn't move or change his expression, just sat forward in his chair and leaned his elbows on the table. They were sitting and staring at him. Get an eyeful, he thought.

"You're sounding like a nigger-lover."

"I don't know what I am."

"We know. We just told you."

"Could be you're right, but they're my friends."

"And they're the very ones who're putting you out of business," Waller said. "That Scoe Loomis. He's the ring-leader who's gettin' them to walk out. You let him get too high and mighty down here. Well, I got news for him and any of the others that walk out. They're gon' have nothin' to come back to. The minute those monkeys strike we'll put our men in and they'll be out on their shiny black asses. They want war in the camp, that's what there'll be, war in the camp!"

Preston thought of all the times he had courted their favors, had overlooked their slights and superior airs. He wished he could vomit it all back on them. It would bury them alive. It had almost buried him.

"I ain't firing them." He stood up. He felt so light he thought he might float up among the ferns. "Yep," he said. "I got 'em, too. My bosses got 'em. My employees got 'em. Principles must be very contagious."

"He don't know what he's saying," Hildebrand said.

Preston looked at him with sympathy. "Why is it that people always tell people that they don't know what they're saying at the moment that they know exactly what they're saying?"

"He's not even making sense," Rasnake said.

"I'm sorry if you gentlemen are having trouble understanding me. It's always been a big problem of mine, being understood. I don't even understand myself, but I know I have to do certain things. If this is gonna be my ship, then I am gonna damn well sail it alone."

"A ship can sail under a different captain, you know."

"I guess that goes for the captain, too."

"You won't get another chance with anybody in this town," Hildebrand said.

"Maybe not," said Preston. "But that looks like a chance I've already taken. Now, if you're finished with the food and finished with me, we're closing up. I make sure all the tables are cleared and dishes are washed before I go home. I may not have a place to run much longer, but I'm gon' run it while I'm here."

Waller was the first to move. He gave Rasnake a nudge, and Rasnake slid out, grabbed his hat, and shoved the cigar he'd been about to light into his vest pocket. Hildebrand dipped his napkin in water and wiped his mouth. All three men stood up and regarded him solemnly. "You made a bad mistake, Vacalis."

"Maybe so. Maybe so," Preston said, "but I can't be bothered with that now. I got work to do. I will leave you gentlemen with this. If you change your mind about the way you want things run, you can get in touch with me by Saturday noon."

Once again they didn't believe what they heard. Waller chuckled dryly, like a dead tree in the wind.

"You're really something, Vacalis."

Then they left, trooping out single-file, but bunching together on the sidewalk, speaking and gesturing rapidly to each other, exploding with the things they had bottled up in The Melba.

Preston walked up to the door. He was no longer light-headed. He was heading heavily back to earth. He had gone against them and said something he felt. He

398

didn't know how he felt now. He didn't feel good. He knew that much. For a moment he thought he might be a hero, but heroes felt better than he did. They knew they were right. He knew only that he was in trouble. He stepped on the scale and received the Free Weight. One eighty-five. That was all right. He was a big man with big bones. He pushed out through the revolving door and stood on the sidewalk. The Melba sign was shining brightly. So were his eyes.

Saturday came around like the end of time. Preston got up, shaved, and dressed, thinking as he put on his clothes, This is what I put on to wear the day they closed The Melba. He wore a blue suit, a white shirt, and a pale gray tie that had a series of almost imperceptible holes in it. It was the one Palmetto had sent him with the nipple attached. He had never worn it. He kissed it as he put it on. Oh Palmetto. She was among the things of his life he hadn't reached out for until too late. Possibly, if he was good from now on, when he died they would lead him to a room where all the things he had loved and lost were stored. He hoped Palmetto would be there. He would like to see her again.

At work things went on as though they would go on forever. Biscuits were hot and fluffy, as brown on top as they were on the bottom. Customers slid their trays down the line, though breakfast was light. It was always light on Saturday. Lunch was where the rush would be, with shoppers and out-of-towners. There was a football game today, and that would pick things up.

Scoe, Elvira, and the rest of them went about their work as though this was not a different day. So this is what it's like, he kept thinking. Things weren't any different than before. It was only the end.

"Need cups and glasses on Line Two!" he yelled into the kitchen as the first of lunch was served. It was almost eleven thirty. He went back into the main room. Sidewalk traffic was brisk. The transit company had put on extra buses to get people to Grant Field. Preston stood watching them for a moment, wishing he were going somewhere too. Then Roy

Al touched his arm.

"How's it going, Presto?"

He was glad to see his brother. He shook his hand. "Going right along," he said.

"Thought I'd come down and see if you needed anything."

"Got all I can handle." He laughed. "Have some lunch."

"If you will."

"Sure. You've heard of the Last Supper? This is the Last Lunch."

It was strange. he ought to feel bad. He wanted to feel bad. Actually, he felt pretty good.

He and Roy Al sat in the round leather booth near the door. Preston looked up at the clock. It was five till twelve.

"Just five more minutes," he said.

"Till what?"

"I gave Waller, Hildebrand, and Rasnake an ultimatum. It looks like they're givin' me theirs instead."

He turned to look at the line that was forming. It stretched almost all the way to the door. That usually didn't happen until twelve thirty. It was going to be a big day. Drew was playing "Embraceable

You" on the organ.

Roy Al put down his fork and looked at Preston. "I don't want you thinkin' this is charity or anything, but I got a coupla hundred if you need it."

They had come a long way, high road and low, and here was Roy Al with his feet on the ground. "I can get by," Preston said. "But I thank you . . . That's from the heart."

Thank God for the corned-beef-hash special. They could turn their embarrassment to that. Preston pierced his poached egg, the yellow drooling slowly over the sides of the mound of hash. He took a bite and chewed. It tasted good. He began to speak, gesturing with his fork.

"You know, I never told this to anybody, but all I ever wanted to be was a free man. No family to worry about. No responsibilities. Just be out in the world somewhere with nobody looking to me or for me. By myself. Of course, I've never lived that way . . . looked down on those who did . . . but it was a wish of mine anyway . . . Foolishness is what it was

. . . Damned if it didn't come true."

He slung some of the yolk on his tie and stopped to put water on it, rubbing it with his callused thumb. He held it up to the light to see if he had gotten it all out.

"With all this delicious food around, I would think you could find something better to dine on than a tie."

It was Palmetto, in Mamie's fox coat. She had it pulled close around her, under the delusion that it reduced the enormity of her pregnancy. She wore a little round hat that had green feathers in it, and there was a yellow silk scarf at her throat. She was nervous, and it made her eyes big. She was afraid she had worn too much lipstick, and she knew the wind had ruined her hair.

She was the most beautiful thing that Preston had ever seen. He dropped the tie, stood up, and rubbed his hands together, his eyes big too, and his throat dry. He began to rock back and forth on his feet. Josephine and Bertram stood clutched together in back of her. They were pleased and anxious.

Roy Al stood up and kissed Palmetto.

"Still pretty as a picture."

"Pretty as a picture and a half," she said, and introduced him to her sister and brother-in-law.

Elvira spotted them from behind the counter. She got Alma to take her place on the line, grabbed a tray, and started toward them. "Howdy do," she said. "Lemme get you folks something to eat."

Palmetto hugged her. She remembered her from her first visit, and she couldn't stop herself. If only she could have gone back to that time she would have done things so differently. Just how differently, she didn't know, but surely she would have managed to have done something right. As soon as the baby was born she was going to change entirely. She was not going to bother anybody, and nobody was going to bother her.

"Oh, Elvira," she said. "How good it is to see you."

"It's good to see you, too. You filling out nicely."

They laughed. Elvira took their orders and told them to have a seat. Preston and Palmetto walked toward the scale. He wanted to take her arm, but he was afraid she would shake him off.

"I'm glad to see you," he said.

"It's nice to see you, too."

"Are you craving anything?"

"I am craving to have some fun. Josephine and Bertram were coming over to see the game, and I just wanted to get dressed up and go somewhere. It would give me the greatest of pleasure to see Tech stomp Auburn."

"I'd put my money on Auburn."

"I might have expected that . . . Nevertheless, do you want to go?"

"If you want me to, I do."

She touched his hand. "Please, let's have a good time today. Let's be friends and forget about being lovers or married or whatever the hell we are. I simply cannot handle all that has and has not gone on between us. But I do like you. I always have. There's something about your company that pleases me."

They should have kissed. They both wanted to. But they didn't. There were too many people. Her stomach was too big. Excuses.

Drew switched to "Everybody Loves My Baby." Palmetto looked around the room. "Oh, it's so good to be back. I missed this place. The good old Melba."

"It's about to be the gone old Melba."

She was astonished. "Oh, no!"

"Yep. I got caught between two sides that wouldn't budge. Make that three. I became a side myself."

She was looking around stricken, her hand to her throat. "But what will happen? What will you do?

"There's nothing I can do now."

She could tell he felt that way and wasn't just saying it. His lips were set into a sad smile. She wanted to kiss him, to hold him in her arms and tell him everything would be all right, but things wouldn't be all right unless he made them that way. She had always wished she'd been a man so she could shake the world around; then she saw how hard it was. "There will always be something you can do," she said. "And if this place is down the drain, well, then it's down the drain. But you're not."

He had never agreed with her more

wholeheartedly. It suddenly dawned on him: She already knew what he wanted everybody to know — that he was Preston Vacalis — A Man — Someone who would never be defeated. He took her hand and led her to the table.

They could finish off The Melba on their own. He didn't like the end of dreams.

Even without the wind there would have been a bite in the air, but with the wind spirits went soaring. Flags and pennants were sailing, and pandemonium prevailed outside Grant Field as thousands shoved into the game. Preston gripped Palmetto as if she might try to escape. He held one hand in front of her stomach, which she found most amusing. He had already shoved away one or two people who had bumped against her accidentally. "It's all right, Preston. It won't hurt him. Let him know there's a world out there."

"I'm not gon' have anybody bumpin' into you. People can look where they are going."

She nuzzled her cheek against his arm.

She liked to be protected. "A couple of years ago I was down in Jacksonville with a bunch of drunks at the Georgia-Florida game. There was a pregnant woman and her husband there, and somebody bumped her. The husband grabbed this guy and said, 'Can't you see my wife is pregnant?' And this guy just looked at him and said, 'Whom do you suspect?' It started a huge fight."

"No call for a fellow to say anything like that about a pregnant woman."

"Well, it was a good remark. You wouldn't punch anybody over me, I'm sure."

"The hell I wouldn't!"

"Would you really?"

"If I had to."

"That's very sweet. I'm sorry about The Melba. What will you do?"

"I'll have to cross that bridge when I come to it."

"That doesn't sound like you at all."

"Maybe it's the new me."

"I'm going to make some changes myself," she said.

He stopped and pulled her to the side of

the crowd. A man was selling souvenirs and mums, big white ones with gold ribbons, Tech's colors. "You want one?"

"Oh, Preston, I'm sure they're expensive."

"That doesn't make any difference. I'll get one for your sister, too. They got yellow ones and whites. I'll get you the white and her the yellow."

She didn't say anything at all, just burrowed into the prickly softness of Mamie's coat. Fur coats made her feel so elegant and graceful, like a swan . . . who was eight months pregnant.

Preston stood over her. He seemed to be sure of everything in creation, except how to pin the mum on her. She smiled up and let him do it. It was hard to stick the pin through the coat, but he did it, though he jumped when the pin stuck his finger. Palmetto took the finger and kissed it. "That'll make it all well," she said.

A little blush passed across his face. She took his arm. The crowd swept them inside the gates, and they started up the ramps. They saw Josephine and

Bertram just ahead.

"Miss Palmy," Preston whispered to her as they started up. She gave him a squeeze.

"Y'all go and sit down," she called. "We've got to take out time."

The ramps were steep, and they had to climb two of them. They stepped to the side so the others could flow past them. It was a happy, noisy crowd, mellow in a bloodthirsty way.

"Are you all right?"

"I just have to take it slow."

"When do they think it's going to be here?"

"Three weeks and two days. Mama thinks longer because we were all late. But you're not going to be late, are you, Junior?"

Preston hadn't even thought about a name, but Junior seemed to be so right. Junior. "That what you're going to name him? He going to be a junior?"

"Oh no. I don't even know why I said that. I think it's wrong to name a person after somebody else. Everybody should have their own name and their own identity. Don't you think?"

He felt small, as though the only contact that had been made was in his imagination. "I never gave it much thought," he replied, wanting to kick himself for having asked.

Midway up the second ramp Palmetto though she felt something, stopped, and looked around as if the answer was in the wind.

"What's the matter?"

"I don't know."

"Must be something. You feel all right?"

"I'm fine. I just thought I heard somebody say my name."

"See anybody you know?"

She looked at the passing crowd. "It was as though they were right next to my ear."

"I think you're hearing things."

She should have been irritated by him, but she wasn't. "Yes, and my mind's going bad, too. You better get me inside before I start screaming and foaming at the mouth."

He smiled and narrowed his eyes when he looked at her. It took her breath away.

You're a pistol ball. That's what you are."

They came off the last ramp and entered the stadium just as the Georgia Tech Yellow Jackets ran onto the field. The crowd had a collective fit. Palmetto screamed along with them, though from her vantage point she had no idea which team was making its entrance. "Oh, I love it! I love it," she said. "I'm just having the best time."

"It hasn't even started yet."

"Oh, I don't give a hoot about the game. I just like being here . . . especially with you."

The crowd was as friendly and deadly as a big lovable bear. The band played "I'm a Rambling Wreck from Georgia Tech," and there was a lot of singing and clapping. The cheerleaders did flip-flops and backbends. There was a really pretty one who kept whirling and twirling, sending her long skirt up so that it circled around her like one of Saturn's rings. She had on white satin shorts beneath it, and great legs. She was showing them off to full advantage. She'd have been arrested at the fair, but it was all right at the football game. The crowd kept cheering her on, and she loved it. A gang of boys from the *Journal* and *Constitution* were taking her picture. What she didn't know was that the right leg of the shorts was snuggled in the crack of her ass and she was giving the crowd more of her all than she knew. Not everybody noticed it at first, but when they did, they all started laughing and applauding. All the women thought she was a hussy who was getting what she deserved. Finally, one of the boy cheerleaders told her about it, and she got so embarrassed that she ran off the field and didn't come back until after the first quarter.

Preston and Palmetto stood at the entrance to their row. Josephine and Bertram were seated halfway down. Preston had trouble making his wishes known to a convivial bunch who were busy trying to open a flash with a stuck top. Palmetto gave up. She opened the fox coat and exposed her enormous belly. "Coming through!" she hollered. "Lady with a baby!" Preston turned so red that he could have blended in with the coat, but Palmetto got results. Everybody on the row stood up, and one man took off his hat.

Palmetto and Josephine hugged as if they hadn't seen each other in weeks. Football games were like that. Bertram leaned forward and handed him a paper cup containing a Coca-Cola that was clear on the top. "Stir it up," he said. "It'll give you a kick."

Preston started to protest, but Palmetto stuck a long finger with maroon polish on the nail into the cup and stirred it, sloshing some over the side. "Go ahead," she said.

He drank. He blinked. It made his eyes burn. "It's not as bad as you think it is," she whispered. "The next one'll go down smooth."

"If I take another swallow of that I'll go down smooth," he managed when he could get his breath. "What is it?"

"It's 'shine, but it's the very best. Some of his tenants make it out on the farm."

"That stuff'll make you go blind."

"That's only if you use kerosene. These people are masters. If they were legal and lived in Europe, this stuff would go for ten dollars a bottle."

He took another sip. She was right.

The color guard marched out onto the field, followed by the band. The color guard carried the flag of the United States of America, the flag of the Sovereign State of Georgia, and the flag of the Confederate States of America. Everybody stood up. The rebel flag got the biggest yell.

The band played "The Star-Spangled Banner" while a girl's drill team performed patriotic acrobatics with emphasis on splits and arches. Everybody had their hats off, and a lot of people were going "Sshhh." Palmetto stuck her hand inside the coat and put it over her heart. Her breasts were bigger than they had ever been before, full of milk. ". . . At the twilight's last gleaming . . ."

She heard it again, just her name. "Palmetto." She didn't want to turn around, because she knew whoever said it wasn't there. She looked up at Preston. He was intent on the flag. So were Josephine and Bertram. Goose pimples were up and down her legs. Everybody here was a stranger to her. She wanted her mama.

". . . Land of the free, and the home of the brave."

The anthem was over. The crowd cheered. The band launched into "Dixie," and they went even wilder. It was fall, all right. Preston's season. He inhaled deeply. There was wood smoke in the air. One of the fraternities had a bonfire. There would be plenty of bonfires tonight once they had stomped Auburn. He had never thought he was part of a crowd, but he was glad to be part of this one. He felt as though he belonged to something. He took another drink of the wondrous Coca-Cola as they began to sit down. He waited until all the people in front of him had taken their seats. For an instant he had a view of the entire stadium, and it was as though he had glimpsed the soul of the South: hot times, hotheads, hot women, and hot dogs.

He yelled as the band marched off the field, and Palmetto leaned over, laughing. "Go easy on that 'shine, sugar. It'll sneak up and get a hold on you."

He put his arm around her. She was the dearest, sweetest thing in the world. Then everybody stood up again for the kickoff, and he forgot she was there.

At the half it was Tech 7, Auburn 6. Palmetto didn't want to brave the crowd again, so they stayed in their seats, eating hot dogs that were passed hand-over-hand and watching the band, which did an intricately marched halftime show. "That band really knows how to spell," said Bertram, and gave Josephine a hug, from which she disengaged herself. "Honey, this hairdo was not free," she said. "See if you can't help me make it last till we get back to Cedartown."

Then they were all standing up for the kickoff. It was a high, high, high, kick; Palmetto concentrated on the ball. It looked as if it was just going to keep on going up. She hoped it would. She hoped it would fly away and become a miracle and be talked about forever. And she could tell her grandchildren she'd been there the day the football took wing.

But it didn't, of course. It came down.

She felt as if she were coming down with it, as if she were growing heavy and being pulled toward earth. Then it happened and she was wet. It was hot but she was cold. Her heart was beating faster than it ever had before, and she couldn't catch her breath. Nobody noticed. Everybody was sitting down. A player had been injured and was being carried off the field. They were giving him a round of applause. One of the band members blew a clarinet, but it didn't come to anything.

A voice came over the loudspeaker. "Number Eleven. Rodney Marshall. Injured on the play."

Palmetto looked at Preston. He was looking at the field. She looked at Josephine. She was looking in the mirror of her compact, tugging at stray wisps of hair. Bertram was uncorking the bottle he carried in his pocket. They didn't know what was happening to her. She had never felt so alone in her life. She tugged Preston's sleeve. He didn't look at her, just leaned. She was afraid she was going to start screaming and nobody would hear her. She was afraid. She closed her eyes tight.

He looked down at her. She had gone completely white. Her eyes were closed. He thought she had fainted. He rushed up through the moonshine dizziness and put his arm around her.

"Palmy! Palmy! What is it? What's the matter?"

Josephine and Bertram looked down in amazement as she opened her eyes and spoke in a small voice. "My water just broke. I'm going to have the baby. It's premature."

She nestled against his big, solid warmth. "I'm scared," she whispered. "I've been scared all along. It's a premature baby."

Preston swooped her up in his arms. "My wife's in labor!" he yelled. "Get outta the way!"

"Oh Lord," Josephine murmured, and slumped against Bertram, feeling faint.

"Good God, woman. Get hold of yourself," he said.

Everybody on the row stood up. Preston carried Palmetto by them, but when he got to the aisle, it was blocked all the way to the entrance. Word spread throughout the area. "Take her onto the field! They got an ambulance!" somebody yelled. Others in the crowd took it up. People were standing up in their seats so that they could get by. Palmetto had had her eyes closed, but she heard some murmuring and opened them. People were waving and blowing kisses.

"Good luck, honey," a woman called.

"If it's a girl name her Georgia!"

Somebody handed her a Tech pennant, and somebody else handed her a box of Cracker Jacks. She wasn't scared any more. They were cheering. She waved. "Thank you! Thank you!"

They reached the roped area to the field. Two policemen came puffing over. "Whoa! Stop right there!"

Bertram jumped down and flashed his Masonic ring. "Got a lady in labor up here."

The cheerleaders picked up on it and rushed over. "Hand her down," the captain said. They made a pyramid and passed her down to the field. Preston jumped down, and Josephine stood, feeling left out and about to whimper; then the cheerleaders decided to pass her down, too. She closed her eyes as she went down. She was sure her dress was over her head and there'd be a picture of it in the Sunday paper and she'd never be able to hold her head up again.

One of the policeman ran for the ambulance as Preston picked up Palmetto again and raced after them. One of Josephine's shoes came off, and she had to stop and take the other one off, puffing and cussing every step of the way to the ambulance.

They had already stuffed the injured football player inside when the door was opened again and Rodney Marshall, suffering freely with pain of a broken ankle, saw Palmetto, Preston, Bertram, and Josephine.

"Got a lady in labor here," Preston said.

Rodney tried to get up, and hit his head on the top of the ambulance.

Palmetto took a last look at the crowd. The referees had had to call time out. The cheerleaders were waving at her. Palmetto waved back. They began a cheer.

"Give me a B," they yelled.

"B!" the crowd answered.

"Gimme an A!"

"A!"

"Gimme a B!"

"B!"

"Gimme a Y!"

"Y!"

"What have you got?"

"BABY!"

What they had was a seven-pound-six-ounce baby. Male. Twenty-one inches long.

He was born three hours after they got her to Piedmont Hospital. He was delivered by Dr. Dunbar, whom she loved.

She didn't want the shot they gave her while she was in labor. She didn't want the gas they gave her when they had her on the table, either. But they gave her both. And it didn't help anything, either. It just made her drowsy, but it still hurt like hell. She thought that if she wasn't so drowsy she could get up and do something about the pain. Oh, Mama, Mama, why didn't you tell me it would be like this? She thought to pray, but God and Jesus had both renounced her. They were men, anyway. And she hated men. What the hell did they know about this?

She had been pushing down as long as she could remember, and still they weren't satisfied. "Push down," they kept saying. She didn't want a harelip or a Mongoloid or something with a big purple birthmark all over its face. Then she heard the cry. It was the only thing she could hear. It was all there was in the world. She closed her eyes. She couldn't look. She would love it anyway. It didn't matter what it was. She would love it anyway. She would, she would, she would, she would . . . but please . . .

"He's a fine boy," Dr. Dunbar said. "Ain't nothin' the matter with him except that he's buck naked and crying."

She struggled up. A nurse with rubber gloves was bathing him. He was crying so loud that she knew there wasn't anything wrong with him. The nurse held him up. He looked all right. Slightly slimy, but all right. "You were in a hurry to get here, weren't you, darling," she said. "Mama loves you." And then she went to sleep.

Preston stayed at the hospital until six o'clock. He saw the baby. He was crying behind glass with other crying babies. He had a son. Well, well. He didn't think he felt anything, but he couldn't stop grinning. Josephine kissed him and cried, and Bertram pounded him on the back. They had already gone, but they'd be back tomorrow with the rest of the family.

He had called Roy Al, and he and Joan and Sarah and Maybelle and Araminthia and a neighbor of hers had arrived at the hospital. They couldn't get a nurse that night. Sarah and Araminthia decided to stay with Palmetto.

Preston had seen Palmetto once. She had opened her eyes. Her lips were dry. He had dipped a rag in the water pitcher by her bed and wiped them off. "He's here," she said.

"I saw him."

"Isn't he wonderful?"

"Yes."

"Do you love him?"

"Yes . . . I love you, too."

"Oh, Preston, I love you too. Whatever will become of us?"

"Something good."

"I hope so. I'm going to save you if you'll let me." She went back to sleep with that thought. It left a smile.

He went into the hall and stood there, blinking. What a day. Then he remembered. He was being struck.

Chapter 16

They walked in single file from the corner of Cain and Peachtree down the length of The Melba and back again. There were twenty of them, all black. Welsh and Greener were nowhere in sight. They carried a couple of signs reading UNFAIR, and they were scared. Scoe and Elvira were in the front of the line. Scoe held his head high and looked straight ahead, seemingly the only one unafraid. It was as if his vision ended at the boundaries of The Melba. He and Elvira shared a sign, their hands almost touching on the splintered wood that held it up.

There was a police car parked at either end of The Melba in the no-parking zone. The policemen had been laughing for a while, looking at them as though they had escaped from the zoo. Now they sat in their cars, chewing gum and listening to the radio. Buses loaded with late-afternoon shoppers slowed as they passed, faces pressed to the windows in disbelief. What would the niggers do next?

City Hall had alerted the police that they didn't want any trouble in front of The Melba. That meant black or white. The legislature was in session, and there was a football game in town. Atlanta's streets were going to be safe. The pickets would be guarded till seven o'clock, and then they would have to go home. There were no plans in case the picketing continued.

Preston stood across the street and watched them parade back and forth. He was trying to decide what he felt, and he didn't know. These people were taking away a thing he loved. He hadn't believed that they would do it. And there were Scoe and Elvira leading them. They weren't his enemies. He sighed. The world had turned out to have more subtleties than he was equipped to fathom.

A preacher from the African Methodist Church was standing on the corner. He was wearing a serge suit as good as any white man had. There were three or four men with him, also in suits. They must be deacons or something, he thought. They were looking gravely at the pickets. There was a car parked beside them, a black Plymouth sedan.

When the clock on the Coca-Cola sign read seven o'clock, one of the policemen got out of the car and walked across the street and said something to the preacher. The preacher nodded. He and the other men got into the Plymouth, drove across the street, pulled up in front of The Melba, and spoke to Scoe. Preston wondered why they had to drive across the street. Why couldn't they have walked? It was one of the things of the night that he never forgot, the preacher and his deacons driving fifty feet across the street.

Scoe turned and spoke to the pickets, but his words were lost in the traffic, and Preston could see only the signs coming down. Two of the women climbed into the car with the preacher. They were dispersing. He would give them a chance to get around the corner; then he would go over. He had some things inside he wanted to take with him.

Preston looked in the windows of the Thompson-Boland-Lee shoe store. There were a pair of oxblood wing tips that caught his eye. He might like to try a pair of them. The only shoes he'd ever owned were black, a businessman's color. Josephine and Sarah had already talked about christening the baby. They wanted to do it in Mamie's parlor and have a reception. What he would do was get the shoes and not wear them till then and see if anybody noticed.

What the hell was he thinking about? Here he didn't know where he was going to get any money and all of a sudden he had two mouths to feed and he was thinking about oxblood wing tips. It would be a cold day before he drank any more moonshine. He looked across the street. The pickets had gone. He walked to the corner, waited for the light to change, and crossed.

He was unlocking the door when Miss Fan ran around the corner. She had always looked fragile enough to break, and as he watched her run he thought that any second she would crumble like a sand castle. There wouldn't be a body to take away, just blond, bleached sand. She was crying.

"Oh, Mr. Vacalis! Mr. Vacalis!"

"Get hold of yourself, Miss Fan. What's the matter?"

"Oh, they got 'em! They got 'em in the alley!"

"Who's got who?"

"There are some men. They're roughnecks. Somebody brought 'em in in the back of a pickup truck. There's about ten of 'em. They got Scoe and Elvira and Fat Boy and some of the others. They got planks and shovels. They gon' kill 'em."

"Get the police!" he shouted, and ran for the alley.

Miss Fan stood slumped against the plate-glass window. "Police ain't gon' come till it's too late," she said, but he didn't hear her.

The alley ran from Cain Street in back of the Roxy and Georgia theaters. The back door to The Melba was there. His pickup truck was there most of the time, but he had left it down the street tonight.

He ran into the alley and saw the men. They were big and unshaven; most of them were drunk. He knew where they came from and who had gotten them. There were men like this every day gathered down on Hungry Corner. They came there and stood. If you needed day labor, you went by there and took your pick. You could get them as cheap as blacks. Hungry Corner was an old place. It had been there as long as he could remember. He had seen Doc standing there sometimes when he was little. They were silent men who rarely even talked to each other, just scanned the faces that came to pick them out, tried to stand a little straighter when the picking began. They went without asking any questions, and most of the time they were back there the next day. The job they had tonight was just a job, but it touched something in them. They were fighting people who had jobs and were walking out. And who were black. Black was the enemy. More than rooms that rented by the night, empty wine bottles, and memories of far-off children with dirt-streaked faces.

"Stop it! Cut it out!"

Preston walked down the alley to the corner, where they had the blacks backed against the brick wall.

He tried to adopt a friendly manner as he approached them. He knew enough to try and make them think that they were one, together in their whiteness. "These folks work for me. They're my people. You got it wrong. They had permission to do what they were doing. Now, if you'll just put down those . . . uh . . . things you got in your hands and let them go on their way, why . . . uh . . . we'll just settle down inside and have a little drink."

They looked at him silently.

"Went to the football game today and got a little drunk. You have to excuse me. Anybody know who won? Come on now, boys. Let's go on inside. Getting chilly out here."

The rock came out of nowhere and bounced off the side of his head. He staggered against the wall and slid against it until he was sitting, his legs spread in front of him. Then the men started on Scoe. They were going to do it one at a time, so they could enjoy it longer.

Preston was just about to try to get up when headlights swung into the alley. He got up quickly and out of the way. A pair of tires came to rest where his legs had been.

"What's going on?"

It was Bootsie and the band coming to work. He had not told them about the strike.

Preston leaned on the hood of the car. Blood was dripping down from over his ear. "Help us," he said.

Another car pulled into the alley. It was the rest of the band.

Elvira screamed. Preston left a bloody handprint on Bootsie's fender as he pushed off from it and headed toward the fight.

"Come on, boys," Bootsie said. He didn't know for sure what was going on, but he hadn't been in a fight for a while.

There was a man with a plank. He had just walloped Fat Boy, and was raring back to hit again. Preston got two of his fingers in the man's nose and pulled him over backward. He felt the cartilage give as the man slumped and hung there for an instant, squirming and squealing. Preston rammed the head into the steel railing that was above a flight of steps leading to the basement. The man lay there.

The band waded into the fight, their satin-shawl lapels getting the worst of it. They fought as they played, a driving force with the emphasis on percussion. But they got the men out of the alley. "Would somebody mind telling me what that was all about? Bootsie said after it was over and they were standing looking at each other, breathless and bedraggled, with the kind grinning exhilaration that comes from having fought and won. There was a momentary bond among them all, and it was strictly primeval.

Preston unlocked the back door, and they went in. They came through the kitchen and found Miss Fan crouched down beside the overturned scale. The place was a shambles. The plate-glass window had been smashed, and several of the figures around the fountain had had their heads broken off. They lay under the water, looking sightlessly up from among the pennies on the bottom, their cherubic expressions unchanged while the goldfish swam over them. Tables and chairs were scattered, and there were cracks in the mirrors along the wall.

"There was another whole load of 'em that came up," Miss Fan sobbed. "They just tore the place apart. Why would anybody want to do a thing like that?"

"They wanted to blame it on us. That's why," said Scoe.

"Well, we know it wasn't," said Preston. He looked around. The Melba was over. He recalled the night he had named the place and he and Sarah had toasted. He thought it was the end of all the bad things in his life, and it had turned out to be just something else that happened to him. The place wasn't even his any more. They could be tossed in jail for trespassing, but that wasn't likely tonight. There were too many tales to tell.

Elvira and Miss Fan went into the kitchen and began to make coffee. Bootsie and the boys sat down. One of the fellows opened a bass-fiddle case and pulled out a bottle of whiskey. He yanked off the top and began to pass it around.

Preston walked to the broken window and looked out. There was a celebration in the streets. Auburn had sneaked by Tech on the flimsy excuse of an extra point, which was a win all right but not such a win that it gave them any right to drive up and down Peachtree Street waving navy-blue and burnt-orange crepe-paper streamers out their windows and yelling "War Eagle!" loud enough to raise the dead.

"I hate to see those folks, win," said Miss Fan, breaking the silence in the cafeteria. "If they knew how to win it would be a different thing entirely."

"What are you talking about?" asked Bootsie. "The football game or the one we was just in?"

"Well, we won that battle," said Preston. "But I think we lost the war."

Elvira was pouring water into the coffee urn. "Mista Preston, it ain't safe you standin' front of that glass. There still might be one of them brick-throwers out there. There's always one of them left somewhere, and you don't need to lose an eye over it.''

Preston walked over and sat at a table between Scoe and Bootsie. Preston and Scoe had avoided looking at each other. Now Preston looked at him closely. His right eye was swollen and cut. There was going to be a black-satin scar from the right side of his hairline to the bridge of his nose.

Miss Fan had made up a tray of ice packs. She walked slowly between the tables, distributing them. She looked at Scoe and shook her head. ''You will have to have some stitches.'' She looked at Preston. ''The same goes for you.''

''Fight germs,'' said Bootsie, and handed him the bottle.

I'm getting to be a drinking man, thought Preston. He didn't want it, but took it and drank from it anyway. He found out that he did want it.

A car of screaming Auburn fans went by, and Preston looked in their direction. He put the bottle in the table, extending it to Scoe. Scoe eyed the bottle. He wondered an instant what the band members would say. You were never sure about people you just knew in a crowd. Hell! It didn't pay a damn thing to think you were sure about people you thought were close to you. Still, there wasn't but one good swig left in the bottle, so he might as well gulp it down. When there was nothing left you didn't have to be bothered with hearing how somebody wouldn't drink after a nigger.

Outside, the wind had sprung up. Lots of people lost their hats at the corner of Cain and Peachtree, and tonight Preston Vacalis had lost his shirt. A truck pulled up on the corner, and two boys started throwing off bundles of bound newspapers. It was not quite nine o'clock. They had started doing it earlier. When Preston was throwing papers they didn't come in till 3 P.M. For an instant he felt he was back there, could feel the fear he had when streetcars stopped running and he had to walk the two miles from home to Elmo Flagg's to get his papers — every shadow filled with terror, every noise the crack of doom.

He thought of Palmetto, crushed that thought; thought of The Melba, crushed that, too; thought of Waller, Hildebrand, and Rasnake, wishing he could crush them. Nothing would stay in his head right now. A new bottle was passed to him.

One of the band members was laughing. "Hell! This is one of the best nights I've spent at The Melba."

Gradually everyone started to laugh. It was a standing joke among the band that the food was good but the crowd was strictly yesterday's mashed potatoes.

Preston joined in the laughter. Scoe watched him. He wasn't laughing. He thought Preston was chasing after their favor. He didn't like this trash in the band who imitated what they heard over the radio. They could fight, though. He had to hand them that. He had been on the ground with a foot in his teeth when the man above him had gotten a clarinet across his face. He remembered the look he gave just before it made contact. Then Scoe was laughing too, not wanting to but doing it just the same, and looking around, surprised, when one of the band members nudged him on the shoulder and handed him the bottle. He took a swig and passed it back, looking away when he saw that the next man didn't wipe the top before he drank. That won't make any difference, he thought. But it did.

Scoe turned to Preston, looked away, then looked back. "What fo' did you come back there to help us?"

Preston shrugged. "I just lost my business. I had to hit somebody."

"You soundin' less and less like yourself."

"From what I heard, maybe that's good."

"Just don't go off the deep end."

Preston laughed. "I should have said the same to you."

"What you gon' do now?"

"I don't have any idea. First time in my life I was ever without a job or a plan. And I got a new baby."

Elvira squealed when she heard that, and Bootsie broke out his personal bottle. Preston told them about the baby and its circumstances. Elvira said "If that don't beat all" three times.

Then Bootsie announced that they were going to have to make it to The Rex sooner or later, but that they wouldn't mind running an errand with Preston if he wanted them to.

For a minute Preston didn't know what they were talking about, but when the idea hit him it gave him a better glow than the whiskey had.

They went out through the front, Preston bringing up the rear. He pushed himself through the revolving door twice, his last entrance and exit from The Melba. It was good while it lasted.

It was nearly ten when Palmetto woke up. With the shot they had given her, she should have been out longer, but a thought penetrated her cloudy dreams and told her sleep was not the place for her to be. Sarah was sitting there in the dark. How sweet she is, Palmetto thought. She felt contrite that she hadn't gotten in touch with her all summer. After all, it was her ring that she was wearing on her finger.

Sarah stood up nervously. "Is there

anything I can get you?"

"I want my baby. Step down to the chart room and see if they don't think it's feeding time."

Sarah left, and Palmetto sat up. Thick. That was the way she felt, especially her tongue. She drank some water and propped the pillows up in back of her. What wouldn't she have given for a hairbrush.

Sarah stuck her head back in the room. "She's bringing him down. I'm going to the sun room."

Atkinson, one of the new girls Palmetto barely knew, brought the baby into the room. He was wrapped in a little white blanket, and he was squalling.

"You had yourself a real howler," Atkinson said.

Palmetto said nothing. There was nothing to say. There was only her baby. She reached out her arms. He fit in them so perfectly. She made cooing noises and nuzzled her cheek to his. Oh, what a beautiful head he had, with two crowns in it. And such beautiful wisps of fine blond baby hair. Some of it would find its way into a blue-satin-covered baby book.

"But, oh, you're so skinny," she said. "So long and skinny. You certainly didn't get fat on all that watermelon I ate."

His eyes were open. "Hello, blue eyes." All the doctors said babies couldn't focus on anything until they were five weeks old. He wouldn't know her from a sack of salt. But, holding him in her arms, she didn't believe a word of it. "You know who I am," she said. "You know who your mama is. My little baby knows who loves him."

She spread her legs and lay him between them on the bed, then proceeded to unwrap him as though he were a gift. He was perfect. There was not a mark on him, just a tiny mole on his left heel. How brilliant. He was born with identification. She felt transported. He was perfect. No nun had ever worked herself to blindness over a tapestry that was more intricate than her child.

He clenched his fists and brought his arms toward his chest as though he were about to cry again, but he didn't, just exhaled as if he had been working very hard, then began to pee. His little baby cock almost stood up with the strength of it as the yellow arc splashed back across his stomach, almost reaching the bandaged navel. Then he cried, and Palmetto cleaned him off with the sheet.

"What a big strong boy I've got," she said. "Let's have some supper."

She slipped the gown over her shoulders, cradled him in her arm, and guided the nipple toward his mouth. He attached himself to her immediately. It hurt her the first moment, and she caught her breath. He *was* a big strong boy. "Take it easy," she said. "These have got to last us."

He grew calm and nursed patiently, as though he had some regard for her. He's a little gentleman, she thought. How perfect in every way. What a marvelous baby. What a wonderful person he was going to be. She wanted to tell him something, wanted to share some beautiful secret that life had kept from her till now, wanted to let him know that things would be all right and she would always be there and life was a beautiful place and time was a beautiful thing, but all her feelings were superior to words. "You're a pollywog," She finally told him. "And a peach."

They got out of the cars, slamming the doors behind them. It was quiet. Visiting hours had ended. They had to cut through a line of brittle shrubbery and walk quietly by the side of the building. It was a narrow space. Miss Fan snagged her stockings on a drainpipe. Every couple of steps one of Bootsie's boys would snort, suppressing a giggle, and another one of them would go, "Sshhh," and that would start them over again, but at last they came to a small garden clearing overlooked by all the sun rooms for the hospital's four stories. They had left their bottles in the cars, but as Miss Fan later said in court, "We were all three sheets to the wind, Your Honor. All of us." And she never drank a drop.

Preston was laughing a lot. He didn't think he had ever felt this good before. He had talked so much about being free, hadn't meant a word of it, and suddenly was free and loved it. He was telling everybody about the way he had met Palmetto and how Piedmont Hospital had played a big part in his life. He had a lot to tell people tonight.

He had sent Scoe, Elvira, and Fat Boy home. They had enough problems without getting involved in anybody's pranks, but Miss Fan had firmly refused to be deterred. "You need somebody to take care of you," she twanged. "Though the Lord knows, I don't know what I can do. I can't drive. I can't play, and I can't sing, but I am certainly not going to miss this."

Bootsie and the boys took their instruments out of their cases, assembled in a serious way, snorted, and leaned against one another for a moment; then Bootsie cleared his throat and raised his hands as though he were going to conduct. This set them off again, Bootsie included.

"Y'all better hurry up before one of the guards comes out and chases us off," said Preston.

That did it. They became very serious. Bootsie raised his hands, lowered them, and the song began. The band played a few bars; then Bootsie turned and faced the wing they had determined was Palmetto's. He took off his hat and held it over his heart, then began to sing. Despite the liquor, his voice was sweet and clear, and it blended with itself as the echo bounded off the walls.

When whippoorwills call
And evening is nigh
I hurry to My Blue Heaven.
A turn to the right
A little white light
Will lead you to My Blue Heaven.

Lights began to come on in the building, magically, as if his voice were setting them off.

Preston and Miss Fan unfolded a piece of brown wrapping paper The Melba had used for storing meat. There was an inscription written on it in marking pencil:

PRESTON LOVES PALMETTO.

Sarah couldn't believe her eyes. Dear God, she thought. He's lost his mind. The strain has pushed him over the brink. She felt as if she ought to hide, but she stayed by the window as orderlies and night nurses rushed up to see what was going on. Then she stopped being ashamed for him. He was her brother. He was like her. Neither of them had ever been young. Tonight there was youth about him. She shed a tear when he unfurled the sign. Nobody would ever do that for her. She turned and ran down the hall.

Palmetto had just wrapped the baby's blanket around him when Sarah rushed into the room.

"Go to the window," she said.

"What on earth —"

"Just go to the window."

Sarah helped her out of the bed and stood at the window, giving her support. Palmetto caught her breath in a shocked gasp. "Preston Vacalis," she said. "Preston Vacalis. Preston Vacalis . . ." She said it over and over. This was a night of wonders.

> *Just Molly and me,*
> *And baby makes three.*
> *We're happy in My Blue Heaven.*

The baby began to cry. She jiggled him in her arm, and the rhythm lulled him into sleep. "Preston Vacalis. Preston Vacalis." She stood at the window, saying his name and watching, until the police came and hauled them off.

Preston, Miss Fan, Bootsie, and the band were lodged in the Decatur Street Jail overnight, charged with disturbing the peace, public drunkenness, resisting arrest, and outraging the public morals (one of the band members had stopped to pee behind a bush). By the time they were arraigned by a judge all charges had been dropped except disturbing the peace. A reporter looking for accident news had been at the hospital and had gotten a picture of the drunken serenade. It made the front page of the *Constitution* that morning under the headline: PROUD PAPA SINGS A SONG. They identified Bootsie as the father and Miss Fan as a nurse.

There were a couple of reporters in the courtroom when the arraignment began. Everyone was in a jovial mood. People like to see their institutions celebrated. There was a air of mock solemnity, except for Preston, who was hungover, unshaven, and almost violent when a flashbulb went off in his face.

"What in hell are you doing, bringing us in here for something that didn't mean anything when those hooligans who beat up my help and destroyed my cafeteria are running free on the streets?"

Nobody expected that. They wanted him to a contrite, happy, dumb, drunk daddy who would fade back to beer and football. But something seemed to have happened to Preston. He wasn't looking for approval any more, and he refused to blend in. The judge told him that what he was talking about wasn't the issue here and that if he wanted to make a complaint he could do so separately. Preston's lawyer tried to get him to shut up, went so far as to kick his shins and give him an elbow in the ribs. Preston elbowed him back. The judge dismissed charges against everyone except Preston and fined him fifteen dollars for instigating the disturbance. Preston called him "a dirty courthouse rat," had an extra fifty dollars tacked onto his fine, was threatened with doing thirty days at the work farm, and was hustled out of the court by his lawyer, who paid the fine out of his own pocket, then threatened to punch Preston right there on the steps. Preston was sorry for that, apologized, and gave the lawyer his hand. There was something about Preston's eyes when he knew he was wrong and wanted to make up. They glistened, turned gentle and hurt. "Oh, shit, Pres," the lawyer said, and turned away, embarrassed. "Just don't ever pull a stunt like that again."

He made the papers under the headline: COURTHOUSE RAT. For some reason this endeared him to Judge Russell, who was waiting at the hospital with Mamie when he got there. He shook Preston's hand and called him "son." Mamie kissed his cheek and stepped aside. Judge Russell wanted to talk about the football game, but Mamie yanked him down the hall with her. Preston stood outside Palmetto's room. He had still not shaved, and his eyes were bloodshot. He had slept in his suit, and he had the feeling that he was beginning to smell more human than he liked to smell. He knocked on the door, heard the gentle "Come in," and entered the room.

Palmetto was sitting up in bed in one of her hope-chest gowns that Mamie had brought over. "It's time to stop hoping and start doing," Mamie had told her. It was a pink gown with an embroidered quilted bed jacket to match. She had a ribbon in her hair. She was not quite satisfied with the way she looked, but if she could have seen herself as Preston saw her she would have been content at last. There were flowers in the room, and the sun was coming in on her. It was the way he always remembered her, all in pink, sitting in the sun, surrounded by flowers. It was her natural state.

"Hi," he said.

"Hi," she said.

"You all right?"

"Fine and dandy."

"How's the baby?"

"Oh, he's just so cute and sweet," she began. She already had a torrent of information about him, though he was less than a full day old. But she checked herself. "I heard all about The Melba. I think it's just awful."

He tried to shrug it off. "It was just a dream."

"Anybody that has one dream can have two."

He exhaled, and seemed to deflate with it. He sat on the side of the bed and looked away from her. "I don't know about that," he told her.

"What?"

"I said that I —"

"I know what you said, but it was the wrong thing to say. Aren't you going to tell me that you love me and try to get me to come back with you?"

"Well . . . yeah . . . I suppose I am . . . But I don't have that much to —"

"Preston! I am ready to be swept off my feet. I don't want to listen to anybody whining."

"I just don't know if I'm much good to anybody any more. I lost my temper down at the court —"

"Dear God! This is not what I expected at all. And it's certainly not what I wanted.'' She crossed her arms angrily and looked out the window. ''Well, don't just sit there like a knot on a log. Open that drawer.''

He opened it. Inside was a birth certificate. It had been filled out, the baby's name written in Palmetto's most official curlicue script: Preston Marlin Vacalis, Jr. The delight jumped out all over him. Palmetto regarded him from the sides of her eyes.

''How about that?'' he said. ''Preston, Junior.''

''Marlin.''

''Well,'' he said. ''I never used that name.''

''That's why I thought it would be so nice for him. We don't want him to start off with a secondhand name, do we?''

He had to smile. ''Marlin.''

''I thought you might like it,'' she said. ''Darlin' Marlin.''

''Don't you go calling him that, now. All his little friends'll pick it up and tease him.''

''Don't you think I have more sense than that?''

"I don't know."

"Preston, I have just given birth and I don't need to be insulted."

"I was just kidding."

"You certainly have a funny way of kidding."

"That's the point of kidding."

"Oh, shut up."

He smiled at her. "What'll you give me. if I do?"

"I don't know. What do you want?"

"What do you think?"

She almost blushed. She looked toward the window. "It's going to be a couple of weeks before that gives anybody any pleasure. Particularly me."

"I'd settle for a kiss."

"I don't know if I want to kiss anybody with bloodshot eyes and whiskers all over their face."

He drew back, and she thought she had hurt him. The fear of it ran through her like an arrow. She lunged forward and caught him in her arms, the day-old whiskers feeling better against her face than anything ever had before. "Oh, Preston," she said. "I just love you so much."

His face was in her thick, sweet-smelling hair. He wanted to cover himself in it. "I love you, too," he said. "I love you so much I don't even know how to tell you. I'm kind of afraid to tell you."

"Don't be afraid."

"But I am afraid. I'm afraid of a lot of things. I used to tell myself I wasn't. A man's not supposed to be afraid."

She smiled at him, then laughed. "Preston, human emotion is for men, too."

"How do you know so much?"

She leaned back against the pillows, the sunlight streaking goldenly across her. "Oh," she said. "We goddesses are close to God."

He lay his head against her breast, the way the baby had, and she was filled with love again. She marveled at the different faces it had. She wanted to tell him about it, but she knew it was hers alone, the unspoken burden of her delight.

Her little bird heart was beating beneath his ear. He wanted to do more for her than anybody had ever done for anybody else. He remembered The Taj Mahal. That was love.

"Did I ever tell you my idea about The Taj Mahal Cafeteria?"

She laughed, but not at him. "That sounds wonderful."

"That's what I think I'm going to do." He sat up. There was a glow about him. "I can do it. I know I can put that together. Hell! I got all the help. Ain't none of 'em working. I ought to be able to come out of this thing with a couple of thousand bucks. What do you think?"

"I think it's wonderful."

"Do you?"

"Yes!"

"So do I!" He grabbed her leg and gave it a squeeze. "And I know just the place for it . . ." Then he caught himself and looked at her. "But I want to take you somewhere first."

"Where?"

"To the World's Fair in New York."

"Preston! That's so expensive."

"Nothing's too expensive for the woman I love."

She took him in her arms again, and

they nestled on the bed. He rubbed the soft, snowy flesh of her underarm. She looked up at him. "The baby looks just like you," she said.

"I thought he looked like you."

"No," she replied. "He'll be like me, but he'll look like you."

He laughed. "I don't know if I can stand that."

She laughed, too. "You'll love it."

"Maybe so," he said, and came toward her again, her arms folding like fronds around him. He snuggled close. "Miss Palmy. Miss Palmy."

She had never felt so good. "Oh, Preston. You'll always have me."

Epilogue

Palmetto was greatly attached to her Kodak, though she never learned the refinements of photography. Her pictures were like life: They turned out by chance and luck.

She had a photograph album. She and Preston bought it in New York when they went to the World's Fair for their belated honeymoon, leaving the baby with Mamie and Alfred. It had a blue cover and was stamped in flaking silver: SOUVENIR OF THE NEW YORK WORLD'S FAIR 1940. It had a hundred pages in it. "I'll never fill this up," she said, and she never did.

The first pictures in it were of the Fair. There was a shot of them outside the General Motors Futurama Building, where they had just been dazzled by the wonders of the coming years. And another outside the parachute jump. Palmetto could hardly wait to go on it. Preston could.

There was one of them with Marlin in his stroller, holding the bear they had bought him. They were looking at him and grinning broadly, trying to make him grin, but he was more interested in the bear. Preston was slightly irritated.

Alfred and Mamie standing on either side of Marlin's highchair. There was a cake in front of it, bearing one candle. Alfred and Mamie posed formally, with no smiles. Photographs were serious things to them. Marlin had just stuck his hand in the icing.

Preston and Palmetto standing together, holding hands. She had on a dress with padded shoulders, and the hem crept toward her knees. Preston had on an Army uniform. His rank was Private. They were smiling, but not with their eyes.

Palmetto in her nurse's uniform, going

back to work. She was holding Marlin, though he was about to be too big to hold. The Russell house was in the background. They were staying there throughout the war.

There was a series of snaps taken when Palmetto went to Boston to see Preston before he went overseas. They were holding on to each other in every picture. There was another couple with them; Palmetto had written on the bottom, "Bob and Jenny Rutledge." They were not seen again.

Palmetto with the baby that was in her when she came back from Boston. Her name was Alma Anna. Marlin had trouble holding her in the pictures sent to Preston. In the last one they were both crying.

A rare one: Preston and Scoe together, with the Eiffel Tower in the background. Scoe had on his Navy uniform. They had run into each other all the way across the world, gone to a bar together, and nobody turned around. Things were different in foreign lands.

A picture Mamie made of Preston when he got off the bus after Japan was bombed and the war was won. Palmetto had thrown herself against him, her face hidden. The children were to the side, bewildered. Preston was almost as thin as Palmetto.

Preston, Palmetto, and the children standing in front of their new house in Atlanta. Mamie said it was no bigger than a chicken coop, but there was a housing shortage. They felt lucky. Marlin was sitting on Preston's head. Palmetto held Alma Anna, who was squirming. She held her because she didn't want to be seen in photographs while she was pregnant.

The new baby, named Ronald, photographed asleep in his carriage. Marlin and Alma Anna were looking in, both wearing hats that belonged to Mamie. She had left Palmetto all her clothes. Palmetto had given them to Elvira, who was good with a needle.

Palmetto was sad in the photographs for a year or so. She gained some weight. But she bounced back. Next in the album came their trip to Florida with the children. Josephine and Bertram were there, too. Palmetto wore a two-piece bathing suit. She had her figure back. Preston knelt in the sand with the children. Alma Anna sat on his head. Marlin and Ronald held buckets and shovels. There was another of Marlin alone, crying. His legs were chafed.

Lemingworth's Produce was a long one-story building where Preston worked for three years. There was a picture of Preston standing on a loading platform with Mr. Lemingworth, who had a stroke a year later and was never able to speak again.

And then there it was, The Taj Mahal. Only it wasn't a cafeteria. It was a drive-in restaurant. Scoe with his head out the window, and Sadie and Fat Boy to the side. Fat Boy had on a turban. Everybody was laughing.

Preston in a turban, Ronald sitting on his shoulder. Preston wouldn't hold them on his head any more. He had begun to lose some hair, and told him it was their fault for having rubbed it off. They were sorry. They liked sitting on his head.

The whole family together at Easter. Palmetto with a corsage of white roses, all the children carrying baskets. Preston had on a Palm Beach suit. None of them was smiling. Preston and Palmetto had just had a fight over whether the Easter bunny should come to see big boys.

All the Vacalises together for a picnic, when Marlin was eleven or twelve. Roy Al and Joan with their three; Araminthia and her family; Maybelle and hers; Louise and her two. Jimmy and Sarah stood together, the only unmarrieds. Palmetto was in shorts and a halter. Preston had disapproved. His sisters all wore dresses. Palmetto had invited him to kiss her butt. They stood at either end of their line of children.

They added on to The Taj Mahal. There was an inside dining area now, and another covered ramp for service.

MERRY CHRISTMAS 1953! It was printed in red on a white card, and showed Preston, Palmetto, Marlin, Alma Anna, and Ronald sitting by the fireplace in their new house, stockings hung, the children combed and brushed — Alma Anna with sausage curls on Preston's lap, Palmetto with her arms around the boys.

Palmetto wearing a navy cape over her uniform, standing in front of Piedmont Hospital with the 1955 graduating class of nurses. She'd been teaching for a year, and she hated it. It made her feel like an old lady at forty-five. She wanted to go back to nursing, but Preston was opposed. He thought she ought to stay home with the children. "Why should I stay home with them? They don't stay home with me," she said. He shook his head and looked away. He had four Taj Mahals to worry about. She invited him to kiss her butt.

Marlin on his first date. He was wearing a rented tux and had a little cluster of pimples on his forehead. He was standing stiffly with a girl in glasses and an evening dress. She wore a corsage. They both looked miserable standing by Palmetto's Oldsmobile.

Preston and Palmetto at a New Year's Eve Party. The year was 1957. They were hugging each other and having a wonderful time. An overweight Preston holding a French '75. Palmetto's hair blonder than before, though she denied it.

Toward the end of the album there were fewer photographs. It was harder to get everybody together. Marlin's high-school-graduation picture, Marlin looking exactly like a young Preston. Another shot of Palmetto and Preston together at the graduation ceremony, she crying, he with his arm around her. Alma Anna and Ronald looking embarrassed. "I'll cry at yours, too," Palmetto had told them, and she did.

Alma Anna, beautiful in her bathing suit and holding a trophy. She had just placed third in the Miss Atlanta contest. Preston decided it was fixed.

Preston and Palmetto in San Francisco for the Restaurant Association Convention. He gave a seminar on how to run a successful drive-in. Preston had lots of information. He had sixteen of them in two states. San Francisco seemed to agree with Preston and Palmetto. They were smiling in every shot, and their arms were around each other.

Alma Anna's wedding, 1961. She was a beautiful bride. There were candles and ferns and lilies of the valley in the church. The bridesmaids wore peach satin dresses with green velvet ribbons in their hair. They carried gardenias. Palmetto's smile was bigger than the bride's. Preston's was not. He thought she was too young. He also thought the wedding cost too much money. The picture that made Preston so mad: a champagne-happy Palmetto sliding down the marble banister at the Piedmont Driving Club in her yellow mother-of-the-bride dress, which was pulled up, showing a great expanse of thigh. Palmetto told him he ought to be glad her legs still looked so good.

Palmetto's birthday, 1962. Preston had his baker make the cake. It was heart-shaped. "No candles on the cake!" Palmetto said. "It'll burn the house down." There was one candle. In the picture she had just blown it out. Preston and Ronald were standing by her.

Preston, Palmetto, and Marlin at the University of Georgia in front of the Sigma Chi Fraternity House. Palmetto made a big hit with the boys. Another shot of them, standing by the car they'd just given Marlin: a red MG with a convertible top. Preston hadn't wanted to give it to him, thought it would be the reason Marlin would flunk out of law school, but Palmetto had insisted.

A picture of Palmetto surrounded by luggage. She was perched on a large trunk, showing off her legs movie-star style. She was off to Europe with some friends, and was going to miss Marlin's graduation. She didn't want to go because of it, but everybody told her not to be silly. She asked Preston to meet her in Paris, but he said he was too busy. Summer was the busiest season. She was standing out in front of the new house with the swimming pool. Preston thought it was too big. Palmetto said they had to have something to lure their grandchildren. Alma Anna didn't mind being photographed pregnant.

Then there was one of Preston and Palmetto together. He kept an enlargement of this framed at his bedside. She was wearing a white dress with a pleated skirt. She had on red accessories. He always liked her best in red. They were at the airport. They'd just promised to miss each other.

Palmetto in Europe, having a wonderful time. On a gondola. With Big Ben in the background. And the last one. Preston didn't like it. She was wearing sunglasses. It made her look funny, he thought, removed somehow, as though she already knew what was going to happen.

And the picture of the crash. It wasn't pasted in the album, like the rest of them, just folded and put inside in the special edition the *Journal* put out the day the plane went down at Orly Field and 130 Atlantans were killed. He wanted to throw it away, but he couldn't. He couldn't do a lot of things for a long time, just get up and go to work and do the things he had to do. The children gathered around and were as sweet as they knew how to be. He loved them more than he ever had before. They were all he had left of her.

Sarah by the pool. She moved back in to take care of him, so that they were just as they were before Palmetto came along. Only they weren't. Nothing was ever the same. At the end of the first year, he was able to get mad at Palmetto. He sat in front of the fire one night with a whiskey and cursed her until he cried, and then he cursed himself. Sarah heard it, but she didn't get up.

Sometimes he thought of Palmetto as still in Europe, still having a wonderful time and spending too much money, having such a wonderful time that she didn't know how late it had gotten and had missed her plane.

Preston with the four grandchildren. Preston with the help at various Taj Mahals. His hair was white and his skin pale. A few buxom widows friends had tried to fix him up with. He made them laugh a lot, and they knew he had money. If he took one out, they went to a nice restaurant.

The picture of Preston that appeared in the *Restaurant News* when he announced his retirement. There was a wondering look about him, as though suddenly things were funny and he couldn't figure out what the fuss of his life had been about. He was never so amused as when he hit sixty-five and saw how funny it all was.

He could not express this to anyone except himself, though Palmetto would have understood. Perhaps she had understood it all along and was just waiting for him to catch up with her. She came to him sometimes, and they laughed about their grandchildren and the widows. "If you marry one of those bitches I'll haunt you forever," she told him.

But he wouldn't do that. He couldn't. He was still married in his heart, which was the only place that counted.

"You'll always have me," she had told him once.

And he always did.